THE RESURRECTION OF JOHN DILLINGER

BY TIM MAHONEY

A tip of the fedora to the early readers:
Kathleen Lewinski, Alison Mahoney and Julie VanLaanen.
This book benefited greatly from their advice and insight.

Other books by this author:

Year of the Rooster
Dead Messenger
Dead Like Lazarus
Dead a Long Time
If the Dead Could Speak
Secret Partners
Jack's Boy
We're Not Here
Halloran's World War

ISBN: 978-0-9908974-4-6

THE HISTORY
BEHIND THIS NOVEL

On March 3, 1934, John Dillinger broke out of jail in Crown Point, Indiana, where he'd been awaiting trial on charges of bank robbery and murder. The exact methods of his breakout have long been debated.

But it's certain that, within days of that breakout, Dillinger drove to Saint Paul, Minnesota.

Saint Paul in those days had a nationwide reputation as a criminal sanctuary. Ranking police officers and elected officials cooperated in this scheme, which by the time of Dillinger's escape had been in place for 30 years.

During Dillinger's time, the master criminal in charge of Saint Paul's sanctuary scheme was tavern owner Harry Sawyer. Harry assigned two of his underlings, Pat Reilly and Bess Green, to help Dillinger find a hideout in the city.

Dillinger arrived in the Twin Cities accompanied by his soon-to-be-infamous girlfriend Billie Frechette. After they settled in, Dillinger rejoined his gang, which now consisted of Tommy Carroll, Baby Face Nelson, Homer Van Meter and Red Hamilton. They hired Bess Green's husband Eddie as a "jug marker" to help them plan bank robberies.

By the terms of the Saint Paul sanctuary deal, that city was off limits for major crime. So the Dillinger gang began pulling off bank robberies in South Dakota and Iowa.

Without knowing who they had in their sights, federal agents stumbled into a gun battle with Dillinger in Saint Paul. Wounded, he sought medical attention and then left the Twin Cities for Chicago. Under the pressure of a J. Edgar Hoover manhunt, Dillinger took a disastrous "vacation" at a Wisconsin resort called Little Bohemia.

The Resurrection of John Dillinger was written in accord with these, and many other historical facts of the last spring of Dillinger's life.

And since early readers have asked, yes, the headlines, news stories and FBI memos are real and verbatim.

Easter Saturday,
March 31, 1934

BLOOD DROPS
IN THE SNOW

BILLIE

Billie Frechette lay in bed, caressing the rough stubbly face of the World's Most Famous Bad Guy. He snored, his lips moved, he uttered a sound like a baby's cry. But nothing awoke John early, nothing.

A rude slam of the front door announced their guests' departure. Billie had waited them out. Breakfast for five? Billie was no short order cook, and besides, there were only two eggs left in the icebox.

Billie rolled out of bed in a white flannel nightgown. She shivered. She had left the window open a crack, John crazy for fresh air, and now it had gone freezing. Although it was Easter Saturday morning, the radiator tooted its winter song. She lifted an edge of the shade. The avenue was covered in snow and tire tracks.

Billie walked out of the bedroom whistling "Beautiful Dreamer."

What did Johnny dream about? Fast cars and baseball games, if she knew him. In the too bright kitchen she lit the gas stove under the tea kettle. She wondered about that Chicago lawyer. He seemed bullshit. Still, she wanted to believe. He had talked to a federal attorney about a deal. Or so he claimed. Amnesty! John would vow to go straight, and his redemption would be turned into a movie. The attorney was angling for a role for himself in that movie. He wanted to call it: The Trial of Handsome Johnny.

Billie must have spent awhile in Hollywood fantasy because the tea kettle was whistling. A bag of Salada tea, a white cup, a squeeze of honey, she was morning happy. She raised the window shade to feel direct sunshine, warm and friendly on her face. She sipped tea, watching traffic in the snow. One egg apiece, soft boiled, and toast for breakfast.

Whenever His Gangster Highness deigned to arise.

With that sip of tea she remembered they were out of cigarettes. Red Hamilton had promised to bring her a carton. But she wanted a smoke now. Hoping to find a stray cigarette, she poked into the living room. Red and his two bedmates had not bothered to raise the Murphy bed, so she lifted it, throwing wrinkled pillows onto the couch. In bed with two sisters, well, Red was quite the adventurer. But he could keep them both. All those girls did was complain. Did they ever pick up after themselves? Did Billie look like their maid?

Heavy knocks at the door. One. Two. Three. Four. She tiptoed, looked into the peephole, couldn't see. A rough voice vibrated through the door.

"Carl Hellman?"

It took a moment for her sleepy brain to recognize that name. John changed names like other men changed trousers. Hellman, right.

Red, such a stupid man, had left the door unlocked and now Billie hitched the security chain. That made a noise. Now she could not pretend she wasn't home. She opened the door a cautious inch, rattling that chain.

"My husband is not in," she called to the strangers in the

hall. "Try this afternoon."

She closed the door. She still hadn't set eye on the intruders.

"Would you be Mrs. Hellman?"

This was another voice from the hallway, smoother, Southern syrup.

"Yes."

"Well, we are officers," said the Southern voice. "We would like to speak to you."

John had instructed her for this situation. She was to open the door and drop to the floor. John would take the cops hostage if he could, or shoot them if he had to. But those instructions were worthless when John was dead asleep.

"I'm not dressed," Billie said.

"We'll wait for you to dress," said the Southern voice.

"No, why don't you come back this afternoon?"

She turned the deadbolt and it made a solid clunk.

They murmured out there in the hall, the Rough Voice and Southern Syrup. Billie, tingling all over, going numb in hands and feet, breathing shallow, held that doorknob to keep herself upright. She cast a terrified look over her shoulder, hoping to see John. He was the coolest man she had ever known.

She trembled like a trapped rabbit. Every step she took toward the bedroom felt like it consumed a decade. When she pushed through the door, Johnny was facedown, bare-assed, hugging a pillow.

She shook his foot.

"John," she whispered.

"Unh."

"Cops."

He rolled over, naked and twisted in the sheets. He glanced at the windows, as if surprised at the sunlight. Then he leaped out of bed and hopped into trousers, cinched the belt around his narrow waist.

"How many?"

"I don't know," she whispered.

He was on his knees at the closet, pulling out the suitcase, piling into it bank-bundled cash, shirts, and belts of machine gun ammo.

He rose to his feet, ripped a starched blue-striped shirt from its hanger and buttoned it over his chest. In three rapid strides he crossed the room and peered through the crack in the shades.

Whatever he saw on the street did not unnerve him.

"All right, Billie," he said. "Keep your shirt on. We're going to get out of here."

He glared at her.

"Well get dressed. Why are you standing there?"

He pulled on shoes and socks while she, sweating, wriggled into a dark purple dress. She picked flat shoes for running. After one sorrowful glance at all her beautiful clothing, she plucked a mink jacket from its hanger. She shouldered her purse. From the dresser she scooped her best jewelry. When she turned around, John was holding the tommy gun, pointed at her, like she was the enemy.

"All right," he said. "Take that suitcase and follow me."

Billie grabbed the suitcase, which was heavy like it was full of stones. She stood behind John in the living room and all of a sudden came an explosion. Shock waves pierced her ears. Her whole head rang like a bell. The air smelled of vile chemistry and flashes leaped out the barrel of John's tommy gun. Bits of plaster stung her face.

John flung open the door. He turned one way and then the other, blasting away with the tommy gun. Billie, that suitcase nearly tearing her arm out, followed him down the hallway. Something down in the darkness flashed three or four times, and a lethal insect buzzed past her ear. John fired toward those flashes, then limped down the stairs. Billie followed, fear gone, exhilaration, intensely alive, the light at the bottom of the stairwell like the glow of Heaven. John pushed out the door, turned to check on her, limped into the snowy driveway.

Blood drops appeared in the snow. John let himself into the passenger side of their Hudson, and Billie, with more strength than she believed she had, threw that heavy suitcase into the rear seat. She upside-downed her purse. Jewelry and makeup spilled out. She saw in that split second their doomed future, shot to death in this car because she, stupid ugly Billie, had forgotten to bring the keys.

But miracle, there they gleamed in her lap. She started the Hudson and backed out. Where the hell were the coppers?

She took a hard left turn on Grand Avenue.

"Take it easy," said John. "Drive slow. We don't want to get pulled over now."

"You're bleeding."

"They nicked me that's all."

"John."

"You drive, I'll bleed, okay?"

"Where the fuck are we going?"

"We've got friends in this town," John said. "Patrick will help us. Drive easy, easy, easy."

SIX WEEKS EARLIER...

Valentine's Day,
Ash Wednesday,

February 14, 1934

PATRICK

Patrick Reilly pushed out of the heavy Cathedral doors and into an arctic freeze. He lit a Lucky. His gray wool overcoat concealed everything but his pale face and short stature. A driver's cap covered his balding head. Upon his forehead, in black ashes, was the thumbprint of a priest.

Memento mori, the priest had murmured when applying the ashes. Pat, having endured seven years of Catholic education, figured this was Latin for *drop dead.* But even on Ash Wednesday, Pat was an optimist. He was young, and up for promotion.

He hustled across the street for his car, an Essex Terraplane, midnight blue, with a new-fangled V6 engine. It once belonged to a gangster who had run off to Cuba.

Despite the cold, that engine fired up with a pull on the choke and the touch of a chrome button.

Pat's wife Dolly waited at the Cathedral's side door, sheltered from the vicious wind. Pat pulled the Essex to the curb and pushed open the passenger door. He loved Dolly, deep and true, although when she wouldn't listen, she drove him nuts. Dolly was a looker: dummy in the kitchen, genius in the bedroom. She dressed fancy, had a sharp tongue, and didn't take no crap off of nobody. To top it off, she was a low-handicap bowler.

At High Mass or in the nightclubs, Dolly dressed the same: rabbit-fur coat, brazen red lipstick, red pill hat. Her beauty-parlor blond hair, short cut, was almost a helmet. Her pale face was punctuated by thick lips and bright blue eyes.

Your Honor, Pat said to his inner judge, *I know Dolly don't have the greatest reputation. But she reformed after we was married.*

Dolly slammed the door, huffed a frosty breath and said, "Any heat in this thing?"

"I just started it."

"Eight degrees," muttered Dolly as she dug into her purse. From it she lifted a packet of tin foil. In there was a thin crooked cigarette. She propped it between her lips. Pat lit it up, flicking his special lighter. A goofy perfume smell filled the car.

Pat spun the Essex around, eager to get away before Mass let out. Of course, just when you need to zoom, there's a red traffic light in front of you. Dolly huddled shivering against the door.

"Florida?" Dolly said. "Am I going to see Florida before I die?"

"Florida's out. I got business up here now," Pat said. "Big business."

From Cathedral Hill, Pat had a sweeping view of the city through the frosty windshield. Pat took a deep drag on his Lucky and his chest swelled with tobacco smoke and pride. Soon a piece of this city would belong to him. No, it wasn't a great city, like Chicago, where he'd been once, or New York, where he'd only heard tell. But these narrow streets, served by a streetcar loop, had hundreds of places where a fella could have a good time: Taverns and pool halls, horse parlors, whorehouses and dice rooms. This wasn't one of those cities run by politicians. Oh, there was a mayor all right, but all he did was make speeches on the radio. This city was run by a sweet deal between the cops and Pat's boss, Harry Sawyer.

"Oh, *big* business," Dolly said.

She was what you could call sarcastic sometimes.

"And don't say nothing," warned Pat as the traffic light turned green. "Because it's men's business and you don't know nothing about it."

Dolly was only cranky because of hunger, Pat figured. A loyal Catholic fasted before Mass and Communion, and Dolly didn't do so hot with fasting. She sucked down one last cloud of perfumed smoke, snuffed her stinky marijuana cigarette in its foil packet, and took out her mirror compact. She blotted away the ashes on her forehead.

"It ain't flattering," she said, "going around with black ashes."

"It marks you as a Good Catholic," Pat argued.

"How about pancakes at the Lowry?"

"Jeez," said Pat. "On Valentine's Day, are you kidding? We'll wait two hours in line. Anyway, look. It's Ash Wednesday, right? Ash Wednesday cancels out Valentine's Day."

"Says who?"

"Ask any priest."

Dolly sputtered.

"We'll get breakfast at the Town Talk," Pat suggested.

"Fine," said Dolly. "Dine with the low-lifes."

"You'll feel better with breakfast in you," said Pat. "You're my Valentine, right, kiddo?"

"For better or for worse," muttered Dolly.

"Oh it's going to get better," said Pat. "Let me tell you."

Pat let Dolly off at McCormack's Town Talk. As she sashayed through the diner's frosty glass door, Pat drove down the icy alley and parked his Essex behind the Green Lantern tavern. From the rear, the tavern looked like a crummy warehouse: chipped brick, rusty gutters, broken downspouts, green paint peeled on the steel door.

But from a dark office in that tavern, Harry played this city like Hampton played the vibraphone.

Chicago had Al Capone, New York had Dutch Shultz, Saint Paul had Harry Sawyer. Capone was in prison, Shultz was dead, but Harry was still going, planning the big snatches and robberies, giving the cops their ten percent, issuing protection orders for gangsters who played fair, laundering cash and bonds with his buddies the bankers, fencing diamonds on Jeweler's Row. Six years Harry had been underworld king and the only time he saw a jail cell was when he was bailing somebody out.

The dirt lot behind the Lantern was frozen hard, so no need for Pat's galoshes. He unbuckled them. A level gangster wore shined shoes, not schoolboy footwear. He set the galoshes in the nasty green puddle that had leaked from the heater.

He stepped out in polished brogans. Pat blessed himself, sign of the cross, for luck. He swaggered in the back door. As dull gray as it was outside, walking into the tavern was like being reborn into darkness.

Bess Green grabbed Pat's arm. She helped him shrug out of his overcoat. She was Harry's Gal Friday, although her official job was running the coatroom. She relieved gangsters of their coats but more importantly their weapons, and Harry depended on Bess to keep gunfights out in the parking lot where they belonged.

Bess was thirty-plus years old, taller than Pat, and stronger, although she wasn't one of those, ahem, gymnastic females. As Pat's eyes adjusted to the darkness he could see her better. She had fiery red hair, enflamed by regular appointments at the hairdresser. She wore a slit green dress, chosen to match her startling eyes, and to display a sexy flash of leg. Those eyes shone with a frightening intelligence.

Bess owned a high school diploma. And it hadn't been clipped out of no magazine, either.

"Crumley's at the bar," Bess whispered.

Pat was going to have to grow up someday, or so he'd often been told. If he was going to take over from Harry, he'd have to get a grip on Inspector Crumley. Pat walked up to the bar and thrust a finger at the big man's ribs.

"Stick 'em up."

Pat didn't feel any actual ribs, due to layers of overcoat and fat. Crumley rattled the newspaper he'd been reading.

"What do you want?" Crumley groused.

To call Crumley fat was an insult to obese men everywhere. No shirt and certainly not his cheap seersucker suit could contain that massive gut. No matter the weather, salty rivulets ran down his spectacular jowls and soaked his frayed shirt collar. He overflowed his own personal barstool, which Harry had reinforced. Crumley had broken three stools meant for normal men.

"Where's Harry?" Crumley barked.

Pat lifted the bridge and passed behind the bar. Crumley bore the ashes of death on his forehead, but faintly. His wife had dragged him to sunrise Benediction.

"Harry ain't around," Pat said. He leaned in, confidential. "He's passing this tavern to me."

"Is that right?"

Pat rocked back, suit-coat open, thumbs hitched in the belt loops of his best trousers. Even indoors he wore his cap sometimes, protection against creeping baldness.

"Not everybody knows," Pat said, "Especially …"

"Oh shit," said Crumley. "Bess? She knows everything, are you kidding me?"

Crumley lay the newspaper beside a cocktail glass that contained two melting ice cubes. He pushed said glass toward Pat.

Pat tossed the cubes into the sink, reached into an ice bucket for exactly two more, dropped them into the glass, flooded it with bourbon.

"Keep going," Crumley said.

Pat nearly overflowed the glass.

"You'll still be treated right here, Jim," Pat said, and corked the bottle.

"I expect so," said Crumley.

"That ain't going to change."

Crumley bent to sip whiskey.

Pat set the bottle before the back-bar mirror. He caught the reflection of a frightened little fella. He straightened up tall. *Errand boy? Are you kidding me? Pat Reilly's the man to see nowadays.*

"Harry's at the farm or in town?" Crumley asked.

"He don't stay in town no more," Pat said. "G-men."

Crumley laughed. "This town been lousy with G-men before, and what happened?" He sipped. "Nothing."

Pat ran a damp rag along the bar. Drinkers needing after-church lubrication would soon push through the doors. Pat might hire a bartender tomorrow, but today he was master and slave in his own kingdom.

"If you need something from Harry," Pat said, "you go through me." He tossed the rag at the sink.

A hostile grin deformed Crumley's jowls. "Oh, well," he said. "If I need to talk to Harry direct, I suppose I can drive out to the farm."

Pat crossed his arms. "What do you need?"

"It's been an awful winter, ain't it?" Crumley said. "I could use a ton of coal."

"A ton of coal," Pat said. "I guess that could be arranged."

"You guess or you know?"

"I'll take it up with Harry."

"Who's the boss here?" Crumley asked.

"It's kind of split right now," Pat admitted. "Between me and Harry."

"And Bess," Crumley said.

"Not Bess," said Pat.

"Ain't what I heard," said Crumley. "You see the nails on that bitch? She'll scratch your eyes out."

Crumley fixed Pat with a stare. "Reilly, do you have any idea how many times I could have took an axe to this place? How many times I've gone to the chief and said leave Harry's joint alone?"

Pat picked up the Daily News.

"If the G-men ain't nothing," Pat said, and thrust the newspaper at Crumley. "Who brought Dillinger back from Tucson in handcuffs?"

Crumley waved that off.

"This time," Pat said, "Johnny gets the chair."

"Unless somebody deposits a sack of money in the sheriff's bank account."

"It's different now with the newsreels," Pat said. "They'll fry Dillinger and make a movie out of it."

Crumley pushed his massive sweating weight away from the bar. The stool dropped, thump, to the floor. Crumley would not, maybe could not, bend to pick up.

"So I'm gonna get my coal, right, partner?"

SAINT PAUL POLICE
HUNT BANDIT DILLINGER,
SAID TO BE ON WAY TO THIS CITY

Crown Point Ind. (United Press) — Upward of 20,000 armed men engaged tonight in a gigantic search for John Dillinger, the nation's foremost desperado, who bluffed his way out of Crown Point jail today with a wooden pistol.

Dillinger commandeered the car of the woman sheriff who ruled the jail he broke out of and gaily drove off singing "Get Alcng Little Dogie, Get Along."

Saint Paul Daily News
March 3, 1934.

PATRICK

Almost three weeks had passed since Ash Wednesday, and Pat had not bumped into Harry Sawyer, not in town, not at the tavern. This afternoon's one-word phone call had been the only communication.

Patrick!

That's all Harry said, and then he hung up.

But it was Harry, all right. His distinctive hoarse bark had given Harry his nickname: The Sea Lion.

Now freezing rain spattered the windshield of Pat's Essex as he bumped along Harry's muddy driveway. Harry swore G-men were spying on his farm, but there was nowhere to hide on this frozen prairie. G-men? Pat had mixed their drinks at the Green Lantern. They drank like sissies, talked like college boys and dressed like insurance salesmen. They could only operate from somewhere comfortable, like a warm office, or a fancy car.

Pat felt cheerful despite the gloomy weather. He imagined a ceremony at the kitchen table, where so many legendary deals had gone down. The names were written in gold in the bank robber hall of fame: Pretty Boy Floyd, Harvey Bailey, Machine Gun Kelly. Hell, Harry's gangsters had ruined more banks than President Roosevelt.

Strong drink would be served after the handover of Harry's

keys, payoff for Pat's years of faithful service. Now would be a great time for Pat's promotion. It would give him almost two weeks to prepare the Green Lantern for St. Patrick's Day. Pat had worked out a name change: The Saint Patrick Tavern. He would celebrate by firing Bess. The new hostess would be Harry's maid, the hot little flirt, Opal.

Pat's dream ended in a groan when he saw, parked at the farmhouse, a Chevy with Illinois plates. This could only mean there was a Chicago gangster in town, and Pat would have to do him favors. He yanked the hard brake, killed the engine. "Same old errand boy crap," he muttered.

Ever since Harry had arranged a certain kidnapping, he'd been laying low. But the man couldn't help it, he was a born fixer. It wasn't just the money. Harry was like the manager of a ball club. Too old and fat to play, he got a kick out of writing the lineup and watching his boys swing the bats.

Pat felt like a fool for driving up with dreamy expectations. With raindrops pelting him like tiny stinging ice bombs, he crossed the porch and barged into the kitchen. Nobody seemed to be home. The kitchen smelled of pork sausage and maple syrup. Said aromas teased Pat's hangover and rang the breakfast bell in his brain.

He pushed open a swinging door for a peek into the dining room. The kitchen was gangster domain, but Harry's wife Gladys ruled the rest of the house like a clawed beast. She had forced Harry to move out to this farm, wanting a country atmosphere for their newly-adopted daughter.

But neither Gladys nor the little girl seemed to be home.

Pat lit a Lucky with his gold-plated lighter. The cast-iron stove radiated heat and Pat backed up to enjoy it.

Footsteps sounded on the porch. Harry burst through the door, swaying with drink. The Sea Lion bellowed: "Opal!" Then he muttered: "Gotta get a handle on that girl."

Harry, with a nod to Pat, pushed through the swinging door and into the forbidden interior.

A thin, pale fellow entered from the porch, whistling a carefree show tune. He'd left his boots out there, walked in stocking feet. He had dark intense eyes and a pencil mustache. His trousers were loose and long, like he'd borrowed them from a bigger man. He shook off a wet Navy pea jacket and hung it on a chair back. He smoothed his plaid shirt.

"How are you, sluggo?" he said. "I'm Johnny."

Pat shook and released his chilled hand.

Through the door walked a stocky, young, dark woman with an acne-scarred face. Her eyes avoided Pat. He figured she hated him on sight.

"Harry tells me," said Johnny, "you played for the Saints."

"Couple of games," said Pat.

"I played short myself," Johnny said, and mimicked a throwing motion. "Might've made the majors. Hurt my arm."

Johnny raised a speckled blue enamel coffee pot from the stove, set it back with an empty clang.

"Rained the whole way up," said Johnny. "Miserable drive. Slippery. Usually I enjoy a good long drive."

An alcove contained a rolltop desk and wooden chair. Johnny's girlfriend huddled there, a shadow against the blue wallpaper. She clutched her black purse against her coat. She sat on the edge of the chair, like she was hoping to leave.

"And this shy creature," said Johnny, "is Billie."

Her lips were painted garish red, which set off her pancaked, pockmarked cheeks. Her lips moved in a silent, reluctant greeting.

"Harry says ..." Johnny began, but the man himself appeared.

"Opal's quit me again," Harry said. "How do you like that?" He glanced over his shoulder. "Can't rely on that girl."

Even before Harry bought a farm, he was the butter-and-eggs man. His farm hands, wife, tavern employees, gangster buddies, all clung to Harry because he understood the magic of cash. Pat had learned a poem from Harry:

> *The man with the dough,*
> *not the man with the gun,*
> *is the fella*
> *who gets things done.*

"No Gladys either," grumbled Harry when he too discovered the coffee pot was empty.

Where had Gladys gone? Pat did not ask. Only cops and rubes asked questions. A level guy would rather not know. Knowledge was danger. If you knew something, and the cops found it out, somebody might call you a stool pigeon. And if somebody called you a stool pigeon, you should chirp out your Last Confession.

Gladys, Pat guessed, had gone crazy, cooped up all winter drinking with Harry. Maybe she had taken little Francine on the train to Florida. If his wife and kid had abandoned Harry, it was more important than ever that Pat stay loyal.

"Pat, I got something for you out in the car," Harry said, and held open the kitchen door. He and Pat in shirtsleeves hustled through frosty rain for a few sloshy steps and ducked into Harry's Packard convertible.

Harry sat in the driver's seat.

In nicer weather, this car gleamed like a showpiece, with cream paint job, tan leather seats and chrome dashboard. But now it was just cold steel, wet glass and leaky canvas. The breath of two chilled humans fogged the windows.

Harry took a nip from a silver flask, did not offer a drink to Pat. He said: "I want these fucking people off my property. Pronto!"

He pulled his wad out of a trouser pocket, peeled off twenties and fifties, jammed them into Pat's shirt pocket. "Keep them away from me. They bring heat from Chicago, that's all they do."

"The regular fix?" Pat asked.

"Deluxe," Harry said. "The car, the cash, the backup. These people are level, guaranteed."

Level meant trustworthy. Level meant you'll go to prison before you'll talk. Some gangsters were on the level, most you couldn't trust. Cops? There wasn't a level cop in the whole world, including J. Edgar Hoover.

Pat looked out the Packard's frosty windows to see Opal slam out the kitchen door. She wore a yellow coat, held a red kerchief to her head, stood under the dripping eaves of Harry's porch.

Like so many of Harry's people, Opal was Irish. Jew and Irish, somehow they got along good. The Saint Paul gang was Irish all the way, except for a few tough Jews left over from the bootleg wars.

"She quit me, but she expects a ride home," Harry grumbled.

Pat lit a Lucky. "You in love with her, Harry?"

Harry sputtered, smacked Pat with a friendly backhand. "You asshole Irishman," he said. "Just for that, you give her a ride home."

"Aw, Harry."

But then Pat began to like the idea. He had learned from Harry that gangster business involved trading favors. If Pat drove Opal home, she'd owe him something.

Harry and Pat slipped out of the Packard and hustled up the porch stairs. "Pat'll take you home," Harry barked at Opal, and thrust a $10 bill at her. "Here, take it. You'll need it."

She snatched the money without looking at Harry.

Then Pat followed Harry into the kitchen, where Johnny sat at the table shuffling cards, Billie looking over his shoulder.

"It's arranged," Harry barked. "Pat's your man in this town. He's dependable, like a gold watch."

Harry's praise tunneled warm into Pat's heart.

"Go ahead," Harry told Johnny, "tell him what you need."

Pat sat at the kitchen table and Johnny dealt him a poker hand. Pat got a whiff of Billie's perfume, nauseous sweet.

"For starters, a clean car," Johnny said. "Big, fast, reliable. I'm not afraid of stylish."

"No jalopies," croaked Harry. "Good Minnesota plates. All the lights working. Top class tires and battery."

"An apartment," said Johnny. "Nice part of town. Furnished. Two beds. Ground floor. Out where the swells live, not downtown. Away from the dives and gambling joints."

Harry pointed his thumb to his own chest, meaning he, not Pat, would arrange the apartment.

Pat glanced at Billie, who stood glum silent. Suddenly Pat felt like this was the chance he'd been waiting for all his life. He became aware of his own breathing and all things around him. An orange cat in the alcove sat on the desk suspicious, swishing its tail. A brass clock ticked over the doorway. The riffle of Johnny's cards. Billie's perfume mixed with the scent of sausage and scalded coffee. Bread crumbs and syrup rings on the checkered table cloth. The peeling blue wallpaper. The rain beating against the windows. The tight feeling in his throat, as if he might never swallow again.

Billie broke the spell, her voice so low Pat had to replay it in his mind: "Polished wood floors."

"She likes," said Johnny, "nice floors. I don't know why, since she covers 'em up with Oriental rugs."

Johnny pushed back from the table, stood behind Pat whistling, and slapped him easy on the back. Pat didn't like that slap. It was the kind of thing you did to an errand boy.

Harry, at the cupboard, poured whiskey into a coffee cup and swigged from it. Then he brought out three more cups and laid them on the table.

The best arrangers kept it simple and told each man only what they needed to know. Johnny would be safe from the cops now, and in return Harry would get a piece of his haul. Nothing was put in writing or said on the telephone. A sip of whiskey was a contract. A nod was a deal. A shrug, and maybe someone was going off level, and would never be seen again. Pat had learned much from Harry, the best arranger in outlaw history, as far as Pat was concerned.

"Billie?" Harry said and handed her a cup of whiskey.

"She don't drink," said Johnny. "She's an Injun."

"I do so drink." Billie put her lips to the cup and blew a little storm into the whiskey.

If Whistling Johnny's last name was Dillinger, as Pat strongly suspected, he was a cheerful fellow hooked up with a moody female. Pat knew what that was like. Where had all the fun girls gone off to?

Johnny wandered to the sink. He washed his hands with a rough bar of Cascade soap. He wasn't a striking fellow, not big, not impressive, not movie star handsome as the newspapers said. He seemed fussy about hand washing. Drying his hands with a red checkered towel, he sauntered to the table as Harry lifted a toast.

"Around here," Harry said, "we call Saint Paul the Holy City. There are things we hold sacred."

Pat raised his cup.

"Like silence," Harry said. "Like loyalty."

"To the Holy City," said Johnny and the three men drank.

Billie picked up her cup. "Shiny floors," she said. "That's all I ask, John, shiny fucking floors."

"You heard the little woman," Johnny said.

CHICAGO AREA COMBED FOR DILLINGER DEN

Saint Paul Daily News
March 5, 1934

PATRICK

Pat hustled past the display windows of Emerald Radio Electronics. Said windows held displays in the truest sense. Outlandish prices taped to the radios insured that no rube would disturb the management, seeking to purchase a Philco.

Pat walked down a cold brick alley and pushed open a rotting wooden door. He entered a dark warehouse, flicked a brass toggle and a dull light revealed a riot of slot machines. Some were shiny, sitting high on tables. Others, like wounded soldiers, lay on the floor, spilling their steel guts.

"Tommy?" Pat called.

"In here, me boy."

Pat tiptoed over a floor scattered with gears, whirl-a-gigs, half-opened boxes. He bumped into dusty pinball machines, passed a rusty safe, its door gaping.

In the office, lit feebly by an occluded sun, stood Tom Filben, dressed like a nightclub emcee. He held some little red device in the palm of his hand. Tom devoted his spare time, and he had plenty of it, to magic tricks.

"By Christ, it's good to see you," said Filben.

"I've been at Harry's."

"Sit down," Filben said, and kicked a heavy oak chair. "How

is our young reprobate, anyway?"

Pat zipped open his leather jacket, fished out a pack of Luckies.

"Harry is retiring," said Pat.

"Christ almighty!"

"He's dealing through me now."

Pat lit that Lucky and tried to figure, through the smoke screen, whether Filben took him serious.

"Well now," said Filben. "That would be quite a promotion. Are you sure you're up to it? What about Big Ryan?"

"Harry will fix me up with the cops." Pat rocked in the chair, felt a thrill run through him.

"When you shake hands with Big Joe Ryan," Filben said, "Red Letter day indeed. Feast of the Assumption."

"Tommy, I need a clean car."

"Try the Lowry Garage."

"I'm not joking. High class, reliable, legit plates, not a speck of dirt on it. I've got an Illinois Chevy to trade, plus make-up cash. This is for a level guy, and I mean level."

He tapped his cigarette. Ashes fell to the concrete floor. Filben shuffled a glass ashtray along the desk.

"I need it today," Pat said.

A radiator whistled.

"That's quite an order," Filben said. "I don't suppose it's accompanied by the relevant bundle of cash."

"Harry pays."

"But he's retiring, you say."

Filben dropped that red object from his hand. The little ball, or whatever it was, reached the end of a string and zipped back into his hand.

"Ever seen one?" Filben asked.

Pat shook his head.

"Defies every known law of physics," Filben claimed. He

shot the little ball toward Pat's face. Pat ducked, but the thing returned to Filben's hand.

"Direct from the Philippines," Filben said. "I've ordered a thousand." He threw the thing and Pat caught it. It wasn't a ball at all, but a fat red wooden disk, with string wound into a crack.

"By Christ, kids love these things. I can't get them away from my nephews. Try it. Stick your finger through the loop, then drop the thing. Comes back to you every time."

Pat let the disk drop. It hung dead, like a man swinging from the gallows.

"Takes a bit of skill," said Filben, and snatched the thing from Pat, demonstrating the drop and retrieve. "They call it a yo-yo. Fantastic toy. I met a fellow last night could do all sorts of tricks. These fellows from Manila are going all across the country demonstrating them."

"Tommy, no joke about that car, Harry's got a new saint and the man needs a halo."

Those had been the code words ever since Pat could remember. A guy under Harry's protection was a saint, and wore a halo that guaranteed he'd be safe from arrest in this town.

"See the thing is Patrick, I'm attempting a graceful exit myself." Filben whirled the yo-yo out. "The days of easy money and bathtub gin are gone."

Filben's game was feigned reluctance, which had the effect of raising his price. During Prohibition, he had made a fortune by "financing" bootleggers' automobiles. When cops confiscated a bootlegger's vehicle, Filben dug out the title and sent his lackey to the impound lot to reclaim it. Said vehicle was returned to said bootlegger for a considerable fee.

Pat smashed his Lucky into the ashtray. "You can't say no to Harry."

"I'll see what Herb's got in the garage," Filben said.

By that Filben meant one of his minions would steal a car to order, and sneak it into Herb's Garage for repainting and new license plates.

Filben dropped the yo-yo, clonk, onto his wooden desk. That desk was the least cluttered surface Pat had ever seen, holding only an ashtray, a calculating machine, and now a yo-yo.

"Somebody's in town?" Filben asked.

"You might have read about him, that's all I can say."

"You want one car," Filben said, "so it can't be the two Shorties coming back to haunt us. No, those brothers would never share anything. I have the feeling we'll never see the Barker lads, their friend Karpis, or their ugly mother in our gloomy Irish city again. Dragging their poor mother along on bank jobs and snatches. Those hillbillies should be ashamed of themselves. No Irish gangster would treat his mother like that."

"This ain't nothing to do with the Barkers," Pat said.

Filben sat on his desk. "What is it about our race, Patrick? Why do we gravitate to the cold and gloom?" He looked out the window. The sun in its heaven may have been a mighty orb, but it gave pitiful illumination to Filben's cobblestone alley.

"I'll bet you," Filben said, "there's not one Irishman in all of Arizona. Our tribe seeks gloomy misery and avoids sunshine and pleasure. If you'd ever visited the Emerald Island, Paddy boy, you would understand. Christ have mercy on that cold, gray lump of rock. It never stops raining there, never. A glimpse of sunshine, why in Ireland, that's a miracle. Equal to the loaves and fishes! It's the climate that made us a cruel people."

Filben shook his head.

"And a corrupt people, Patrick. Once you behold that accursed island, you understand why we're a race of drinkers."

A stray pulse of sunshine flooded Filben's office, and Pat blinked.

"Tell me this," Filben said. "Why in all the world has no Irishman ever emigrated to the Philippines? Is it the sunshine that offends the Irishman? The warm weather? The cheerful natives? By Christ, we find grimy Liverpool attractive enough. We're thrilled to clean the toilets of the hostile Yankees of Boston. We embrace the cockroach slums of the Bronx. And Saint Paul! Christ almighty, how did we discover this igloo? It's the one city in the world with worse weather than Dublin. By Christ, I've half a mind to settle in Manila and start exporting yo-yos. Think of it Patrick, the sunny beaches, the beautiful girls, an Irishman sipping from a sweet coconut instead of a pint of bitter stout."

Filben was beginning to sweat into his starched collar.

"But all you want is one car," he said, and his flush ebbed. "I suppose I can find you one spiffy car. But then I'm out of this game forever, tell Harry that. Don't come around looking for the old Filben, for I'm a new man tomorrow. Enough of these gangsters. Yo-yos, Patrick, yo-yos are the future."

Out on Wabasha Street, Pat wound his wristwatch. It was a gold Longines Harry had given him, traded in by a Chicago gangster in return for a month's protection.

Said watch informed Pat that Opal would be getting off work soon.

The day after Opal quit Harry, she started waiting tables at the Town Talk. Harry had arranged that job for her, imagine that. Harry couldn't help himself, gruff gangster with a big sloppy heart.

Pat waited in the alley beside the Town Talk and when Opal pushed out, he took her arm, hustled along Wabasha, a mad mix of cars, pedestrians, trolleys and even horse-drawn wagons.

HAMM'S

That neon beer sign was like a magnet. Pat opened the grimy door of the Saint Paul Recreation Lounge.

Said lounge was actually a pool hall.

"Is it clean, Patrick?" Opal asked, but stepped in.

Opal, unbuttoning her coat, seemed mesmerized by the Selectophone. She looked tiny before this massive machine. She ran a bright fingernail down the list of song titles. "You got a dime?" she asked Pat.

That was good for two songs. This seemed expensive to Pat, a whole nickel for something invisible that lasted maybe two minutes. The first song Pat had never heard before: *Blame it on My Youth*. As it started playing, Opal said: "They got no dancing in here?"

"Unless you dance on a pool table," Pat said.

He hung up her coat, led her to the bar. Her uniform bore the grease marks of a lunch shift. She ripped a paper napkin from a dispenser, wet it with her tongue, dabbed at her uniform.

A kid bartender seemed irritated by their presence, although he had no other drinkers to take care of.

"A draw for me," said Pat. He flopped his cap on the bar. "Coca-Cola for the lady."

The bartender, an Italian kid, wore white, like he was working a hamburger stand. Bartenders, in Pat's opinion, should never wear white.

"You remind me, kid, so don't remind me," said Pat.

"Huh?"

"Of my humble beginnings," said Pat. "I used to be with the Saints, you know."

Pat looked to Opal for approval, but she only groomed her uniform.

The kid set the beer before Pat, who ducked his head for a look over the rim.

"Bad pour," Pat said.

"What do you want?" said the kid.

"A head," said Pat. "Tilt the glass. Don't you know nothing?"

The kid snatched the glass, poured the beer into the sink.

"Clean glass," said Pat. "Don't use that one."

The kid picked up a clean glass. "I know how to pour beer," he muttered.

"There's three people in this town who know something," Pat said, "and you ain't one of them."

The bartender delivered a beer with a head, and Pat sipped through the foam. "I said Coca-Cola for the lady, didn't you hear me?"

The kid fetched a bottle of Coca-Cola and a glass loaded with ice cubes.

"Some day, kid." Pat fished in his suit-coat pocket for a Lucky and his lighter. "Comes a time when you stop taking orders and start giving 'em. That's when you know you're a man."

"Is that so?" said the kid, lips curled.

Pat tapped his Lucky on the bar. He held that cigarette up, unlit, and stared at it. It seemed important, not just another cigarette. He lit it with his gold-plated lighter, which was shaped like the Statue of Liberty. The flame came out the torch end.

"I got this lighter at the World's Fair," Pat said. "In Chicago."

"Statue of Liberty," said the kid. "Ain't that in New York?

"That don't matter," said Pat. "Chicago. It's a big-time city. I'm going again this summer. Sally Rand, that's what I want to see."

Opal sipped her Coca-Cola. Her head swayed in time to the second song she'd ordered: *Embraceable You.*

"Me, I want to see a Broadway musical," said Opal. "Ginger Rogers, I want to see her dance on stage."

"Who?"

"Don't you go to the movies?" asked Opal.

"Dancing movies?" Pat said. "I ain't got the time." He asked the bartender: "You play ball, kid? I played second base for the Saints, back in '29."

"You did not," Opal challenged him.

"Before your time," Pat insisted.

Opal shook her head with an amused smile.

"I never seen your name in the box scores," she said.

"You want another Hamm's?" asked the barkeep.

Pat hadn't been aware that he'd drained his beer. It had bum-rushed his throat without pestering his taste buds.

"Yeah," said Pat.

As soon as it was delivered, he sucked off the foam, swiveled to face Opal, stared into her blue eyes.

"Opal, it's really swell to look at you."

She cast her eyes down to her greasy uniform.

"You're a married man," Opal muttered.

She rested both elbows on the bar, lips poised above lipstick-marked soda glass.

"I'm scared of you," she said, leaning toward him, eyelids batting.

"Of me?"

Her wide eyes held his, steady. "I kind of like you but I'm scared of your friends. You keep bad company."

Pat realized he'd been breathing heavy. From what? Sitting on a barstool?

"Look, Opal, I mean business. I ain't one of them romantic rubes. I'm a happy married man, my wife, everybody knows her and me. Guys like to look at you, that's all it is. You're cute like a pixie doll. You've got the face I need up front when the rubes walk into my tavern."

"I had my heart set on dancing school," said Opal.

"Great! Nights, you work at my tavern, days you take dance lessons."

"The Green Lantern?" Opal said. "It's such a rough crowd. There's men in there that ..."

"We're going to class the joint up. Harry's got a hostess now, you know Bess, you know how bossy she is. I need new blood.

Think it over. Take all day." He swiveled off that barstool. "I'll be right back."

As he padded toward the restroom he glanced out the big windows and saw Bess. In black coat and high heels, she crossed Wabasha from the streetcar stop.

Pat spun around, rushed the bar, picked up his cap, fished a five-dollar bill from his wallet and threw it toward the bartender.

"Big business," he whispered to Opal. "Be right back."

Pat stumbled onto the street to watch Bess Green duck down Filben's alley. He lit a Lucky and paced amid the streetcar rubes. The Como streetcar went by. The Randolph car screeched to a halt and idled. He glanced backward, worried that Opal, inside the tavern, was amusing herself on his money, playing every dancing song in that record machine. Pat had smoked three Luckies down to their nubs before Bess emerged from Filben's alley.

Pat hailed her underneath the Hamm's sign. She cast him a nasty look.

"Been shopping for a radio?" he said.

She eyed a streetcar like she wanted to hop aboard.

"Or maybe you had another reason to talk to Filben," Pat said.

"I need to catch this streetcar," Bess said.

"You still ain't learned to drive?" Pat called as Bess hustled toward the departing streetcar. Something nagged at him, but he couldn't put words to it.

Was it even possible that Harry might backstab him and give Bess the Green Lantern?

Impossible. The boss of the Green Lantern was the most feared gangster in town. Never in a million years would gangsters take orders from a woman. Never in two million years would a level gangster be caught dead on a streetcar.

Bess swung up on the rear step, lost herself in the crowd

aboard the streetcar. What she was doing downtown was easy to figure. Obviously, Harry wanted Bess to rent an apartment for Saint Johnny Dillinger. So Bess had gone to see Filben, a magician who could conjure up any kind of paperwork, including a fake driver's license. She would rent that apartment under whatever name Filben came up with. The hard thing to understand was: Why hadn't Harry trusted Pat to rent the apartment?

As Pat watched that streetcar roll away he felt betrayed by Harry. It was the worst feeling in the world, the double-cross. It made Pat feel dizzy, like he'd come loose from everything. All those Luckies had left a harsh taste in his mouth and he needed another beer. He walked into the taproom, where Opal, pouty, was working into her coat.

"How about we walk down and get a Coney Dog?"

Opal looked him over. "You shouldn't abandon a girl in a tavern. I look cheap in here all by myself."

"Coney's got private booths," he said. "We could talk better."

He took Opal's arm. He had to admit it wasn't just business, it was kind of a thrill, walking beside a gorgeous young girl. He appealed to the stern judge who ruled his mind's courtroom:

I know what it looks like, Your Honor,
But I swear it was a business deal.

S.D. BANDITS
KIDNAP 4 GIRLS
BANK RAIDERS
USE STOLEN SAINT PAUL AUTO

Using a car stolen in Saint Paul, six machine gun bandits lined up the police chief, a patrolman and 40 others in the Security National Bank, Sioux Falls, S.D., today, looted it of $15,000, kidnapped four girls and one man, critically wounded a motorcycle patrolman and then headed back toward Saint Paul.

One of the bandits closely resembled John Dillinger, witnesses said.

Saint Paul Daily News
March 6, 1934

PATRICK

Pat had been a pin-boy once. Bat boy, pin boy, altar boy, delivery boy, he'd been every kind of boy. So when he edged into the German-American Club, the crash of pins and thud of rolling balls spiked his memory. Pin-boy, Pat had enjoyed. Good tips! But a fella got exhausted, jumping lane to lane, and it was so loud that next morning you answered every question with "huh?"

So Pat had worked his Irish-Catholic connections to become bat boy for the Saints. It was a thrilling promotion. Those boozy rowdy team bus rides were as much fun as the games.

Homer Van Meter was bowling at lane 12, closest to the door. He had not warned Pat about the female. This girl was so small she rolled a child's red 12-pounder. She stood at the foul line watching as the ball thunked down the alley and clipped the 10-pin. She danced back to Van Meter, who sat at the bench, spread-armed, laughing. She play-slapped him.

Van Meter waved Pat in with his long arms, like he was directing a boat into a dock.

"Hey, Mickie," he said to the girl. "Fetch us some fresh beer."

"Well, give me the money," said Mickie. "Stingy."

From his floppy trousers, Van Meter pulled a packet of bills that had a bank wrapper around it. "Don't flirt with the barkeep," he said, and slipped her two fives.

"Little bitch." He watched her trot off in knee sox, short skirt, white blouse. He sighed. "I believe I've found the love of my life."

Pat slipped onto the bench. "I didn't know this was going to be a ladies social," Pat said.

Van Meter cocked his head. "Want to bowl me? Ten cents a pin."

"Um," Pat said.

"You afraid of me, Reilly?"

In a way, Pat was. All the Dillinger gang was red hot now, and that South Dakota bank job had only fanned the flames.

Maybe it was dumb, but Pat was spooked because they looked mismatched sitting together, with Van Meter tall enough to play basketball for the Gophers. Maybe somebody would be staring at them and say hey, the tall goofy guy, I've seen his picture in the Daily News. Pat's gaze fixed on the bleached spot on Van Meter's forearm where a Chicago quack had dulled but not erased the tattooed word HOPE.

Every cop in the country now was looking out for a guy with HOPE on his arm. Except for Saint Paul detectives, they were blind to lots of things.

Pat couldn't stop his legs from twitching. "I just want to get out of here," he said. He peered over his shoulder. He was getting like Harry now, every stranger looked like a Fed.

"Relax," Van said. "Have a beer with us."

Pat's eyes fixed on a bowling bag, dark red leather, set underneath a chair. Van Meter stood, snatched a ball from the return slot, and all gawky limbs, ambled to the foul line. He fired a ferocious rumbling rocket that sent pins flying and endangered some cowering pin boy.

"The pins are like cops," said Van Meter. "You never want to leave one standing." His eyes sparkled as Mickie approached balancing a tray. It held three schooners of beer and a bowl of popcorn.

"That's my girl," said Van, and handed Pat a flat, lifeless Hamm's beer. Hamm's had brewed better beer during Prohibition. Nowadays, they were rushing the brew, and it tasted green.

"Want a tip?" said Van.

"Yeah," said Mickie.

"Nellie Bell in the fourth race."

"Ha ha," said Mickie. "Heard that a million times."

"You ain't heard nothing," said Van. "Hell, you were a five-and-dime girl when I swept you off your feet."

"I was tired. It was the end of a long day."

"Get me a pack of Old Golds."

"What am I, a dog? Fetch this, fetch that."

"I give you two tens," said Van.

"Two fives, asshole."

"Keep the change," Van said. "And take your time. We got men talk here."

Mickie flashed him the middle finger and, slowed by her own defiance, backed toward the concession stand. She taunted Van Meter, cupping hands at ears to mime eavesdropping.

"Crazy about that girl," said Van Meter. "I wanted you to meet her. Ain't she cute and sassy?"

"Is everything set? Because I gotta go."

"Aw, she's all right," said Van Meter.

"This dough is from South Dakota? They'll want to know. They don't want no ransom money mixed in."

Van Meter nodded.

"Pure bank," he said.

"How'd that job go?" asked Pat.

"It went stupid," said Van. "Don't you read the papers? But we got the dough. Little Jimmy went crazy and shot up the town, but we's all right."

By "little Jimmy" he meant Baby Face Nelson, or so the newspapers called him. Little Jimmy was so brave it was stupid, always the first guy to let the bullets fly.

Van Meter gulped beer, snatched popcorn. "Got us a cop. One less prick in the world. Good guys one, cops nothing." He tilted his head and dribbled popcorn into his mouth.

"I'm going," said Pat.

"You just got here."

"If everything's all right, I'm going."

"It's all right, just like I said."

"Then I'm going."

Pat picked up the red bowling bag just as Mickie arrived with a pack of Old Golds.

"Nice to meet you ma'am," said Pat.

"Well you ain't sociable," grumped Mickie.

Pat slunk off. He didn't know Homer Van Meter well enough to trust him. The number one fear of every level gangster was betrayal. The cops weren't smart enough to snag you without help from guys you counted as friends.

Even among guys he trusted, Pat tried to be the least memorable man at any meeting. That habit had so far kept him out of jail, so he wasn't worried about the opinion of this Mickie Conforti, a Chicago five-and-dime girl.

Pat Reilly, was he there?

I can't rightly remember, your honor.

As Pat lugged that bowling bag into the dark cold parking lot, he thought of his mother and father, and what a lifetime in the family laundry had done to them. Washed out! It had killed his old man. Only two fates awaited the Irish: death by drink, death by hard labor.

But maybe there was another way. Since 1900, the O'Connor brothers, God bless them, had showed that Irishmen with wit and courage could run a city from the backroom of a tavern. Politicians and cops begged for an audience like the O'Connors were Twin Irish Popes. Money, that's all it was. The O'Connors proved that a couple of sharp Irishmen could take over a city without firing a shot. When the O'Connors turned senile, it was Harry Sawyer and Big Joe Ryan who took over the grand tradition.

Pat sat behind the wheel of his Essex sucking down deep breaths, that bowling bag on the seat beside him. He'd bought this Terraplane on credit from Filben. It had belonged to one of Harry's errand boys, a guy named Powers, who had disappeared to Cuba. Pat hadn't been crazy about a used car, but the Essex company boasted that its Terraplane could reach 83 miles per hour.

Pat could get only 78, floored. Still, the Terraplane could outrun any police jalopy.

Pat started the car and gunned the engine, his gut gurgling out a warning of backroom police beatings and shackled walks down Leavenworth's corridors. With shaking hands he zipped open the bowling bag and lifted out one bundle of bills wrapped in a white cotton sock. He pinched out a few bills and stuffed them into the pocket of his flannel shirt. He zipped the bag shut, breathing like he'd just run down a dark alley.

Pat opened the bag again and pinched another wad of money.

I needed it to feed my starving family, Your Honor.

He zipped the bag closed and patted it firm. He slipped on leather gloves and motored away from the grimy neighborhood, past brick compounds belonging to Minnesota Mining and Hamm's Brewery. In ten minutes, he arrived at the swell-elegant Rice Park. The park, its fountains dry for the winter, was surrounded by the new library, the opera house, the Wilder Charity Building, the Hotel Saint Paul and the Federal Courthouse. Pat parked in a shadowy alley behind the hotel. It gave him the creeps to do business under the nose of the G-men. He hustled along the alley as fast as he could without looking too guilty.

They were burning the lights late, the G-men men on the second floor.

At the hotel entrance Pat dodged the bell captain and mixed with the crowd: women in furs and swagger suits, and men whose fedoras cost more than Pat's wardrobe. Pat carried that bowling bag nonchalant through the marble lobby, across plush rugs and up fire stairs to the third floor. No guest rooms occupied this floor, only offices with pebbled glass doors. Said offices belonged to lawyers and dentists and accountants and gamblers. This last one, in a dark alcove, had been rented by Big Ryan. In black letters it said on the glass door:

SAINT PAUL PROTECTIVE ASSOCIATION

Pat opened his wallet and removed a brass key. Nobody lurked in the hallway, so he slipped the key into the lock and nudged the door with his foot. Without crossing the threshold, he slid the bowling bag into the dark office, pulled the door shut, locked it, made a quiet exit down the fire stairs.

Somehow, Pat had a thirst for a highball or maybe ten highballs. Deliveries to Big Ryan made him nervous. The danger was getting robbed or losing the bag. That would be your last appearance on this unholy earth until they dragged your bloated corpse out of the Mississippi.

A thousand people claimed to know Big Ryan, but he had no close friends. Harry and Filben and the late Serious Bobby had dealt straight with him, but everybody else kept their distance. Big Ryan rarely appeared at his office. Errand boys brought him cash, which was divided according to a secret formula, among cops, politicians, jailers, judges and prosecutors. Harry was the most important gangster, but still, most of the cash flowed to Big Ryan, who took it in, and dished it out.

Pat pushed through the revolving brass doors of the Grill Room. Oh this was a theater-mad town. The pretty people got plastered at the Grill Room and sometimes you'd even find Hollywood stars in town to flog their latest mule of a movie. Oyster stew and strong cocktails, starlets and stagehands all randy after the play, that was the Grill Room. But any so-called gangsters in here were pretenders who went home to mama at night.

Pat pushed past black curtains that glittered with tiny silvery stars. He took two steps toward the massive oak bar and then stopped. Sitting with her back to him was Dolly, in a lame' dress, talking to some sandy-haired guy in a cream-colored suit. Pat saw her through the haze of cigarette smoke, his heart beating like a racing engine, his lips moving to a tortured language no tongue could speak. His Irish temper was the exact reason he never carried a gun, even on money runs.

Again! Dolly, you two-timing, fat-ass tramp.

His teeth ground in rage and he hustled blind through the revolving doors and whoosh into the cold night.

This is the thanks you get, marrying a Carey. Married by a priest and behaving like a whore! Pat rushed to his Essex and sat behind the wheel. You can't do nothing with beaten-down love, and Pat knew it. You can't drink it to death, cry it out, sing it away, punch it senseless. Maybe you could jump off the Empire State Building but nothing else worked to crush this horrible sick feeling.

Betrayed by the love of his life! Dolly and Pat were meant to be, here on earth and in heaven for eternity, except that Dolly ... Pat dug out a Lucky and lit it with his Statue of Liberty.

He started the Essex. The fan on the dashboard, supposedly a defroster, only drained the battery, so Pat pulled a bandana out of his side pocket. Scattering loose tobacco and small change, he wiped the foggy windows so he could see clear to drive. He was having no fight with Dolly in the Grill Room, where the swells would laugh at him.

He drove down Fort Road, a strip of dive bars, pawnshops and cheap hotels. In the mirror he saw the same car behind him once or twice, it had one flickering headlight. If the Feds were on his tail this would be the prefect rotten ending to an awful night. He made a quick turn and lost that car. He stayed parked for exactly one smoke, rolled down the window, tossed the Lucky, and resumed his journey of anger toward Swede Hollow.

They were renters, the Careys, of the last shabby house on Maria Avenue. Said domicile, clad in asphalt siding, was sagging toward its date with the wrecking ball. One rusty steel chair sat on its peeling porch. Directly across the street was a Lutheran Church, and beyond that a cul-de-sac servicing fine homes at the rocky ravine known as Swede Hollow Park.

No light shone from the Carey house, but his mother-in-law Nora was in there, squirming with the gut-knowledge that Dolly was out late in danger town. Was this what she wanted? A divorced Dolly, playing with strangers?

Pat parked in the moon-shadow of the Lutheran Church, yanked the handbrake, waited. Patience is a virtue, Pat's mother loved to say, although what good came of virtue she never explained. All Pat wanted now was to see Dolly's guilty face and hear bullshit excuses roll off her lying lips.

The moment Dolly sneaked home, Nora would be up in her tattered robe, so Pat readied a barrage of curses. His mother-in-law was always nagging her daughter to find a man, any man but Patrick. We're in love, Pat muttered as if Nora could hear him. We'd work it out if you'd leave us to hell alone.

His worries were interrupted by the shine of a single headlamp. Pat knew what he would see next: the face that wallpapered Hell's waiting room, Inspector James Crumley.

Crumley waddled to the passenger side of Pat's car, and Bulldog McMullen rapped with a heavy ring. Pat cranked the window down.

"Was I speeding, officer?"

"He's a funny guy," said Bulldog over the roof of the car to Crumley.

Crumley, gasping and sweating, plopped himself into the passenger seat. The car springs groaned as the Essex leaned to Crumley's side. His entrance knocked the hat off his head, and he fanned his sweating face with it, although it was near freezing.

"Give the Inspector a fucking heart attack," said the Bulldog, "making us chase you all over town."

Crumley coughed into a handkerchief.

"What the Inspector means to say," McMullen said. "Is we're feeling left out."

He tweaked Pat's ear.

Crumley croaked: "I see the boys brung a piece of change back from South Dakota."

"It's my favorite state," said McMullen. "Especially this time of year. Don't you like it, Jim?"

"I ain't never been there."

"Still, you like it, right?"

McMullen hammered Pat's shoulder. Pat's head filled with squeaky music like from a $5 Philco. His shoulder stung, mule-kicked. Pat had been hit by a line drive once, but McMullen's punch packed more sting.

"Where's our piece?" said Crumley.

"You get yours from Big Ryan," Pat said.

"That's where you're wrong, partner," said Crumley. "We been cut out of the action."

From his overcoat pocket, McMullen drew a dull revolver and handed it to Pat. Too late, Pat realized he should not have touched it.

"Oh, no," said McMullen. "Are we looking at a gun charge, Jim?"

Crumley grabbed the pistol out of Pat's hands, inserted three brassy ammo rounds and said, "Loaded, too."

He twirled the cylinders.

"You know we have to make it safe for the citizens of this fine municipality. Is that how you say it, Bulldog? Mew-nish-aw-pal-it-ee?"

"Nope," said Bulldog. "There's no pal in municipality."

"How do you say it then?"

"Ninety days and a hundred dollar fine."

"That's how you say it," said Crumley. "It's a crime. Deliver a fat bag to Big Ryan and you forget Jimbo and the Bulldog."

Crumley's jowls moved in waves.

"What do you guys want?" asked Pat.

"You know the city don't give us no clothing allowance, now," said Crumley. "We gotta pay out of pocket. New wardrobe, overcoat and all, what's that go for, Bulldog?"

"Hundred bucks easy," said McMullen. "Including shoes."

"Just a couple of bills out of Big Ryan's bag," said Crumley, "that's all it is. He'd never know it was missing."

"I'll see what I can do," said Pat.

"In the meantime, Bulldog, keep that pistol. Take it to Tierney, see if he can find prints on 'er."

"Come on, Reilly," said Bulldog. "How much did you keep for yourself? Anything less than five hundred, you're a sucker."

Pat gripped the steering wheel with both hands and said: "I'll see you boys tomorrow."

"Damn right," said McMullen.

"One way or the other," said Crumley

HOUDINI OF THE OUTLAWS
CONTINUES GAME OF
HIDE AND SEEK WITH OFFICIALS

INDIAN GIRL BILLIE FRECHETTE
IDENTIFIED AS GIRLFRIEND
HER WISCONSIN HOME UNDER WATCH

Saint Paul Daily News
March 10, 1934

BESS GREEN

Bess watched, amused, as Eddie gorged on deep-fried frog legs. Even in dim candlelight, his calloused hands, red knuckles, greasy lips betrayed him as a ruffian. When they'd first met, sled dogs couldn't have dragged him to a candle-lit dinner.

"Not hungry?" Eddie asked.

Before Bess sat a Caesar salad, barely ruffled. In Bess's business, a girl needed her figure, and anyway, she got self-righteous satisfaction from watching a caveman turn his dinner into a pile of bones.

Sam Tanaka wheeled a stainless-steel dessert cart to their table. "Something wrong with your salad, Mrs. Green?"

"No, Sam, please pack it up for me," said Bess.

Sam, like all Hollyhocks waiters, was entombed in a tuxedo. He set the salad on the cart, whisked away Eddie's frog bones and potato skins. He lay a long-stemmed, thorny yellow rose across the white tablecloth.

"Dessert will be courtesy of Mister Peifer."

"Just coffee, please, Sam," said Bess.

"I heard about your bread pudding," said Eddie, wiping his lips with a napkin. He was cute in that moment, Bess thought, with curly dark hair, eyes shining like a dog's in hopes of a treat. Bess could only love a man she pitied, and she was beginning to fall for Eddie.

Sam poured coffee from a graceful silver pot, served Eddie bread pudding in a chalice of cut glass, then retreated.

Bess held Eddie's rough hands, stared into his eyes. Although a born criminal, his eyes reflected a basic decency, a contradiction she could not explain. He was a laid-off iron worker, a miracle mechanic who could fix anything. He only needed that job for appearances, anyway. He had hot money stashed all over town. In Bess's future, there was a place for a man like that.

But he was reckless in his choice of friends.

"Eddie, those hillbillies ..."

She meant the Barker-Karpis Gang, but these days, it was wiser to keep their names off your lips.

"They're gone," said Eddie.

"They'll be back," said Beth.

He scooped pudding with a silver spoon. "Fred treated me level," he said.

Eddie had lapses in judgment, which was why he needed Bess. The spooky eyes of Karpis, the drunken vacancy of Doc, the dangerous mama's boy Freddie — didn't that hillbilly gang give Eddie the creeps? My god, those vicious punks left men bleeding on the sidewalk, burned women in their cars. Eddie was just a jug marker until Fred Barker thrust a tommy gun into his hands.

"I've got a plan," began Bess, but Sam Tanaka slapped six casino chips on the tablecloth.

"Good luck from Mister Peifer," Sam said.

Eddie snatched the chips and stood up. His tie was askew, his coat flung open, no suit fit him gracefully.

Bess shook her head.

"What?" said Eddie.

Bess sighed. Eddie could not recognize a sucker game. Sure, $6 in chips to lure you upstairs, where you'd lose everything in your wallet.

But Eddie needed action. The man could not sit still. So Bess followed him up a wide staircase. They entered a smoky room, gamblers crowded around tables for craps, blackjack, poker and a whirling roulette wheel. The crowd included quite a few of the alleged civic leaders of Minneapolis and Saint Paul, and their alleged wives, too. Losing money in a gangster casino apparently gave them the illusion that they were living dangerously.

Eddie stood at the craps table, working the chips in his hands, staring at tumbling dice as if he could divine the secrets of the great god Chance.

Bess scanned the room for the king, Jack Peifer, and his queen, Violet. Jack was a stocky man past forty with greasy black hair, pale skin and penetrating dark eyes. Violet was much younger, a Scandinavian beauty, built like a tennis player, with short blonde hair and blue eyes. He wore a tux, she a sleeveless shimmering gown. Bess wriggled through the smoky crowd to reach them.

Violet averted her eyes.

"My but you do look fabulous," said Jack, taking Bess's hands.

"Your husband," Bess said to Violet, "is so full of it."

Violet parceled out a smile.

"Can I see you in my office?" asked Jack. "I've got something for you."

Bess rolled her eyes at Violet and followed Jack into a back room. It featured a cigarette-scarred wooden desk, a huge iron wall safe and a sleepy Rottweiler chained to the desk.

Jack sat at his desk, braced his hands behind his head, a man about to divulge a secret.

"How's Harry?" he asked. "Want a drink?"

"No thank you," said Beth.

"Mind if I do?"

From a desk drawer Jack fetched a glass and a bottle of no-label whiskey. He poured a heavy shot and examined the amber liquid in the light of a brass desk lamp.

"I can tell if it's been cut just by looking," he said.

Bess believed that. Jack had made a fortune diluting good liquor.

"Dillinger," he said.

"What about him?"

"Hunch," said Jack.

"Do you know something?"

"Me?" Jack sipped whiskey. "Nah. But let's say a certain guy pulls in from Indiana. He's your basic tourist. Doesn't know the territory, needs a local jug marker ..."

"Eddie's staying away from those guys."

"No matter who marks the bank," Jack said, "they'll need a laundry. I'd rather it be me than Harry."

"Noted," said Bess. Now she realized what those casino chips were about: Peifer wanted her to carry a message to the Dillinger gang.

"You go broke selling steaks and salads," Jack said. "Say, I'm hearing bad things about Harry."

"Such as?"

"Maybe he's disappeared."

"Oh, he's around."

"Do tell."

"I catch a glimpse of the great man now and then."

"You know what friends we are, him and me," said Jack.

Bitter rivals, Bess supplied, but only in her head.

"Just when this town cooled off," said Jack, "he pulls this stunt."

Jack meant the kidnapping, two months back, of a millionaire banker. The family, it turned out, were financial supporters of President Roosevelt. It was the dumbest crime Bess had ever heard of, kidnapping the son of the President's friend. Now there were so many G-men, lawyers and newsmen in town, you could hardly get a hotel room.

Bess and Jack both knew a secret that J. Edgar Hoover was furious to uncover: Harry Sawyer had arranged that kidnapping, and the Barker-Karpis gang had pulled it off.

"I'd like to talk some sense into Harry," Jack said.

By which he meant ...

The Rottweiler alerted, dragging her chain toward the door. Jack put a finger to his lips. G-men had tapped the Hollyhock's phone, or so Jack had been informed by his courthouse sources. Suzy the lazy Rottweiler lived in this office so no G-men could sneak in to bug it.

Whoever was out there moved down the hall, and Suzy relaxed, chain clanking.

"I've driven by the house," whispered Jack. "No Harry. He's moved to the farm?"

Bess ran her hand through her hair. "I don't know what the Sawyers do, Jack, they don't consult me."

Jack aimed a pack of Chesterfields toward Bess. "Smoke?"

"I'm trying to quit," said Bess.

"I always considered you and me to be great friends," lied Jack.

"So have I," Bess lied.

Nobody knew for sure, but it was probably Jack who conspired with the Barker-Karpis gang to burn up two women snitches in a car. That was, oh, two years ago. Bess had once chatted with these women at the Green Lantern. She could hazily recall them: a chubby Indian and a skinny Jewish girl. But her most potent memory was a Daily News photo of the women's corpses, burnt to cinders.

Jack wedged his feet against the desk and tugged at his black boots.

"I could be looking for a hostess."

"You can't do better than Violet."

Jack grimaced. He rose from his chair, twisted open the blinds to reveal a night view: streetlamps, bare trees, the long black void of the Mississippi.

"She loves me," Jack muttered to his reflection in the window. "She hates my business."

Or maybe it's just the opposite, Bess thought.

"You've got to convince Harry to blow town," Jack said. "The kidnapping, it's causing all this Federal noise."

Bess shrugged. "I'm supposed to tell Harry to beat it?"

"You're a clever woman," Jack said. "I've always admired your class and brains."

Jack slid open a desk drawer and brought out a small revolver, stainless steel with a white grip and hidden hammer. He opened the chamber and spun it.

"Don't you feel it?" Jack asked.

Bess swallowed. "Feel what, Jack?"

"The heat."

A knock came at the door. Jack slid the pistol into his suit-coat pocket. The dog barely looked up from her snooze.

Eddie stuck his head in.

"You kids having fun?"

"I'm sending you away ..." Jack said, and from behind his desk grabbed a liter of champagne. " ... with a token of my esteem." He handed Eddie the bottle. "And my wishes for an early spring."

"Gee, thanks Jack," said Eddie. He squatted to pet Suzy, who submitted sweetly.

Jack escorted Eddie and Bess to the casino staircase. Jack was waylaid by Saph, his punch-drunk bartender. Eddie and Bess descended to the porch, where, in summer, diners might admire the mighty river. But it was frosty on spring nights, and Eddie and Bess shivered alone, hidden in the gray shadows. Eddie popped the champagne cork, sipped the bubbly overflow, handed the dripping bottle to Bess.

She poured the champagne over the railing.

"What the hell's wrong with you?" said Eddie. "That's good champagne."

Bess tossed the empty bottle into a remnant snow bank.

"Eddie, these gangsters are no good for you."

"It's a bottle of fucking champagne," said Eddie.

"Harry Sawyer," Bess said, "is giving me the Green Lantern."

"What do you mean *giving* you the Green Lantern?"

"He can't operate there any more. Ever since that kidnapping, the Lantern is swarming with Feds."

"So why would he give it to you?"

"Ten percent kickback."

She dug into her purse. From a crumpled pack of Viceroys she drew one last cigarette. Eddie lit it, match flame steady.

"What about Reilly?" he said. "I thought Pat was his, what do you call it, heir."

"Pat will never be another Harry." Bess grimaced against harsh smoke. "Pat will be taken care of in other ways."

"What the hell do you mean by that?"

"Maybe he can tend bar on weekends. We'll run the place right, Eddie, you and me. Bootlegging's over, even if half the characters in this town can't admit it. We'll run it swell, no sporting girls, no gambling. That gives the cops nothing to get their greedy hands on. We'll take a lesson from Jack and run a class joint. Steak and oysters and high-class booze. I want you to be my partner."

"Partner?"

"I'll need a tough guy." She draped her arm around Eddie. "You're my tough guy, aren't you?"

DILLINGER BELIEVED TRAPPED
IN PORT HURON, MICH.

Saint Paul Daily News
March 16, 1934

BESS

When the streetcar squeaked to a stop at Cretin-Derham Catholic School, Bess stepped off. Parked just up Randolph Street was a green four-door Studebaker, washed and polished at Herb's Garage. Bess passed it with a pat on its gleaming fender. Gangster life could be good. She admired Tommy Filben, thief that he was. He delivered a beautiful vehicle every time.

Outside the brick school lay a baseball field surrounded by a black iron fence. Bess gripped the cold bars and looked past a flabby coach, who was batting out fungoes. Her eyes focused on Lincoln, who slumped on a green wooden bench. It stabbed Bess's heart to see her virile son reduced to a spectator in uniform. He'd been a star first baseman, his dreams fixed on the Gashouse Gang, aka the Saint Louis Cardinals. But a collision at home plate, and a swollen knee, had benched him for his senior season.

She waved. He looked away. His mother embarrassed him.

Linc, glove tucked under his arm, slapped hands with his teammates. Shoeless and wearing sanitary stockings, he limped across a field of dormant grass, just emerged from snow.

He was lanky, like Bess, with red hair, like Bess, and a bad attitude, like Bess. Lincoln, born during his father's brief employment as an auto salesman, had been named after the car, not the president. Bess had insisted on James for a middle name, since Catholic children deserved a saint's protection.

Lincoln was no saint. At thirteen he started running with Payne Avenue punks, drinking, stealing bikes, shoplifting, breaking into garages. Every time the cops brought him home, Bess plunged into a sick despair. But Lincoln quit that gang once he'd made the team at Cretin-Derham, the state's prestige baseball high school.

Bess stood beside the Studebaker, dangling keys.

"Fancy car," Linc said. "Who'd you steal it from?"

"You are hilarious," Bess said. "It's cold. Where's your jacket?"

"None of your business."

"Drive," she said.

Linc fired up the Studebaker. Bess turned on the radio, hoping for jive music. Half the reason she worked in nightclubs was her love of this low-down, joyful music. Bennie Moten! His music proclaimed: *We don't care what respectable people think, we're having fun.* She would be first in line if he ever played the Boulevards.

"What else can you pull in?" Linc twisted the dial. "The Cubs?"

Had he been any other man, she would have slapped his hand away from the dial. As the engine warmed up, he reached into a rear pocket, pulled out a tin of Red Man.

"No chewing in this car."

"Ma, you're living in the dinosaur days."

"Dinosaurs chewed tobacco?"

Linc slipped a pinch of tobacco under his lip.

"Where's supper?"

"Lindstrom's," said Bess.

"Fish?"

"It's Lent, remember?"

"So now you're holy?"

"Yes. Yes I am. I'm your holy mother, and I have good news. I talked to Father Mack ..."

Linc groaned.

"Father Mack can pull strings at Saint Thomas."

"Ma, why is it always pulling strings?"

"Because, Einstein, you don't have the grades to get in."

"If I can't get in on my baseball," he said, "I'm not going."

"There's nothing wrong with having a priest speak up for you."

"Father Mack? He's just off the boat."

"Well, you're part Irish too, so ..."

"Yeah, way back."

"I know, in the dinosaur days. Look, honey, I need to make a stop first. I'll only be gone a couple of minutes."

"That's what you always say."

This mild rebuke, hinting at a deeper neglect, wounded Bess. For male leadership, Linc had seen only weakness. When his father realized it wouldn't be a hoot to raise a child, he left for Los Angeles. Then a couple of bootlegger "uncles" turned out to be rats. Then Robert, who spent like a banker and earned like a newsboy. Then came Eddie, whom Linc despised. Linc's hero was Ducky Medwick, baseball star, and Eddie was ... well, short, not exactly handsome, a bad dresser with no social graces.

Eddie was an energetic lover, a shrewd and daring gangster, and had money stashed all over town, but none of that was any business of Lincoln's.

Bess had worked long hours and late nights during Linc's childhood. She rarely prepared a home cooked meal. Linc had been raised with the help of baby sitters and aunts, and lived with an aunt now. Her neglect of this boy now caused her flushes of shame. But she was only 17 when he was born. She had chosen the the exciting life of a speakeasy flapper over the dull duties of motherhood. Was it too late to repair that damage?

"All the way down the avenue, please," she said.

"Where to?"

"You'll see."

Linc sped down Summit, Saint Paul's fanciest avenue. Its elms and oaks were bare, its mansions set behind broad lawns framed by crusts of snow. Linc lowered the window and spit tobacco juice. Was this contempt meant for her, or for the poo-bahs who ran this corrupt little city?

"Eddie stole this car, didn't he?" Linc accused her.

"It's *borrowed.*"

Where Summit Avenue ended, at the Mississippi River, Saint Thomas College rose in red brick buildings set on frosty lawns.

"Okay, Ma, I get it."

"Take a good look. You'll be here for four years." She pointed. "Maybe that will be your dorm room."

"I don't know, college? If I don't make it in baseball, maybe I want to be a cop."

"A policeman? Over my dead body."

"Law and order, ma."

"An ignorant, rotten policeman? You're saying this to shock me, aren't you?"

"And all your shady friends."

"Okay, wisenheimer, turn around. Lexington and Grand. And since you're going to be a cop, I expect you to stay well under the speed limit."

After enduring two miles of rude silence and purposefully reckless driving, Bess said: "Park here please."

Linc steered the Studebaker rumbling across cobblestones and streetcar tracks. When he parked and cut the engine, Bess handed him two dimes. "Buy a soda. Play pinball. I'll be back as soon as I can."

"Bribery, ma. I'm not even a cop yet, and already you're

bribing me."

She sighed. "Lincoln, it's not a world of baseball heroes and cute girls, as you seem to imagine. It's a jungle full of gorillas who'll do anything to survive. I have to live in that jungle."

"That's your excuse, mom?"

"And that's the reason you need an education, okay? We don't need another gorilla in the jungle."

He made kissy lips to taunt her, eased out of the Studebaker, and slammed the door.

She watched him saunter down the street, and it seemed even his leisurely pace was defiant. He opened the glass door of Grand Rexall Drugs. Linc the ballplayer had become diet conscious, and had switched vices, from beer to pinball machines. What was it about men? Sex, games, drink. That was all they cared about.

She had a shameless crush on her own son, six foot three, shaggy hair, engaging when he wanted to be, sullen the rest of the time, a wild boy, a tease, but never vicious. Bess would throw herself in front of a speeding locomotive if it would save him.

Imagine, the son of a speakeasy flapper, graduating from Saint Thomas College.

Bess reached into her black leather shoulder-bag and fumbled for her wedding ring. She hadn't worn it since Linc's father booked the sleeper for the Coast. She wedged it on, not quite the skinny teenager who'd married the old con man. She let herself out of the Studebaker, careful to lock it in a town full of thieves.

She lit a cigarette, needing this one last smoke to calm her nerves. Dodging a streetcar, she crossed Grand Avenue. She buttoned her coat. Saint Paul was warm only in the sunshine at this time of year.

She strode with purpose. What Harry wanted, Harry got.

From Harry flowed the dark money and secret favors that had run this town for years. How could she refuse him and expect to take over the Green Lantern?

Bess paused before a fine brick building. A sign pounded into dead grass announced:

LUXURY APARTMENTS. INQUIRE WITHIN.

Someone had inked in the words:

Now Furnished.

She squashed the burning cigarette underneath her high heel shoe. A middle-aged landlady answered her knock at the office. The woman had dull, frizzy hair and gray eyes, wore a starched white blouse and prim skirt.

Her voice rasped with irritation: "How can I help you?"

"I called about the apartment. I'm Mrs. Carl Hellman."

Bess reached into her shoulder-bag for the fake driver's license. Filben had bought it through his statehouse sources. It gave her name as Elizabeth Hellman, with the address of a vaudeville theater downtown.

The license had cost $50, wasted, because this landlady barely glanced at it. She reached for a pegboard where keys hung from brass hooks. She selected a key and led Bess over a black-and-white tiled floor and up the stairway to the third landing.

"Nothing's available on the ground floor?" Bess asked.

The landlady opened an apartment door and stood aside like a soldier at attention. Bess entered a sunny, well-furnished parlor with gleaming parquet floors. Good, the wood floors. Bad, an upper story. Bess walked toward the steaming radiators and the windows. They overlooked Lexington and Grand, with its classy shops and cafes.

"Living room, bedroom, kitchen-dinette," the landlady said and folded her arms. "How many are you, Mrs. Hellman?"

"Pardon?"

"How many people?"

"Just my husband and myself."

Bess glanced into the bedroom, where an iron bedstead held a bare mattress and two striped pillows.

"It is completely furnished," the landlady announced. "Everything but linens."

Bess noted a dark vanity with a big mirror, a deep closet, and a wall hung with two framed Norman Rockwell magazine covers: ice skaters; a boy fishing. She pushed through a swinging door and into the kitchen-dinette, which featured a gas cooking range, modern refrigerator, Formica table with four yellow-padded chairs, and white-painted steel cabinets.

"Pots, pans, utensils included," said the landlady.

The kitchen windows looked across a courtyard into another apartment. That wasn't ideal for privacy, but Bess couldn't imagine Dillinger spending much time in the kitchen.

"What does your husband do?" the landlady inquired.

"He is in the steel business."

"The what business?"

"Iron and steel" said Bess, louder.

"I see," said the landlady. "This apartment is not suitable for children."

"No children," said Bess.

"Do you have children Mrs. ... what was your name?"

"Hellman. No. No children." She felt like a fraud, denying not only herself but her son.

"Good," the landlady said. "Because we don't allow them." Now her frost melted to mere slush. "I am Mrs. Daisy Coffey, owner."

"You don't have anything on the first floor?" Bess asked.

Mrs. Coffey rattled her keys. "Sixty dollars a month," she said. "Steam heat and hot water included. Tenant pays electric, and phone, if he wants a phone." She cleared her throat. "We're not stingy, as you can see, with the heat."

"But nothing on the first floor?"

"Oh my dear, those are more expensive. I don't think we have any salesmen on the first floor. We have a dentist, an accountant ... professional people."

"But do you have an apartment available down there?"

"Where?"

"Downstairs. My husband makes an excellent income."

"Where did you say you were from?"

"Originally? St. Louis."

"Ah. I've a cousin down there. What part of St. Louis?"

"Near the river. Mrs. Coffey, do you or don't you have apartments on the first floor?"

"Of course we do."

"Are any available right now?"

"Not until May."

As Bess retreated to the living room, she spotted a handle built into the wall. She pulled down a Murphy bed, all platform, no mattress.

"We'll want the mattress," Bess said.

"You did say there were only two of you."

"Yes, but we might have guests."

"Well, I would have to order that mattress from Minneapolis."

"I really would like to have it. Surely if you ordered it today they could deliver it tomorrow."

"Hmph," the landlady said.

Bess followed her down the stairs, through the lobby and into the damp basement office. Mrs. Coffey sat behind a desk. Rising from its clutter: a flagpole bearing a starched Stars and

Stripes. As Mrs. Coffey rolled rental forms into a typewriter, Bess spied the afternoon's Dispatch on her desk.

CHICAGO COPS CLOSE NET ON DILLINGER

A few months ago, nobody in Saint Paul knew Dillinger from Douglas Fairbanks. Now he was getting front-page coverage any Hollywood star would envy. Bess had kept company with hoodlums, gangsters, bootleggers and fixers for years, and had never seen anything like it. She had never met Dillinger nor his suddenly infamous girlfriend Billie. But the hysteria that surrounded them filled her with swirling dark feelings.

One thing she knew: The Chicago cops were wasting their time. The Houdini of Outlaws was working his magic in Harry's territory now. Like the Barker Gang before them, the Dillinger Gang would pay ten percent of its haul to Harry, who would arrange for police protection.

Mrs. Coffey's typewriter tapping ceased.

"We don't allow parties. You're not party people are you?"

"Of course not," said Bess.

But Eddie, Bess suspected, would not be able to resist the Dillinger gang. When those mad-dog Barker boys and their creepy friend Karpis had blown town, it was like getting rid of the plague. That relief lasted but a week, and now who shows up but Dillinger?

Mrs. Coffey proofread the rental agreement under lamplight, then pushed it forward.

Bess signed in a shaky hand.

"Are you feeling all right Mrs. Hellman?"

ALL SAINT PAUL JOINS IRISH
TO CELEBRATE FETE
OF ST. PATRICK.

ALL GIVEN 24-HOUR RELEASE
FROM LENTEN RESTRICTIONS

POLICE SCORE ZERO IN
ROUNDUP OF GANGSTERS

Saint Paul Daily News
March 17, 1934

Saint Patrick's Day, Saturday, March 17, 1934

PATRICK

Pat reminded himself he didn't own this tavern ... yet ... as he nailed a huge paper shamrock to the door. Harry hated Saint Patrick's Day. Every March 17th, when the crowd got unruly, Harry would clear the tavern, leaving green-clad revelers shivering out on Wabasha Street. Although he was master of the police force, Harry, strangely enough, feared a cop raid more than anything.

By nailing up this shamrock, Pat felt he was restoring this tavern to its Irish origins. Dapper Dan Hogan, its founding genius, might be paroled from Hell today, in honor of the Irish rebirth of the Green Lantern. By the grace of Saint Patrick, Danny Boy's legs might be restored to him, poor fella, imagine: a belly full of breakfast, a turn of the car key, and boom, separated from his legs and this world by a cowardly bomber.

Many suspected Harry of hiring the bomber who blasted Dapper Dan to Kingdom Come. Pat wasn't among them. There was only one crime in Harry's world: disloyalty. If you turned stool pigeon, Harry would arrange for you to be shot, like a man ought to be, with a memorial drink for your friends afterwards at the

Green Lantern.

Pat carried hammer and a paper bag of nails into the back office. Here sat Harry's most potent weapon, an adding machine, along with a two-ton safe and two black telephones. One of those phones had a number secret from even the cops, thanks to a payoff at Western Telephone.

The newest item in that office was a golf bag Johnny D had left at Harry's farm. It held golf clubs, all right, along with two Remington Model 8 rifles. These were apparently Dillinger's backup weapons, and Pat was to hold them in case of emergency.

A lot of times, a guy in Pat's position, you had to know what to do. Harry wasn't going to explain. That's why Pat had risen in Harry's esteem. He knew what to do without being told.

Pat locked the office and peeked into the kitchen, where Lillian was boiling vats of aromatic corned beef and cabbage. Pete, the chef and a one-legged refugee from the Great War, had refused on French principle to boil beef. Wouldn't Saint Paddy's celebrants be surprised to learn that their Irish feast had been cooked by a Colored woman?

Pat felt as ready as could be for Saint Paddy's, with Bess signed on for fourteen hours in the dining room, Lillian in charge of the kitchen, and Jackie Gannon and two cousins coming in special to mix drinks and pour beer.

Pat let himself out the front door and locked it. The Green Lantern would be closed until after the parade. He would sell a drink to no man who hadn't marched to honor Ireland's greatest saint.

Pat drove his Essex toward the Capitol, the bleached edifice that blocked sunlight from his neighborhood. Saint Paul's greatest buildings, Capitol and Cathedral, were built on adjacent hills, like two glaring hockey players at face-off.

When the road got clogged with parade traffic, Pat parked on a rooming house lawn. That was okay since any ticket he got could be cheaply fixed. He hustled through a mob of people dressed in fool's green. He was dressed respectfully, like a businessman, in gray suit, white shirt, and tasteful kelly-green necktie.

Saint Patrick had granted this crowd a fine day worthy of Ireland itself, fifty degrees and misty with passing sunshine. Pat climbed the Cathedral steps, and heard organ music leaking out of high Mass.

Dreadful!

As an altar boy, he had acquired a hatred for ritual. All he could remember from his altar boy days was muffing the Latin, and earning glaring rebukes from the priest.

"Christ almighty," called Tom Filben from atop the Cathedral's stone steps. "The prodigal son returns."

Pat shook Filben's hand.

Filben, whose usual wardrobe covered the spectrum from white to beige, today dressed in top hat and black tuxedo. A green carnation was pinned to the lapel.

"I don't suppose you're marching," Filben said.

"I do suppose," said Pat.

"Then you honor your name saint. It's a proud thing to be Irish, Patrick. We belong to the most intelligent race God ever placed upon this sorry and suffering earth. By Christ, did you know an Irishman invented the wireless, only to have an Eye-Talian steal it?"

Pat stood beside Filben and watched the assembling crowd.

"Marconi was merely a simpering in-law of the great Guinness clan," Filben claimed. "Aye, it was Arthur Guinness himself who put up the money to develop that infernal device. Patrick, we're a wonderful people for inventions, if we'd ever get any credit for it."

The Schmidts Brewery had sent a horse-drawn wagon filled with beer kegs to lead the parade. The red wagon was papered over in green, as if Schmidts' owners were Irish and not a bunch of

Kaiser-saluting Germans.

On the road between Cathedral and Chancery, men in top hats, along with baton-twirling colleens, gathered at the Holy Name Society float. It featured a statue of Jesus anchored in a truck bed of hay. Jesus held up two fingers, like He was ordering a couple of beers.

"You're chummy with Big Ryan," Pat said. "I know you fellas own lake property up north. Good fishing, I heard."

"And what are you fishing for, Patrick?"

"Big Ryan should know that Crumley and McMullen are working their own game. With Harry retiring, they figure they can make a dope out of me."

Filben sighed and tipped back his top hat. From an inside pocket he produced a white meerschaum pipe, carved into the figure of a man's head. It was packed with half-burnt tobacco. Filben re-lit it.

"Patrick, you're a god-fearing ... " He blew a smoke ring ... "dead-earnest Irishman, so take advice from your Uncle Tommy. Avoid like the plague the intrigues of the Saint Paul Police."

"They came to me. I didn't go to them."

"Regardless. Crumley should avoid challenging Big Ryan. Greed and gluttony, Patrick, only lead to damnation."

Filben blew a puff of smoke out of the bowl of his pipe.

"Now McMullen, he's another one. Never trust an ex-pug Patrick, they've had their brains scrambled. I shouldn't be surprised if the Bulldog sends love notes to Big Ryan, chapter and verse on the doings of his supposed friend, Inspector James P. Crumley. Oh, the treachery! Which is why I advise you, Patrick: Scoundrels with badges are to be avoided entirely."

Men from the Teamsters Union guided a grocery truck into the parade line and Filben flashed them a look of contempt.

"There's nothing worse than an Irishman in a labor union, Patrick. Hard work is what's kept us down all these years. Why glorify wage slavery? You know how these Protestants think. Christ almighty! If you can't afford a mule, get an Irishman."

Pat started to respond but Filben held up his hand. "Big Ryan is a necessary evil, Patrick. I go fishing with the man on occasion, as you may have heard. He's a greedy fisherman, I can tell you that. Never throws one back. The tragic history of Ireland informs us, Patrick, that the greedy and ruthless run this world and always will."

So Filben ... Pat tried to dope it out ... Filben was fishing buddies with Big Ryan. Filben and Big Ryan were partners in lakefront property, and God knows how many other investments. Slot machines? Nightclubs? Did Filben help Big Ryan run the Saint Paul Protective Association? What kind of man was Filben? Slippery. Yet Filben was somebody in this town. Filben, who never worked an honest hour, had so much dough he gave it away.

"Big Ryan," Filben said, "at least he's one of us. Without the likes of him, we'd be bullied from that Capitol. Behold that monstrosity, Patrick, squirming with Scandinavians, Free-Thinkers, Lutherans and Communists. Christ almighty, they'd reduce us Hibernians to potato peasants."

"So what do I do about Crumley and McMullen?"

Filben stared at his pipe, which had gone cold. With a glance over his shoulder he saw the parade was starting. He tapped Pat on the shoulders with his baton, as if he were bestowing knighthood.

"Rogue cops never double crossed Harry, and do you know why?"

Pat shrugged.

"Remember Blinky Wong, the Chinese cop?"

"Worked out of Rondo," Pat said. "Horse patrol."

"Whatever happened to Blinky Wong?" Filben asked.

"Killed himself."

"Did he now?" Filben asked.

He rapped his baton three times on the Cathedral's stone

steps.

"And what event transpired before he killed himself? Don't strain the mental apparatus, Patrick, allow me. Blinky collected police tribute from the Negro speakeasies until December, 1929, when he claimed to have been robbed of his collections while on the way to pay off Harry. On Christmas Eve..." Filben put a gun finger to his head ... "boom.

"Coincidence? Perhaps. And let's consider Mick Powers, who ran rum and favors for Harry for a decade. Then Mick was seen exiting the private quarters of Harry's main rival, Master Jack Peifer. Poor Mick! He hasn't been seen for months now."

"Powers is in Cuba."

Filben laughed.

"So they would have you believe, Patrick. If Powers is in Cuba, it's because his corpse floated down the Mississippi and across the Gulf of Mexico."

Filben shrugged. "It doesn't matter who committed any of those atrocities. What matters is that people *believe* Harry was behind them. Belief generates fear. Fear of crossing Harry. A fear, Patrick ..."

He poked Pat with his baton.

"No one fears you, Patrick, and that's your trouble exactly. They think the world of you, they'll buy you a thousand beers, they'll slap you on the back, they'll tip you off on a horse race, but they don't fear you and they never will."

Pat puffed up. "Okay, I ain't never been the schoolyard bully but ..."

"Patrick, we may fool others but we must never fool ourselves. Ask yourself: Do you have the cold, stony heart to murder a man who has three little children? To place a bomb in a rival's car? To send assassins after a policeman on Christmas Eve? That's what it takes to be head gangster in this town. If you can do such ruthless things, you're Harry's true heir. And if not ..."

Filben's face took on the look of a man watching a sad movie. "Don't allow your fondness for Harry to persuade you that he is a benign ruler, Patrick."

Pat shoved his hands in his pockets and looked at his shiny shoes, thinking maybe Filben had scored half a point.

"Excuse me," Filben said. "I'm to be conveyed by float, which happens to be filled with young colleens."

Pat followed him down the stone steps and toward the parade floats. Over his shoulder, Filben said: "Patrick, just march in the parade, me boy. You don't need to be the Grand Marshal, just march along and enjoy the parade while it lasts."

Pat stood at the curb as Filben clambered aboard the Hibernian Twirlers float. Someone blew a whistle and Filben, a great smile on his face, put his arm around a pretty, green-clad girl.

GOOD FRIDAY MARKED BY CHURCH SERVICES AND SKIING

LATE WINTER SNOWFALL, TWO DAYS BEFORE EASTER

Saint Paul Daily News
March 30, 1934

BESS

Bess held a tommy gun by its barrel, as if it were a stinking dead musky.

"Imagine I'm a policeman, Eddie."

Behind her was her bedroom, scattered with cardboard boxes and suitcases.

"That braggart is going to lead the G-men right to our door. We are moving. With or without your help. I've signed the papers."

"Where?"

"Marshall Street," said Bess. "It's not as nice, but ... " She handed Eddie the tommy gun. "Try not to shoot anybody."

"Ah," Eddie said. "The artillery is strictly to scare the rubes. You spray the street, they run like hell. You grab the money and get away clean."

Eddie lay the tommy gun on the coffee table. "What has you all riled up?"

"Eddie, read the papers. There are 20,000 cops looking for this man. Every theater shows a newsreel warning people to watch out for him. How long before they find him?"

Eddie parted the window blinds to peer out. He wore a

sleeveless t-shirt, fine worsted trousers and was barefoot.

Bess sat on the couch, tore open a carton of Raleighs.

"I thought you were quitting," said Eddie.

"I need the coupons," she said. "I've got my eye on a lamp."

"I'll buy you a lamp if you quit. Ashes all over the house."

"I'll get my own lamp," said Bess, her lips around a cigarette. "With coupons."

"What do they drive," asked Eddie, "a Hudson, right?"

Bess blew smoke. "What happens when they trace Dillinger to this apartment? Federal prison, that's what happens. They just opened a new one, Eddie, in California. It's on an island. Surrounded by sharks."

Eddie waved that off. "Yeah, I heard."

"Every dollar we've got can be traced to a bank job."

"Here they come," said Eddie. It was gray skies and swirling snow outside. Eddie had turned the radiator cocks to full open, explaining that their honored guest had been in prison, and now got the chills easy. Eddie said he wouldn't be surprised if the Dillinger gang someday retired to a warmer place, like Florida. From the closet he selected a Hawaiian shirt, sky blue with palm trees.

Bess encircled him with her long arms. He was short but solid with the honest muscles of an ironworker.

"You promised, Eddie. No more banks."

He lifted her hands, kissed them, escaped her embrace. "Bessie, I hate to bust your dream. But gangsters ain't gonna what you call, patronize, a tavern owned by a woman. They don't trust women. Women talk too easy."

"We won't be running a gangster tavern. Gangsters are finished. I want swells."

High heels sounded on the back stairs. Bess eased open the door and a woman slipped through. She held up two greasy white bags. "Surprise!" she said. Bess closed the door behind her.

"Chinese food!" the woman said.

This was Bess's first look at Billie, she of sudden fame. What a disappointment! Mother Infamy had chosen a dumpy Indian woman who wore exquisite clothes without grace, whose face was a minefield of acne, whose hair was coarse, whose voice was squeaky and harsh. Her eyes were striking, though: soft, warm, beautiful, all-consuming. Little Johnny had grown up without a mother. Now, Bess suspected, he had found his warm-eyed mama at last.

Billie plopped the greasy bags on the dining table, strode to the window, flashed the blinds.

"He's a little slow since he took a bullet," said Billie. She sighed. She was jeweled up with a pearl necklace and three diamond rings. Her dark blue dress, flecked with tiny stars, extended to mid-calf to hide chunky legs.

Bess sniffed at the bags. She had set out the good China, resurrected the silverware out of its velvet coffin, tent-folded the linen napkins, and for this?

"One's chop suey, the other's chow mein," said Billie. "Don't you just fucking love Chinese food?"

"It gives me the hives," said Bess.

"Oh cocksucker," said Billie. "I didn't know. John wanted to bring steak. But there's not one steakhouse open on Good fucking Friday."

"I'm not hungry," Bess said. "But Eddie loves this slop."

Billie was distracted from that insult by the sound of Johnny, gimping up the stairs. She opened the door. Johnny, in a tailored light-gray suit, loud purple shirt and white tie, drew himself up and surveyed the room. He handed his hat to Billie.

"Sorry we're so goddamn late," said Billie. "We got lost coming over."

"No sense of direction," said Dillinger.

"Too many fucking lakes in this city," said Billie. "None of the roads go straight."

Dillinger flopped onto the couch. A smile of wry amusement played across his face. "I could live here." He spread his arms. "This reminds me of our place in Chicago, doesn't it Billie?"

"What John?"

"Doesn't this remind you of our apartment in Chicago?"

"Eh," said Billie.

"We brought Chinese food," announced Dillinger.

Eddie handed him a sweating can of Schmidt's beer and a magazine.

"I thought you'd get a kick out of it," said Eddie.

Dillinger set his beer can on the gleaming wood table, disregarding the cork coasters.

"Why, I haven't seen this," said Dillinger.

"Just come out," said Eddie.

"Houdini of the outlaws," Dillinger muttered.

He turned pages, let out a soft whistle. "That's all?" he said.

Billie mussed his thinning hair.

"Don't take it personally, John," she said, and then to Bess and Eddie: "He hates when they mention his father. Poor old man, he doesn't know whether to shit or go blind." Billie leaned over Dillinger's shoulder and read: *"Johnnie's a good boy, said the elder Dillinger."*

"Shut up," said Dillinger.

"I was just..."

Dillinger pushed her bejeweled hand away, took a swig of beer.

"Should we eat?" said Bess.

"I'm starved," said Eddie.

"They called our whorefucking lawyer," said Billie.

"Who called your lawyer?" asked Bess.

"Hollywood," Billie said. "Those whorefuckers. They want to make a movie. Can you fucking believe it? Me and John?"

Dillinger flipped to the cover of the magazine, Startling

Detective Adventures. A photo showed the jail in Crown Point, inset with the face of a male guard and female sheriff. An arrow painted on the photo showed the path of escape.

"Bullshit," said Dillinger. "They can't get away with writing this kind of crap." He threw the magazine down in disgust. "It shouldn't be legal."

"Take it with you," suggested Eddie. "Read the whole thing later. There's good parts."

Bess bit her lower lip. The good part, as far as she was concerned, was the magazine's naming of the new Dillinger gang: Tommy Carroll, Red Hamilton, Homer Van Meter, and Baby Face Nelson. Eddie, who planned every detail of the robberies, was the invisible man.

Billie, at the dining table, studied her reflection in a serving spoon. "I always wanted a sterling set," she said. She called to Dillinger on the couch. "Did you hear that John?"

"What?"

"I always wanted sterling."

"I heard you the first time."

"No you didn't," said Billie. "These he-men and their guns, it's ruining their fucking hearing."

"Would you ladies care for a cocktail?" asked Eddie.

"Can you make a gin fizz?" asked Billie.

"Why sure," said Eddie. "Honey?"

"My stomach's staging a riot right now," said Bess.

Eddie bashed through the swinging door and into the kitchen.

"I'm starving," said Billie. She piled two plates with white rice. "Did you hear the one about Father O'Brien's rooster?"

Bess peered into the chow mein container.

Billie said: "Father O'Brien's rooster ran away, so at Sunday Mass he says: 'Has anybody got a cock?' All the men stand up.

" 'I meant,' said Father O'Brien, 'has anybody *seen* a cock?'

All the women stand up.

" 'I meant,' said Father O'Brien, 'has anybody seen *my* cock?' And all the choir boys stand up."

This joke cracked Eddie up. Delivering the gin fizz to Billie, he spilled sticky drops on her dress. Bess laughed, although she didn't care for jokes against the Church, especially on Good Friday. Dillinger kept his face hidden behind Startling Detective Adventures.

"John's heard it before," said Billie, using the good linen to wipe gin spots off her breast-swollen dress.

Dillinger slapped the magazine on the coffee table, drained his beer, slipped off his suit jacket. Sweat rings surrounded the armpits of his purple shirt. A shoulder holster, tan leather, held a dark automatic pistol with a gray grip.

Dillinger rose, faced the widows and the snowstorm.

"We're going to bust out Mac," he muttered. "Before summer."

"Aren't you hungry, John?" asked Billie.

"I know exactly where they've got him," said Dillinger.

He walked to the dining table. When his hands gripped the back of a chair, his knuckles turned white. His lips twisted. "If any uniforms get in the way, well what's the difference?"

He coughed.

"No difference now."

This seemed to satisfy him and he sat alongside Bess. The chow mein was cold and the gravy congealing, but Billie and Eddie were scarfing it down. Dillinger's sullen mood cast a pall at the table. When Eddie finished eating, he said, "Say, I know," and slipped into the parlor. He returned with the Daily News. "Let's see what's playing."

Billie looked over his shoulder. "We saw that. Fashion Follies of 1934. William Powell and Bette Davis."

Dillinger said: "You don't want to see that, Eddie. It gives the girls expensive ideas."

Billie gave Dillinger a playful slug on the shoulder.

"It Happened One Night," suggested Eddie. "Clark Gable, Claudette Colbert."

"Seen it," said Dillinger.

"Red," suggested Eddie.

"Huh?" said Dillinger.

"The movie. Red. Harlow and Gable."

"How can one man be in two pictures?" asked Billie.

"They make 'em all in the same town," explained Dillinger.

"What do you think?" said Billie. "Do movie stars take the streetcar to work?"

"Anyway," said Dillinger, "I've seen it."

"John will be in the movies someday," said Billie. "Playing a handsome gangster."

"Man's Castle at the Cameo," said Eddie. "Spencer Tracy, Loretta Young."

"Seen it."

"Palooka," said Eddie.

"Who's in that?"

"Jimmy Durante."

"Aw," said Dillinger. "I guess it's Palooka. It's playing in the theater near our apartment."

Billie arose, attracted by a crystal ball atop the sideboard. She fondled it.

"Where'd you get this?"

"World's Fair," said Bess.

Billie rubbed her hands over it. "We're going to the Fair again this summer. Let's all go together. We'll take the train. Chicago's such a great town."

Dillinger inspected the newspaper's front page. "No hogwash from Hoover."

"It's nice to be off the front pages for a change," said Billie.

"You see," she said to Bess, "they paint us like a bunch of criminals."

"We *are* a bunch of criminals," said Dillinger. He tapped a Camel out of a pack and lit it from a matchbook, bending the match over and striking it to flame.

"We're not so fucking bad," said Billie. "At least we're not a bunch of kidnappers."

Bess stacked messy dishes. "That'll be next," she said. "That's when I'm out."

She bumped the door with her ass and slipped into the kitchen.

"What's wrong with her?" asked Billie.

Eddie shrugged.

Billie said: "John got out of prison without hurting anyone. Tell them John."

"They know."

"Well," Billie said. She moved regally to the couch, settled in, crossed her legs. "I thought it was clever."

Eddie studied the newspapers, his lips moving.

"We drove right through a couple of roadblocks," said Billie. "On the Mississippi."

"She knows how to distract a copper," said Dillinger. "Your average copper … " he pointed to his head, shaking it.

"John treats me like queen shit."

"Now now," said Dillinger.

"I couldn't ask for more," said Billie.

"I can operate hot," said Dillinger. "I'm used to it by now. But of all the outlaws in this country, why do they pick on me? Houdini of the Outlaws? You don't see that stuff about Van or Jimmy."

"It's your fault, because you're so goddamn handsome," said Billie.

Bess pushed through the swinging door. "Quit posing for

pictures," she told Dillinger, "and they'll stop taking them."

Dillinger gave her a wry smile. "Your woman's got my number," he said to Eddie.

"Who's going to play me, John?" Billie asked.

Dillinger gave her a quizzical look.

"In the movies."

Dillinger said: "There's nobody beautiful enough to play you, Billie."

Billie blushed.

Bess rolled up the stained tablecloth and muttered: "Oh, brother."

SAINTS WELL SET FOR FIRST
ENCOUNTER WITH BREWS

Hot Springs, Ark. -- Manager Bob Coleman was
preparing to apply the final touches today to the
St. Paul baseball club for the opening of the spring
exhibition series with the Milwaukee Brewers.

St. Paul Daily News
Friday, March 30, 1934

PATRICK

Pat stood at his dresser, tossing a baseball. Set on a lace doily atop that dresser was a photo of himself and Max Murphy. In the photo, both Pat and The Murph wore the baggy gray flannels of the Saint Paul Saints. Pat was kneeling, a pile of bats and gloves at his knees. Murph had his arm draped around Pat's shoulders. Both squinted into the Hot Springs sunshine.

Arkansas, spring training. Hot Springs was the one town Pat had ever seen that rivaled Saint Paul in booze, gambling and friendly females. And the Saint Paul Saints were heroes in that town, even the bat boys.

Those were the days.

Pat tossed the baseball and caught it, smack, in his mitt. Said mitt had that oily, dusty leather smell. Pat examined the ball, signed by Murphy and every one of his Saints. Pat wished he could stop that moment, live it forever, kneeling at the dugout steps, watching the boys round the bases. The miracle of photography, if we could live in its world, captured, still and perfect.

It was The Murph, the teetotalling, foul-tongued, tobacco-chewing Saints manager, who had introduced Pat to Harry Sawyer. "Most dependable kid ever," said The Murph. He was only trying to boost Pat into an off-season job. Murph, dead now of cancer, never imagined he was turning Pat into a gangster.

Pat tossed the ball into the glove and enjoyed that satisfying sound.

On the Saints he'd only been a bat boy. He'd been sort of a bat boy in gangland too. But inheriting Harry's tavern was a job for a man. Most of Harry's work had nothing to do with guns or beatings, Pat reminded himself. The profit was in cleaning up all that lovely cash generated by bank robberies and ransoms. Dark money was filtering into Saint Paul from all over the nation. This city was like Wall Street for bank robbers.

Harry knew the deepest secrets of this world, and would reveal them to Pat once the tavern changed hands. Filben was wrong. Pat did not need to be a stone-eyed killer in order to take over from Harry. Most of that rough stuff was gone, Prohibition had bred it, and it would die with Repeal. Gangsters were becoming money men now.

As Harry's heir, Pat would step up into a world of respect. He would shake hands, firm, with Big Ryan. Then it would be Pat who granted halos to gangster saints. A jealous Dolly would beg to run the Green Lantern's dining room.

Pat imagined him and Dolly, running the most level tavern in town. Free-spending rubes would mob the place, hoping to see famous gangsters, just like when Harry was in charge.

Pat wrapped the ball in the glove, tied the glove with twine so it would keep its shape around the ball. He put the glove in its sacred place, the dresser's top drawer, then glanced out the windows.

A face dodged past the window across the alley. Since when did they allow Mexicans in this neighborhood?

This Mexican across the alley seemed awful nosey. Pat had caught him five or six times now, staring. Since when did single Mexican guys rent three-bedroom apartments? And what kind of fella was home night and day? He didn't look right in his clothes either. His hair was too neatly combed, as if he ought to be wearing a suit, not khakis and rough shirts. Fred Gomez, that was supposedly his name. Pat, asking neighbors, could discover no more.

"What are you, Gomez?" Pat muttered. "Homo or G-man?"

"Maybe both," Pat concluded. According to underworld rumors, J. Edgar Hoover was a homo. Maybe he was hiring his own kind now.

Pat took from his refrigerator two cans of Hamm's beer. This fridge, Dolly had begged for. She hated not only the icebox but also the leering pervert iceman. So Pat buys her a brand-new Saint-Paul-made Bohn refrigerator and what does she do? Moves back to her mother's!

He ambled down the stairs, across winter-killed lawn, and into the lobby of the brick apartments next door.

The brass mailboxes had paper nametags. They read like a Dublin law firm: McCann, O'Rourke, Sullivan, Mannix and Lafferty. The single exception was 301, Gomez.

Pat mounted the stairs and, with the lip of a beer can, tapped on the door of 301.

A tall, slender man with slick black hair answered. He was pale, wore tattered sweatshirt over gray tweed trousers. His face was pinched by dime-store eyeglasses. He was thirty years old, maybe, clean shaven, sharp faced.

Pat held up the beers like they were trophy fish.

"I saw you were home," Pat said.

"You are ... ?"

"Neighbor," said Pat. "Across the way."

The man opened the door a little wider.

Pat glanced in. "Your wife's not home or nothing, is she?"

"She's not in town yet," said Gomez, if that really was his name. "She's back in California."

"I thought you'd enjoy a beer."

"Just a minute."

Gomez closed the door. In less than a minute he opened it and allowed Pat in. Pat's first impression was bright sunshine and bare wood floors, an apartment with almost no furniture. In the living room, an army cot topped with wool blanket. In the dining room, a cheap card table and exactly one folding chair. Curtains had been draped only on the windows facing Pat's apartment.

Pat, at the card table, produced a church-key from his pocket and opened the beers. A game of solitaire had been laid out on the table, beside greasy white deli paper that had recently held a sandwich.

"Yeah, I figured maybe you were killing time over here," Pat said, examining the card game. "That's why I came over. California, huh? What brings you to Saint Paul?"

Gomez hefted beer can to lips. It was then that Pat noticed the polished shoes. They clashed with the shabby appearance Gomez was trying to put on. Pat could almost see J. Edgar Hoover's reflection in those shoes.

"Gomez, that's like Mexican, right?"

"Spanish," corrected Gomez. "I'd offer you a better place to sit ..." He turned the folding chair toward Pat. "But our furniture hasn't arrived."

"No, I'll stand. Been sitting."

Pat looked toward the window and noted just how clearly he could see his apartment, the street, the lobby entrance. He decided that in the future he would use the alley door. He could have sworn he had spotted, when Gomez first opened the door, black binoculars on the window sill. They were gone now.

"Lucky you missed our winter," Pat said. "What a bitch."

"So are you married, Mister ... ?"

"O'Hara. O'Hara's the name. Yeah. In fact, there's my mother-in-law now."

Nora, wrapped as if it were deep winter, trudged up from the streetcar stop, disappeared into the apartment lobby.

"She lives with you?"

"Oh no," Pat said. "Not her. It's just me and the little woman. And my mom. But mom's never home, she works like, oh, a sixteen hour day."

Pat stared out the windows, swigged beer and said: "Nice to meet you, Gomez. I got to see what my mother-in-law wants."

Mission accomplished, Pat felt, descending the stairs. Maybe he was truly a level gangster now, if he had his own personal FBI spy. He congratulated himself on getting information and giving away nothing that "Gomez" didn't already know.

When Pat reached the third floor landing of his building, he found that Nora had let herself in with Dolly's key.

He opened the door, found his mother-in-law rifling the bills his mom had piled on the dining table.

"Dolly's not here," he said.

"I know very well Dolly's not here. New radio, I see."

"Yeah," said Pat, and walked to the set. "You can listen to police calls."

"So that's how you waste your money," Nora said. "Spying on policemen."

Pat sighed. He gathered empty beer cans from the couch so he could sit.

"Dolly and I," Pat said. "We have it worked out."

Nora set her purse on the dining table, which was polished to a luster and set with a silver candelabra. The dining room was a shrine to hope. Pat's sainted mother, bless her laundry-steamed heart, had splurged on fine china, trying to raise the family from Shanty to Lace Curtain.

"I can take your coat," Pat said.

"I won't be staying," she said. "Patrick ... " she dug into that purse. "My daughter does not wish to continue this marriage."

"Since when?" said Pat.

From her purse Nora dug a sheaf of papers, rolled and tied with a black ribbon. She threw it into Pat's lap. He leaped up and waved it in her face.

"I ain't taking 'em," he said. He rushed to the window, flung it open, threw the papers out. "That's what I think of your summons."

"It was not a summons."

"Any papers you can draw up, I can get crushed. I know judges."

"You've stood before them head bowed, that's how you know judges."

"You have an awful nerve coming to my house with this bullshit."

"Do not use your barroom language with me."

"Where's Dolly? Where is she?"

"She's in my home, her forever home, and she's never coming back to you."

The phone stood on a sewing machine near the window and Pat leaped for it. He dialed, glaring at Nora.

"Answer, Dolly, answer," muttered Pat and finally slammed down the phone.

"You get out of my house."

"It's your mother's house, not yours. And I'm going nowhere until you sign that decree."

"Never!"

"Dolores wants you to sign and then she never wants to hear from you again."

"She knows you're here?"

"She sent me. She begged me."

"You," Pat pointed at her. "You're the instigator."

He rushed into his bedroom, grabbed his chrome revolver

from the sock drawer, then returned to confront Nora.

"Get out of my house, you troublemaking bitch." He pointed the gun at her, gut level. "Take your phony divorce decree with you. I don't believe Dolly signed it. If I see you near this building again I'll shoot you dead."

"Go ahead and shoot," said Nora and thrust her chest out. "You ruined my daughter, why not kill the rest of me? Shoot. Shoot, you coward!"

The gun trembled in Pat's hand. His finger twitched and a tremendous explosion hit him like a shock wave.

His mother-in-law screamed and ran out the door.

The smoke cleared. His ears stopped ringing. Pat thrust his finger into a singed hole in a sofa cushion.

How was he going to explain a bullet hole to his mom?

DEBAUCHERY, CHEATING
AT ALL-NIGHT BARROOMS
UNDER PRESENT POLICE REGIME

Saint Paul Daily News editorial

March 1934

FATHER MACK

Father McCarthy O'Sullivan loved glorifying the Lord at a fragrant Benediction or a joyful Baptism. But he loathed serving as the Archbishop's glorified altar boy at High Mass. So when Daisy Coffey phoned on Good Friday, he was happy to leave High Mass duties to actual altar boys.

Together he and Mrs. Coffey rode a nearly empty streetcar around the Loop to the Federal Building. The streetcars were drafty, the heaters feeble. Mrs. Coffey, a dignified woman well past forty, was dressed for the chill in massive overcoat and pull-down purple wool hat.

"They are gangsters, I am certain of it," said Mrs. Coffey.

He patted her black-gloved hand. Normally, Father Mack had little sympathy for landlords. In the Ireland of his youth, landlords were dual agents of Satan and the British. Many a good Catholic families had been run off their farms by the landlord class.

But we're not in Ireland anymore, Father Mack reminded himself. And Mrs. Coffey was a stalwart of Saint Patrick's Pence. As a landlady she turned a stern face toward her scheming renters.

But if not for her generosity, many a child would be hungry or cold.

So he owed Mrs. Coffey this indulgence. Father Mack suspected she'd called him because of the rumors: He was supposedly the Archbishop's ambassador to the underworld.

The holy day, and the late spring snowstorm, had emptied downtown. The Archbishop had fearsome influence over this city, and most merchants closed for Good Friday. Only a few job-starved men haunted Rice Park.

Mrs. Coffey slipped off the streetcar, and Father Mack grabbed her arm, saved her from tottering into a snow bank.

He escorted her past the River State Bank. The corner office belonged to Mister Richard Alt, bank president and latest kidnapping victim of Saint Paul gangsters. The Alts were Catholics, so the bank was dark. But Mrs. Coffey stopped to admire an American flag in the window, beside a heroic photo of Franklin Delano Roosevelt.

"The shame of it," Mrs. Coffey said. "A town so infested with gangsters. A fine Catholic like Mister Alt. A college man. In this town, a decent man can't take a taxi without being abducted."

Heavy wet snowflakes pelted Mrs. Coffey's purple hat, flecked her black coat. She followed Father Mack to the Federal Building, which resembled a German castle. Mrs. Coffey informed Father Mack that she had been on bad terms with Germany ever since the War. Herr Hitler had done nothing to improve her opinion of the Hun character.

Once inside the Federal Building, Daisy Coffey stopped to point out the sparkling American cleanliness: marble floors, mahogany paneling and wide open stairways.

An elevator girl, in crisp uniform, piloted them to the second floor. Mrs. Coffey and Father Mack marched to corner offices, where bright glass doors were labeled:

DIVISION OF INVESTIGATION
DEPARTMENT OF JUSTICE

Father Mack pushed into an office where three young ladies pounded furious at typewriters. Wisps of cigarette smoke hung over their bobbed heads, floating past a scowling photo of The Director. Mrs. Coffey unbuttoned her coat, puffing with pride. "G-men," she whispered. "Father, I believe they will clean up this rotten town."

She cleared her throat. "We're here to see Mister Clegg," she announced to the nearest typist. The girl led them into a private office.

A husky man with oiled-back hair invited them in. He was dressed in a tailored gray pinstripe suit and red tie, wore eyeglasses, had a cleft chin. This was no ordinary G-man, but J. Edgar Hoover's emissary from Washington.

The typist hung their coats on a wooden rack. Mrs. Coffey sat, smoothed dark skirt over stockinged legs. Father Mack stood behind her, admiring the G-men's view of Rice Park and the city's better hotels and theaters.

"Kind of you to come see us," said Clegg, in a deep, syrupy voice. Mrs. Coffey seemed mesmerized by his big, manicured hands, his discreet gold cufflinks. He flipped open a book on his desk that contained thick pages pasted with photographs.

"Kindness had nothing to do with it Mister Clegg," said Mrs. Coffey. "If those people are gangsters, I want them out of my building."

Clegg nodded.

"Father O'Sullivan can attest to my character," Mrs. Coffey said.

"I wonder if you might explain to me, Mrs. Coffey, why you believe them to be gangsters?" Clegg's voice hinted at an aristocratic upbringing in a gentle climate.

"Inspector Clegg, normally I have little trouble renting my apartments, but in these uncertain times, I am required to furnish them extensively. Tenants have become quite choosy."

"Mmmm," said Clegg.

"While I was installing furniture in an apartment across the courtyard from number 303 ... "

Clegg jotted into a leather-bound notebook.

" ... I noticed the tenant in the kitchenette ironing. She had black hair. But the woman who rented the apartment had flame-red hair."

Clegg stared, expecting more.

"They are not the kind of respectable people we usually accept as tenants, Mister Clegg. They seem rather sneaky. They keep the shades drawn all day. They use the back stairway. They come and go at all hours. I believed I was renting to a husband and wife but I have seen five or six different people coming and going."

She paused. "They're very quiet, I'll give them that. I sent my janitor to their apartment to install a toilet paper holder. They refused to let him in."

She leaned toward the desk. "Mister Clegg, these people don't have jobs. They don't keep regular hours. I would call our local police but ... "

Clegg waited.

Mrs. Coffey pursed her bright red lips. "You read the Daily News, I take it?"

Clegg nodded.

"Finally someone is telling the truth about the police in this city. Bravo, I say for the Daily News."

"Mrs. Coffey, I shall show you photographs, and I'd like you to tell me whether you've seen these men or women around your building."

Mrs. Coffey studied pictures as Father Mack looked over her shoulder.

A beady-eyed man, severe side-wall haircut.

A creepy looking fellow, dark hair, thick lips.

A snarling convict in sleeveless t-shirt, numbered board around his neck.

A young strumpet posing near a lake.

Mrs. Coffey's head slowly shook as Clegg flipped pages. "None of those," she said. "I take it these are kidnappers."

Clegg smiled like a polite border guard. "We want them for questioning," he said.

Clegg stood, clearly disappointed, and escorted them to the door.

"I'm afraid to go into that apartment," Daisy Coffey said. "It's my property, and I am afraid."

"We shall investigate, Mrs. Coffey, you can depend on that."

Daisy Coffey walked the marble hallway toward the elevator. "Well, I'm highly impressed," she said, voice echoing in the federal cavern. "Father, the United States is the leading nation of the world now-a-days. After speaking with Inspector Clegg, I can understand why. Such a quality man. It was men like him who defeated the Kaiser, father. And now President Roosevelt is rescuing the banks and putting idle men to work. You are a Roosevelt man, aren't you, Father?"

Father Mack smiled. It was the rare Catholic who didn't need the approval of the nearest priest.

"Aye," said Father Mack. But in Ireland he had witnessed the terrible price of patriotism, and his political loyalties only went so far. "So long as Roosevelt's for the workers, I'm for him."

"We defeated Germany, Father, and we will prevail against the gangster element."

The elevator bell dinged just as she proclaimed:

"It makes me proud to be an American."

FINAL HOLY WEEK
SERVICES SET TODAY

St. Paul Pioneer Press

March 31, 1934

FATHER MACK

Father McCarthy O'Sullivan sat in blessed isolation at the Chancery's kitchen table. Before him lay the world's most optimistic newspaper, the Daily Racing Form. In the Sixth at Hawthorne next Wednesday, a contest at a mile and a sixteenth, a mare named Skibbereen caught his eye. Why, Father Mack might bet this horse on sentiment alone.

Skibbereen.

He sighed. He drank the dregs of a cup of Barry's Tea. No priest could hope for peace on Easter Saturday, so Father Mack cherished these stolen moments.

Skibbereen had run twenty-two times, the poor thing, winning only three contests. She was just a claiming mare who'd be lucky to earn her feed bill. None of the racing writers preferred her, which endeared her to Father Mack. Any punter could pick the favorite. Father Mack, a born contrarian, loved the longshot.

"Father McCarthy?" probed Mrs. Bold.

"Aye."

"Mrs. Nora Carey to see you."

Mrs. Bold was round, a grandmother, white haired, and wore thick, pearly eyeglasses. Her selection as housekeeper led to little temptation for sex-deprived priests, and minimal fodder for parish gossips.

"Very well."

He handed the Racing Form to Mrs. Bold.

Nora Carey appeared in the doorway, wearing a black dress. Father Mack stood as Mrs. Carey seated herself across the gleaming table. Mrs. Bold set a place mat, poured tea for two in humble silence, retreated.

"Father." Nora cleared her throat. "I wanted to ask you about divorce."

Father Mack reached across the table. Mrs. Carey's delicate bony hand disappeared in his. Her breath smelled faint of liquor. Her eyes looked bleary.

"Now Nora, things in a marriage are rarely as bad as they seem."

"It's not about my marriage, father. My husband is no longer with me. I'm here about my daughter."

The daughter, Dolores, whom the tavern class called "Dolly," was a favorite of Father Mack's. She was a perfumed hussy who reminded him that underneath his black robes roamed a male animal. It was dreadful blasphemy, but Father Mack preferred Mary Magdalene to the Blessed Virgin.

He had often heard the confession of Mrs. Nora Carey. Her sin was a cardinal one: *Ira,* or wrath. Nora, poor soul, aspired to lift her family above the taverns, the street life, the factory floor and into the hazy realm of afternoon teas, literary discussions, and fine linens. All her modest ambitions had failed. Having survived a drunken husband, Nora had one precious hope remaining: the daughter Dolores. God help this suffering mother, her dreams had crashed when Dolores married a man of the gangster class and started answering to the tavern name Dolly.

As if she sensed his sympathies, Nora launched a barrage aimed at Pat Reilly.

"He drinks and shoots pool all weekend, then brings home his gangster friends and they sit around gambling."

"Now, now, none of us are without sin."

"What can I do, Father?"

"The Church in her wisdom forbids divorce."

"But Patrick Reilly is ruining us!"

Father Mack kept book on rogue Catholics, and reviewed the short chapter on Patrick Reilly. Harmless, feckless, gregarious, eager to please, not repulsive but certainly not handsome, bad teeth, no sartorial sense whatever, fond of those dreadful flat caps that made him look like a bookie. Reilly was no of particular credit to the Irish race, but neither was he the devil incarnate. He was an ordinary lout of the class you might find in any factory or tavern. What a temptress such as Dolly Carey saw in him, well, that was one of Our Lord's Mysteries.

"Are there no exceptions, father? For divorce?"

"In rare circumstance," said Father Mack, and immediately regretted it.

"For instance?"

"Marriage under false pretense. If one partner was not Catholic, it may have never been a true marriage, and so may be annulled. Still, there can never be divorce, because what God ..."

"I know father, but Jesus wrote the Bible a long time ago."

From her purse, Nora's trembling hands fetched a sparkling blue rosary that ended in a silver crucifix.

"I'll go to the Archbishop if I need to."

"Well ..." said Father Mack. His prime duty was to keep the Faithful from pestering Archbishop McMahon. His Excellency was a frail man of scholarly dignity, with no desire to be among the people. His business was conducted exclusively with priests, or laity of high station. *Aquila non capit muscas,* as they said in Rome. An eagle does not capture flies.

Any priest who displeased His Excellency might be exiled to a one-man parish, out on the windy prairies, ministering to tundra farmers and their pie-baking wives.

"Archbishop McMahon," Father Mack said, "is a very busy man."

"If I ever get my hands around that man's neck..."

"The Archbishop's?"

"Patrick Reilly!" said Nora. "If I had a gun, Father, I would be tempted," her lips quivered, "to commit a mortal sin."

Father Mack walked behind Nora and lay his strong hands on her thin shoulders. She shook with sobs.

"The church might consider," he said, "annulling the marriage of a husband who refused all support of his wife, or a man imprisoned on a serious offense."

In truth, annulments were rarely granted, but it was his priestly duty to prevent murder.

"He never gives Dolores a dime," Nora cried. "He never spends money on anything but his own bad habits. He's a Near Occasion of Sin, Father."

"We will require," said Father Mack, "documentation."

Oh the Church, She was wise. It was easier for Catholics to suffer a bad marriage than to endure years of ecclesiastical paper shuffling.

"Bless you, Father," said Nora, and kissed his hand.

He escorted her out the doorway, then, alone, crossed the library toward the Archbishop's quarters. In a city rife with bank robbers, Public Enemies and kidnappers, Archbishop Daniel McMahon believed himself a kidnapping target.

Perhaps this fear was realistic, and not merely the product of a half-senile priest's brain. The Archbishop was a friend of two wealthy Saint Paul families that had suffered a kidnapping in the past year. Why, it had been a scant two years since the infant Lindberg's brutal murder. At 6-foot-5 and well over 200 pounds, Father Mack was a comforting presence, posted in the library each night. Under such comforting guard, the Archbishop was finally sleeping until daylight.

Father Mack climbed a spiral staircase, reached a high-polished double door and discreetly tapped.

"Excellency?" he said softly.

Mrs. Bold peered out of the kitchen. "He's away for a few days."

"Away? Away where? He didn't mention any travels to me."

Mrs. Bold, humble, ignorant, cast a glance at the floor.

ST. PAUL GUNNER
IDENTIFIED AS DILLINGER

It was John Dillinger, "the cop killer" who blasted his way out of a St. Paul apartment building Saturday with a hail of machine gun bullets that forced two federal agents and a St. Paul detective to seek cover.

Minneapolis Sunday Tribune
April 1, 1934

PATRICK

In the history of the Green Lantern, no direct ray of sunlight had ever penetrated Harry's office. Sheltered from the glaring sunshine of an early spring Saturday, Pat did pencil work by the weak illumination of a desk lamp.

Pat's task was to dope out the Kentucky Derby, that hoof-pounding event to be held four weeks hence. Pat, until last year, had worked part-time at the Royal Cigar Store, taking bets at a teller's cage. He believed this experience gave him special insights into horse racing.

He and his pencil were vacillating over the fortunes of Mata Hari, Peace Chance, and Quasimodo when the phone rang.

Harry's secret phone.

Pat cursed, threw down his pencil, stretched to open the closet door. He picked up the phone and summoned his manliest voice: "Go ahead."

"We need you," Bess said. "Now."

He held the phone away and glared at it. "Since when do you give orders?"

"Patrick, don't make me explain on the telephone."

"All right," said Pat.

"Pronto," said Bess. "Emergency."

Pat sighed. "If you say so."

He grabbed his leather jacket and backed out of the office, locking up.

"Pete, I'm going out."

Pete, in the steamy kitchen, held up a hand.

"Who's your Derby horse?" Pat shouted.

Pete shrugged.

"Yeah, ain't no French horse running," Pat teased him.

He hopped into the Essex, drove up Cathedral Hill, shot out on Marshall, the road steamy with melting snow. With all this blasted sunshine, the car felt as warm as a greenhouse. He dialed the radio to KSTP, hunting for sensational news. Tinny orchestra music rattled the speaker. All was dull-normal in the known world, but something was wrong in Pat's secret world, because here he was doing fifty on city streets. When he crossed the bridge into Minneapolis he slowed down. The cops in said city were unpredictable.

He detoured into an Esso station and waited, just to be sure he wasn't tailed.

When he rolled past the Greens' apartment, he spied Dillinger's black Hudson, with yellow wheels and yellow accent stripe along its hood. It was parked in the alley, half-hidden behind trashcans. Nobody was in the Hudson that he could see.

Pat parked a block away. Hands in his jacket pockets, cap pulled low, he walked like a man in no particular hurry. He circled the Hudson and peered in. A hand beckoned.

Pat opened the door and slipped behind the wheel.

Saint Johnny Dillinger was hunkered in the passenger seat.

"Nice to see you," said Johnny.

"I got a call from Bess."

"Well, because I'm bleeding," said Johnny.

Pat, sun-blinded, could see little but Dillinger's grimacing face.

"How bad?"

"It's nothing," said Johnny. "Billie's worried, though. We're trying to find a doctor. You don't know a doctor do you? A doctor who will stand up."

"Maybe," said Pat. But his mental calculator was trying to figure out how Johnny got wounded. There was no bank job on the weekend's schedule. Dillinger's gang was supposedly laying low. Maybe, Pat guessed, the gang had gotten heated up into an argument. Jimmy and Van hated each other, and maybe Johnny the peacemaker had gotten between them. Pat wasn't going to ask. Harry had taught him: You ask questions, you start sounding like a cop.

Johnny wasn't wheezing or moaning, so wherever he'd taken a bullet, it wasn't going to kill him.

"Well, get going, will you?" said Dillinger. "I've only got so much blood in me."

Pat eased out of the car and drummed on the roof. He stared up at the windows of Bess and Eddie's apartment. A dark figure appeared at the half-open blinds. Pat ran up the back stairs and pounded on the door.

Bess opened it a crack.

"Your friend needs a doctor," she whispered.

With a glance over her shoulder, Bess slipped into the hallway and shut the door of her apartment.

She grabbed Pat by his jacket. "You brought them here. You get rid of them. They're your problem."

She let him go with a shove.

"Where's Eddie?" Pat asked.

"I can't get hold of him."

`"Okay, I'll take care of it."

"Back stairs," commanded Bess.

"I know."

Bess opened her apartment door. Billie burst out into the

hallway. She was dressed for the nightclubs in mink wrap, a dark dress, a yellow kerchief wrapped in her hands. She followed Pat downstairs and they slinked toward the Hudson.

"Are you a good driver?" Pat asked as he opened the car's door for her.

"She's an ace," said Johnny.

Billie commandeered the driver's seat, Pat wriggled into the back. Out toward Hennepin and Lake they drove. The traffic was mad, Easter shoppers scrambling on and off the streetcars, autos dodging and swerving. The streets looked gritty, the shoppers ragged on this last day of Lent. The Hudson was a yellow streak with frosty windows powering down Lake Street, trolley lines above crackling.

From the back seat, all Pat could see of Billie was white knuckles on the steering wheel, black curly hair. Beside her, Johnny writhed in silent pain, ice in a bloody rag wrapped around ruined tan trousers. Billie had pinned a silver crucifix to the roof fabric, just above the windshield. Pat prayed that Jesus would guide them, although a man nailed to a cross, he figured, had problems of his own.

Dillinger turned to tell Pat: "It's a swell car." He winced. "You're a level guy, I won't forget that."

"Left," Pat directed. "Then left again." He instructed Billie to park in an alley behind a cream-brick office building.

"Keep it running," Pat said, then leaped out and pushed through a back door.

In a bright glassy office, Pat bull-rushed Doctor May, who was fetching his coat and bowler hat from a rack.

A gray haired woman dressed in white stepped in front of him. "Sir, do you have an appointment?"

"Harry says hello," Pat shouted over her.

Doctor May's face registered shock, horror, intrigue. He was a slight, balding middle-aged man dressed in a tan three-piece suit and bright blue tie. He replaced bowler and coat on the rack.

"I'll see this man," he told the nurse.

He invited Pat into an exam room. In its half-light, Doctor May seemed grotesque, even threatening. Of all crimes against the Church, none was more sinful than abortion, Pat believed. Harry had run a lucrative side business arranging abortions, but there would be none of that in a Catholic Reilly regime.

I didn't have nothing to do with no abortionist, Your Honor.

"Where is our young woman?" asked the doctor.

"There is no young woman," said Pat. An office visit was $2, an abortion up to $500, in consideration of the legal risks. Pat counted twenty-dollar bills out of his wallet.

"Gunshot wound," he said.

Doctor May stared at the cash.

"It's not a bad one," said Pat. "There'll be more if it turns bad."

Doctor May snatched the money.

"Bring him in."

"Not this guy," said Pat. "You don't want him here."

Doctor May stared at Pat. "I want to talk to Harry."

"Harry's mute at this point."

"He's what?"

"Mute."

Pat counted out five more twenties. "Here, come with us, we can pay."

They crowded into the Hudson: Bleeding Johnny and nervous Billie up front, Pat squeezed into the back with the dapper little doctor and his haggard nurse. Billie, following the nurse's directions, turned down a side street, up a dirt driveway, into a snow-muddy yard between two crummy gray houses. Billie parked within inches of a back door. Dillinger, limping, was helped up the rear stairs by doctor and nurse.

They all jammed into a bedroom-clinic and Billie and Pat gawked as doctor and nurse snipped Dillinger's bloody trousers with a scissors. The doctor pronounced it a flesh wound and chased Billie and Pat out.

They settled on the sun-warm porch. So this is it, Pat realized. A secret abortion clinic. He hadn't imagined that this Mortal Sin would be committed in an ordinary home. Maybe in a basement, he'd figured, or a demon-haunted cave.

Pat used his Statue of Liberty to light Luckies for himself, for Billie. They smoked in dead silence until the cigarettes were glowing nubs.

"Why are you so glum?" Billie asked. She ground out the nub between porch floorboards and her purple high heels. "I'm the one who's got problems."

"You have problems?" said Pat. "You don't have The Bitch for a mother-in-law."

"Shit," said Billie.

"I had to chase her off with a gun," said Pat. "That's what it's come to in our so-called family."

Billie sat in the streaming sunlight, which revealed the highlights of her dark hair, and reflected off her pearl necklace. Staring at the gleam of those pearls, Pat experienced one of those moments where his life made a sort of magical sense. Pat Reilly, fixer, center of the wheel, had found his destiny at last. People would see him on the street and whisper: *You'd never think it to look at him, but he's the Secret Mayor of Saint Paul. He's the guy got Dillinger out of a jam.*

He felt he'd been born for this moment, his soul flooded like this porch was flooded in sunlight. This was no ordinary sunshine, Pat believed. He was overwhelmed by the Grace of the Father, Son and Holy Ghost. Goosebumps!

His mother, his mother-in-law, his wife, the Saints ballplayers, his teachers, the priests, the nuns, the bootleggers and gangsters, all had been wrong. Harry had been right. There was a use for Pat Reilly, a reason he had been born on this Earth. And of all crazy places for the Enlightenment, here on the porch of Satan's abortion clinic.

Doctor May stepped into the sunlight. "He'll be a asleep a while," he said. He looked from Billie to Pat. His bloody white coat hung open on suit and tie. "Don't worry, he's a tough guy."

Doctor May touched Billie's bare shoulder and sneaked a glance into her cleavage. "Before he fell asleep, he asked for fried chicken."

"That's John," Billie said, her eyes brightening. "He's okay!" Her hands tightened around her purse. "We're going back to Chicago. I'm going to need all new clothes."

Pat, feeling shabby beside a woman in mink and pearls, walked Billie up Lake Street. They stopped at the show windows of A-LINE MODERN CLOTHING and Billie stared at mannequins in furs.

All Pat noticed in the window was reflected traffic, which he scanned for police cars.

"What happened back there?"

"The cops busted in," Billie said, gawking at furs. "What the fuck do you think happened?"

"That was a clean apartment Harry arranged for you."

Billie sputtered.

"Who tipped the cops off?" Pat asked.

"I don't know, but if John finds out, it's their funeral."

"If you want to stay here, I can find you a better apartment."

"I don't know," said Billie. "Your lousy police department can't mind its own fucking business. I thought the fix was in here."

"That wasn't our cops I guarantee you."

"Shit," said Billie. "What good does that do me?"

She opened the shop's brass door and Pat followed her in.

She took the sleeve of a sealskin coat in her pudgy hands. "I left some beautiful stuff back in that whorefucking apartment," she whispered.

A lanky, bored shop-girl, in pigtails and bright lipstick, muttered: "May I help you select something?"

Billie eyed this young woman. A Scandinavian blonde, she was blessed with long limbs and a gorgeous figure. She wore a plain navy dress off the $2 rack, accented by a cheap gold-plated bracelet.

"There's nobody but you to help me?" Billie asked.

The shop-girl flushed and stammered.

"Because excuse me honey," Billie said, "you don't exactly dress with style."

"I'll get the manager, he's in back."

"Don't bother, I buy my furs in Chicago."

Billie swept out the door, an embarrassed Pat behind her.

Two doors down, Pat opened a storefront door under a sign that read: SECURITY LOANS AND FINANCE. He led Billie through a narrow office set with desks at which nobody ever worked. He opened a door into a much larger back room. It was rank with cigar smoke. Scurrying clerks made chalk notations on a grand blackboard.

Pat approached a clerk at a barred window.

"Chartreuse, Hawthorne," he said. "Ten to show."

A bearded man in ragged coat looked up from a bench and rattled his Racing Form. "Cowards bet to show."

"Aw shut up. Punch that ticket, kid," Pat said.

He and Billie ogled the big board. The columns underneath Belmont and Hawthorne and Tanforan listed the horses and jockeys in chalky script. Pat did not need to study these, since he had gotten a call last night from his Chicago tout. Chartreuse, the tout said, twenty-to-one in the morning line, across the board. Pat ignored said strategic advice and made the most cautious bet. He calculated a $40 show payoff, more than the workers at his family's laundry made for a week of steamy work.

"Buy you a drink?" Pat asked Billie.

"Oh I don't know, it's early. Do they make a gin fizz here?"

"If they don't, we'll go across the street."

Pat approached a narrow cage. Behind it a schoolboy bartender was loading an oak bucket with ice from a huge galvanized tub.

"Say kid, can you make a fizz?"

"Does your mother wear underpants?"

"You could get your face slapped for that."

"I dare you," said the kid.

"Tough little monster, ain't you? Can you make a gin fizz or not?"

"I made a thousand of 'em."

"Well make two more," said Pat. "And don't be stingy with the gin."

He put a buck on the plank, added a dime for the kid. He looked over his shoulder at the board just as a scratchy voice came over the loudspeaker.

"Two back now..."

A drink in each hand, he walked toward Billie, the only well-dressed woman in the room. The crowd was held in 70 seconds of suspended hope as an announcer called the horses at the quarter pole, the half pole, into the stretch.

"Dark Mane, There I Go, Chartreuse..."

Pat handed Billie her fizz.

"Dark Mane drifting out, There I Go full of run, it's There I Go first to the wire."

The loudspeaker went to all static for a moment.

"There I Go over Dark Mane for second, Lemon Soda up late for the show. Prices in a minute."

"Shit," said Pat and stared at his worthless ticket.

Billie shrugged. "It's only a horse race."

"No it ain't," said Pat. "It means my man in Chicago lost his touch. It ain't the same since they took Scarface to jail."

"It's better if you ask me," said Billie. "The Italians are a bunch of pricks. No class. You can't trust 'em."

"Yeah well." Pat shrugged. He set his fizzing glass on a side rail, ripped his ticket and let it fall, wounded butterfly, to a littered floor.

It wasn't his lucky day. Maybe there was no Father, Son or Holy Ghost, no such thing as Grace. Certainly no sunlight strayed into this dark, secret parlor, where enlightenment entered as sparks over the telegraph.

Loser sparks.

"Just like my so-called wife," Pat said. "She finished out of the money too."

"Who?" said Billie, sipping through a straw. The drink brought a flush to her face.

Pat hung over the steel railing, looking at photographs of horses, trainers and jockeys. Unlike Pat, they were winners.

"If Johnny was a milkman," Pat asked, "would you still go for him?"

"What do you mean?"

"Women don't fool me. Used to, but not no more."

"Oh boy," said Billie.

Pat drank off his fizz, rattled the cubes.

"You gotta be a big man," said Pat. "That's what the ladies want. Little fellas don't count for nothing."

"If it's gonna be a speech, make it short, like the Gettysburg Address."

"Nah," said Pat. "A priest hears my confessions."

"I've taken a lot of shit from men," said Billie. "Not from John. Never from John. He is a gentleman. That's why I love him. It don't have nothing to do with his, you know, occupation."

"I didn't realize it until Dolly moved out on me," Pat said. "I took her for granted. I stayed out nights. I ain't no tomcat, see, I stay out with the boys playing cards and such. I should have paid her more attention."

Billie put a hand at the back of Pat's neck, squeezed the tight muscles.

"You're all like little boys and that's why we love you so. It's just as much pity as love. You're helpless without us, like a bunch of diaper shitting babies."

Pat nodded.

"Not John, though. John is the only real man I've ever met. He is not afraid. That man is not afraid of anything."

"I'm taking over Harry's place," said Pat. Dillinger's courage inspired his own. "Dolly will come back to me. She'll be queen of the place. And Bess, I will throw her ass out on the street. Her and Eddie can buy their own joint or blow town."

"Preferably," said Billie, "the latter."

"Yeah, preferably," said Pat.

"Bess?" Billie said. "What an asshole. She's been so cold to John. And her cocktails taste like rubbing alcohol."

She looked around. "Say, don't they have a ladies powder room?"

"The men piss out back," said Pat.

"Swell," said Billie.

"The joint across the street," said Pat. "Tables for ladies it says. Let's get away from these losers."

MACHINE GUNNERS ESCAPE; NET SPREAD OVER MIDWEST

Leaving behind a confusing trail of mixed-up automobiles, phony addresses and conflicting descriptions, the machine-gun gang which Saturday morning blasted its way out of a police-federal trap successfully eluded pursuit.

Saint Paul Daily News
April 1, 1934

St. Francis Cafeteria
Easter Sunday Dinners
50-cents

Turkey, steak, roast loin of pork, mashed potatoes, kernel corn O'Brien, head lettuce, Thousand Island Dressing, pie, pudding.

Saint Paul Daily News ad
April 1, 1934

FATHER MACK

"No Patrick?" Father Mack asked. "He promised to bring a friend."

"His friends," said Nora, "are vile criminals."

"Mother," said Dolly, "it is Easter. Please."

Priest, mother and daughter pushed through the gleaming bronze revolving doors of the St. Francis Cafeteria. Father Mack had hoped that Patrick's "friend" would be the notorious Mister Dillinger, who sometimes showed up brazenly in public. Was it Dillinger who yesterday shot it out with G-men on Lexington Avenue? Rumors said yes, rumors said no.

Father Mack selected a weepy slice of lemon meringue pie, filled a teacup at a steaming copper samovar. The Carey women pushed their trays along stainless steel tracks, assembling their Easter dinners.

Was Dillinger Catholic? Father Mack hoped so, and had prepared a debate over the morality of bank robbing. It might be categorized as a Venial Sin, provided no one was hurt and a generous donation was diverted to the poor. He had sympathy for a good Catholic gangster. Back in Ireland, McCarthy had been a tough guy right up to the miracle of his conversion. Patriot, terrorist, saint, gangster, folk-hero, outlaw — in the struggle to free Ireland, they were much the same thing.

In any event, apparently Patrick and his mysterious friend were spending Easter elsewhere.

Nora, tray laden, grumped at Dolly: "Find us somewhere quiet to eat."

Dolly led them to a bright window table. It overlooked a slushy street jammed with autos and pedestrians. A ragamuffin at the curb held up a newspaper and shouted sensational headlines. A rumbling streetcar created a minor earthquake that rattled silverware and shimmered windows.

They set their trays on gravy-spotted linen, alongside a white lily in a cut-glass vase. Nora had burst out of Lent's darkness into a yellow dress, punctuated with hothouse carnation. Dolly wore a frilly pink blouse with dark skirt. Her outfit did not meet Nora's approval.

"You'd think we were dining with a bookie in a cocktail lounge," Nora muttered.

"What mother?"

"Nothing."

Nora unloaded her platter, piled with both turkey breast and pork loin, along with a volcano of mashed potatoes oozing gravy lava. Side dishes overflowed with string beans almandine, and mixed corn and peas. A wedge of lettuce was surrounded by pink dressing. Another plate supported a slice of apple pie. Nora snapped her fingers at the busboy, who removed trays, poured water and coffee, performed a theatrical bow.

"That young man," pronounced Nora, "is going places. Unlike your Patrick, who cannot manage to show up for a free dinner."

"Maybe I should marry the bus boy, mother."

Nora, occupied by mashed potatoes, ignored this.

Dolly set her straw bonnet on the table. In its pink ribbon was trapped a white Easter lily.

"Father, you're not eating?" asked Dolly.

"I'm to have dinner with the Archbishop."

Nora glared at Dolly's rib-eye steak. "No vegetables," she observed.

Dolly cut into her steak.

"Ahem," said Nora. "Father?"

Father Mack blessed himself. "Bless us oh Lord and these thy gifts which we humbly receive through Christ Our Lord, amen."

Nora prompted Dolly: "Amen?"

"Amen, amen, amen."

"The impertinence!" said Nora.

"I see you got your fifty cents worth," said Dolly.

"What are you talking about?"

"For somebody who didn't want to eat here, you sure loaded up your platter." Dolly chewed. "Town full of slaughterhouses, and you can't get a decent steak."

Father Mack sipped hot strong tea. Hearing confessions had taught him that irritation was merely the rough edge of love. When the shadow people in the confessional found fault, it was usually with those closest to them. With this thought, Father Mack armed himself against mother-daughter bickering.

"Who ever heard of Easter Dinner in a cafeteria?" Nora asked. "Did you ever hear of such a thing, Father?"

"Look around, Ma," countered Dolly. "See all these people? Every single one has heard of Easter Dinner in a cafeteria."

"It's not respectable," said Nora. "Do you think the Blessed Mother ate Easter Dinner in a cafeteria?"

"The Blessed Mother was busy rolling back rocks on Easter Sunday, right Father?"

Nora muttered: "Don't take the Blessed Mother's name in vain."

"Excuse me," Dolly said, "but does anybody give a damn about the Blessed Virgin these days?"

"Blasphemy!" squeaked Nora.

"It's old fashioned. The Rosary. Lent. The whole thing. You're living in the middle ages, Ma. Even priests drive cars and go to movies. We don't need to live like monks in a monastery, praying and burning incense all day, no offense, Father."

"I raised you a Good Catholic."

"I am a Good Catholic. I'm just not medieval. Just because a Pope said bla bla bla in 1492 doesn't mean you have to live by it now. Did I want to go to church with you this morning? No. Did I go, yes. That makes me a Good Catholic, doesn't it?"

Nora glared at Dolly, then began a serious assault on the slabs of turkey.

"You should eat your salad first," said Dolly.

"Where's your salad?"

"I don't take a salad. That's how well you know me, Ma."

Dolly unfolded a Daily News and began scanning the front page.

"We're in the presence of a holy man," said Nora "and you're reading the newspaper?"

"I am no holy man," Father Mack protested, "merely a sinner who has taken vows."

Dolly smirked. "John Dillinger. The newspapers say he's in Saint Paul, Ma."

"Who?"

"Dillinger. They think the shootout yesterday, that was John Dillinger."

Dolly let the newspaper fall to the table.

"Ridiculous." She whispered: "If Dillinger was in town, Pat would know."

Dolly looked around, as if maybe even a whisper was too loud.

"I'm curious," said Father Mack. "Did you mean Patrick would know absolutely?"

"Oh, it's all arranged, Father," said Dolly. "Don't believe

what you read in the papers. If Dillinger is here, he came by arrangement. The fix is in."

Nora said: "Shooting up the streets? Machine guns! What if they had hit an innocent child?"

"Calm down, Ma, it wasn't Dillinger. The cops in this town couldn't bust up a poker game, never mind do battle with Dillinger."

"John Dillinger," said Nora. "He's a monster, that man. I believe he killed the Lindbergh baby.

"Okay, Ma."

"Little innocent baby Lindberg."

"Don't cry in public, Mother."

"My heart breaks for Colonel Lindberg. The bravest man on earth, and look what your gangsters did to him."

"So somewhere in your twisted mind, Patrick is responsible for the Lindberg kidnapping. What else, Ma? What other ..."

Nora slammed down knife and fork. "I demand that you divorce Patrick!"

Her eyes implored Father Mack for backup.

Dolly adopted a softer tone. "Must we always talk about upsetting things at dinner? No wonder I have indigestion."

"It's because you don't eat vegetables."

"You have a gift, Ma, for making me feel ten years old."

"I've been to see Mister DeCourcy the lawyer. Here are the papers."

Nora fished in her purse for a thin sheaf of papers and threw them onto the table. "And now I have a holy priest as a witness."

"I'm not divorcing Patrick, Ma."

"Why not? You don't love him, do you?"

"It's not worth divorcing him. We're not really man and wife anymore ..."

"Your bedroom life is not to be discussed in the presence of a holy priest."

"The last thing I want is another husband, so why bother with a divorce?"

"He buys you presents, that's why you won't divorce him. He gets drunk, feels bad about how rotten he treats you, and buys you presents, and you fall for it every time."

"It's no wonder you don't understand Patrick, Ma, he don't even understand himself. He tried to be a ballplayer and ended up a bat boy." She lowered her voice. "When the Barkers came to town he tried to be a level gangster. They laughed and sent him on errands. All his life he's been trying to prove himself a big man, but he ain't cut out for it. He's an errand boy, Ma, that's all he is."

"Then find yourself a real man."

"You know why Patrick can't be a gangster, Ma? Because he has a beating heart. He can't shoot a man in the head, like some of his so-called friends can do. He's a boy all right, but I'd rather be tied to him than the mean sons of bitches ...."

"So you admit he's a gangster."

Dolly glanced at Father Mack.

"Ma, Patrick runs a tavern. Taverns are not patronized by saints and angels... which you would know if you ever left the house. So take that divorce decree off the table. I'm not signing it. Patrick may be a lousy husband, but he's mine. You didn't make such hot choices yourself."

"Your father was injured on the job while trying to provide for his family."

"He fell off a boxcar drunk, the day after they fired him for stealing."

"Your father was an excellent provider."

Dolly snorted.

Father Mack had a sudden insight into this prickly young woman. It was clear now that she had chosen Patrick in rebellion against her mother. And if anyone sympathized with rebellion, it was Father Mack.

So, he realized, Dolly stayed with Patrick because she could live with him on equal terms, and just as important, her mother disapproved. Dolly, like Father Mack, was a born rebel, and in a strange way, life with Patrick was her declaration of independence. Just as enrolling in seminary was McCarthy O'Sullivan's rebellion against the heartless brutality of Ireland's civil war.

Father Mack finished his lemon meringue pie and checked his wristwatch. As he was evolving his exit excuse, through the cafeteria's doors pushed the Crumleys. Mary entered first, then the tall gawky son and the gimpy polio-leg daughter.

Inspector Crumley squeezed like a wedge of blubber into the revolving door and extracted himself with a whoosh of air. He passed the cash register without paying.

Mrs. Crumley, rotund but half the size of her husband, selected a table as the Inspector worked the room, patting backs, shaking hands, waving like the star of a particularly low vaudeville act.

"Inspector Whole Hog," muttered Dolly.

"More to be pitied than scorned," said Father Mack. "A fellow so gluttonous is trapped by constant dissatisfaction. A full belly distracts him but for an hour. He knows he's missing something, but cannot imagine what. His entire life is a quest for satisfaction, and he is doomed never to achieve it."

"I suppose so, Father," muttered Dolly, and threw her napkin over a half-eaten steak. "Don't you ever get tired of understanding people? To hell with them. They're not worth understanding."

She glared at the Crumley family. "We're just lucky we got here early. The Crumleys will wipe the place out."

"Your sniping has ruined my appetite," Nora said. "I'm sorry, Father. We've disappointed you. All the squabbling."

Father Mack forced a priestly smile as they all stood. Dolly, in cheerful bonnet, led them out the revolving doors and into an

Easter afternoon of swirling, fast-changing weather.

The wind blew eye-stinging dust, newspaper pages, and a man's cap through the narrow manmade canyons. One moment it was sunny, then slanting cold rain, then the wind calmed and the rain turned to snow. Just as abruptly, sunshine burst out again. All those changes happened as Father Mack escorted Nora and Dolly two blocks to the Wabasha Bridge. Saint Paul wasn't much of a city for vistas, and a bridge over the Mississippi was about as scenic as it got.

They walked with one hand holding their hats against the capricious wind, but on the bridge the weather became calm sunshine. The Mississippi, churning with spring mud, looked like a river of chocolate.

"We'll miss our streetcar," complained Nora.

"There'll be another one," countered Dolly. "I love the view from this bridge."

Dolly leaned on the concrete railing and stared. The great river snaked toward a hazy horizon.

"What's downriver, Father? Saint Louis and New Orleans, right? I so wish I had been born to the traveling class. I'd love to take a steamboat, believe me."

Father Mack leaned over the rail beside her. In the struggle for his Eternal Soul, priest and rebel wrestled. He wanted to throw his arms around her, press her warm body to his, plunge into a deep desperate kiss, carry her aboard a Pullman car and wake up beside her in New Orleans.

She turned to him. "Why can't I leave, Father? What is it that keeps me here?"

Traffic roared behind them and an unsettling vibration rumbled through the bridge.

"I've no answers," Father Mack said. "Some of us are born loyalists, some are born to rebellion. Others are born merely selfish, with nothing but greed in our hearts. Why God has created us so, and why He loves us regardless, I've no idea."

A gust of wind stole Dolly's Easter bonnet. With a lily flapping in its pink ribbon, it floated like a huge butterfly over the Mississippi, hung suspended, then tumbled as if wounded into the river.

"Oh, baby, your bonnet," Nora said, and rubbed her daughter's back.

Dolly watched it float out of sight, first a hat, then a smudge, then a speck, then nothing.

"Happy Easter," said Dolly, then burst into tears.

SAINT PAUL POLICE SCRAMBLE
AS DILLINGER DISAPPEARS
JAIL 30 PERSONS
FOR QUESTIONING

Saint Paul Daily News
Monday, April 2, 1934

FATHER MACK

Father Mack chose to deliver the Petition for Annulment in person. Provosts rarely ran their own errands, but the prospect of encountering Dolores Carey again was enough to get him into his plain black Plymouth. He'd endured a restless night at the Chancery. He'd been tormented by imagined scenes of the life he had rejected, with a lusty woman like Dolores, his evenings devoted to rowdy nightlife, instead of just plain devoted.

Oh, he was no eunuch. Young McCarthy had been all for the pubs and the lassies in Ballydehob.

Dolores, however, was absent. Nora, alone in her pristine living room, was washing windows.

"It's a brand-new product," Nora proclaimed at the sparkling bay window. She shook a silver can labeled WINDEX. "The hardware man said it works wonders, but watch out, Mrs. Carey, he says, it's like gasoline, you can't smoke around it."

She swiped at the window with a rag.

"I told him, I said, I am not some filthy smoker, sir."

She looked at Father Mack. "You never smoked, did you, Father?"

Father Mack squirmed. What expectations of purity these

Catholics invested in their priests. It was as bad here as in Ireland. But cherished beliefs were the most stubborn of human forces, and he was not fool enough to challenge them.

"I may have sneaked the odd puff in my youth," he evaded.

"It's true, isn't it, Father? You were a prize fighter in Ireland."

"There wasn't much in the way of prizes."

"You're such a modest man, Father. I heard you were a holy terror in Ireland."

"Most of us have every reason for modesty."

Nora capped the can of Windex. "Oh, Father, I do wish she'd come home. I worry about that girl so."

She lay the Windex can on a lace-covered table beside her black leather purse. She snapped open its brass clasp and drew out a dark pint. "It's for my nerves, Father." She showed him the label: LYDIA PINKHAM'S VEGETABLE TONIC.

"Mister Rosen at the pharmacy says I should take it three times a day."

As she tilted her head back for a long swallow, a black car pulled up, framed by those sparkling windows. Nora gagged. Father Mack rose from the easy chair.

That black Dodge rocked and out lumbered the massive Inspector James Crumley. Trailed by a man of normal size, Crumley trudged up the concrete path hatless, his coat flapping in the breeze. Nora's gnarled arthritic hands grabbed the brass knob, pulled the door open.

"Inspector Crumley. A delight to see you! I apologize about the mess."

Father Mack suppressed a smile. Nora's home was as antiseptic as a surgery parlor.

"Let me take your coat, Inspector and yours too, Detective McMullen. Of course, both you men are Good Catholics, you must know Father O'Sullivan."

McMullen tipped his fedora. Crumley sat in an easy chair, hands on his knees, like a school principal about to reveal that Nora's mischievous daughter had been expelled.

"How about a nice cup of tea?" Nora asked.

"We'll take one," said Crumley.

Had the man ever turned anything down?

When Nora retreated to the kitchen, Crumley said: "Father, I been meaning to ask about the Nine First Fridays. If you take Communion on nine First Fridays in a row, you're guaranteed safe from Hell, no matter what your sins. Right?"

Crumley glanced at McMullen.

"But they gotta be in a row," Crumley said. "McMullen here says it's any nine First Fridays and they don't got to be in a row. So which is it, Father?"

"This must be an American notion," said Father Mack. "I have no idea how such things get started."

"But the nuns told us, Father," said Crumley, looking to McMullen for support.

McMullen pulled a flask from his inside jacket pocket and held it, like it was a sacrament, in both hands.

Father Mack said: "I doubt the existence of a free pass to Heaven."

"Not even from the Pope?" said Crumley. "I heard this comes straight from the Pope."

Father Mack changed the subject to horse racing, which proved a perfect defense against pious insincerity. He enumerated the prospects of the top Derby horses while Nora carried in a silver platter, complete with a lemon, a pitcher of milk, lightly toasted white bread, jam and butter.

McMullen spiked his tea with whiskey.

In a quavering voice, Nora said: "Inspector, I fear this is not a social call."

"I need to see Dolly."

"Dolores?" Nora sank into a chair opposite Crumley. "What did she do now?"

Tears rimmed her eyes. "I sit up worrying all night. I hate the ring of the telephone, inspector."

"My daughter worries me too," said Crumley. "We live in dangerous times."

Nora pulled a handkerchief from an apron pocket and dabbed her eyes.

"I tried everything with Dolores," she said. "I had her put with the nuns ..." her eyes shifted to Father Mack, "and she ran off to spite me."

"Dolores means sorrow, right, Jim?" McMullen said.

"Huh?" said Crumley.

"Dolores," said McMullen, "it's Latin for sorrow."

"I wasn't no altar boy, like you were, now. We got a priest here who knows Latin."

"How about it, Father?" said McMullen.

"Sorrow. Sorrow indeed."

Crumley blew into his teacup and asked Nora: "Do you know when Dolly's coming home, now?"

"Inspector, may I be bold?" Nora asked.

Crumley shrugged.

"I want you to arrest Pat Reilly."

McMullen laughed.

Crumley said: "Why?"

"For crimes against my daughter."

Crumley winced. "We got nothing to take to a judge," he said. "Do we, Bulldog?"

"Nope," said McMullen.

"He is a thief," said Nora.

"The town's full of thieves," said Crumley. "Honest men have to steal to get along. That's how it is in these times."

"Oh, please, Inspector Crumley," Nora said, "if Reilly goes to prison, Father Mack will grant Dolores a divorce. Won't you, Father?"

"There's nothing quite so simple..." started Father Mack, but Nora trampled his words.

"He has committed enough crimes to go to prison ten times over."

Some subtle noise drew her eyes to the windows.

"Well, here she is now," said Nora and rushed the door. "Where have you been young lady? Where is your coat?"

Dolly held shimmering silver high heels in hand. Her stockings were crazed with rips and runs, her purple skirt disheveled, her blouse stained, perhaps with beer.

"Ma, can it will you?" Dolly nodded toward Crumley. "What's His Majesty doing here?"

"You're so rude!" complained Nora.

"Go, get the hell out of my house," Dolly barked at the cops. "I've got nothing to say to you."

She focused on Father Mack.

The primal male inside Father Mack admired her: fallen, sexy, bold and bad.

"Oh, the busybody Irish priest, I see."

That hit Father Mack like a punch to the gut. *Busybody?*

Dolly dropped her high heels in the dining room, stomped into the kitchen, followed by her mother. "Got anything for lunch in this joint?"

"You apologize right now," demanded Nora.

"Let them bring me to the police station," said Dolly. "I've been there before." She flung open the icebox. "No cold cuts?"

Crumley filled the kitchen doorway.

"You're crowding me," Dolly told Crumley. "What did I do now? Beat the streetcar out of a nickel?"

"This is a friendship visit," said Crumley, and attempted a smile.

Dolly sputtered. "Cops ain't my friends."

Nora shouted: "How did you become so brazen and coarse? I sacrificed everything to send you to the Sacred Heart."

"Let's all settle down," said Crumley. He leaned against the doorjamb like he owned the place.

Dolly buttered an end crust and devoured it.

"I came around to tell you," said Crumley, "the federals have put you both on a list."

"What list?" shrieked Nora.

"Shit list," said Dolly.

"They'll be watching you," said Crumley.

"Mister Hoover's men? Watching us? The Carey family?"

"Oh, now, ladies, just play it safe. Don't tell them nothing. Don't give them no names."

Nora winced.

"We in Saint Paul can handle our business, now," Crumley said. "We don't need Hoover's men from Washington. And we will hear everything you say to them Federals. Their office leaks like a retread tire, don't it Bulldog?"

"Leaks something terrible," McMullen agreed.

"Remember, now," Crumley said, "in a couple of weeks these G-men will go back to Washington, but we will be here the rest of our lives."

He winked at Dolly. "Won't we?"

Then he waddled into the living room. "When you've got your health, you've got everything, ain't that right, Bulldog?"

"Sh..." said McMullen, but with a glance at Father Mack, cut the vulgarity short and twisted it into "yeah." He tipped his fedora on the way out.

"Thank you, Inspector," called Nora.

When the door closed, Dolly spat: "Thank you, Inspector? Mother, you are such a fool. The man is a criminal with a badge. Don't you know a threat when you hear one?"

Father Mack stood bewildered. His reflexes had always been a touch slow. In Ireland these slow reflexes had cost him a championship. And he cursed himself as slow now. The detectives were driving away when he finally realized what had transpired. Standing at the window he stared at the disappearing police car.

"I can hardly believe it," said Father Mack. "The temerity! A priest sitting here as a witness, and police issuing veiled threats."

Dolly sputtered. "That's how it works," she said. "The crooked cops run this town. This ain't Catholic school."

She glared at Father Mack. "You're a horse racing fan, Father," she said. "Take the blinkers off and look around."

DILLINGER STORIES CIRCULATE, HE'S REPORTEDLY SEEN IN DULUTH

Saint Paul Daily News
April 2, 1934

BESS

Bess stared through wet glass into a heavy rain. She had chosen this apartment for its class: the most modern, cleanest, warmest place she had ever settled. The neighborhood was fashionable, with brick apartment buildings on the corners and cute bungalows in between. Two blocks away stood the city's better shops, theaters and restaurants. She had hoped to make a quiet, sane life here, in a respectable place that Lincoln could visit when he needed a break from studying ... what subjects did they teach in college?

Her living room was a maze of cardboard boxes. Elegant furniture, draped in white sheets, had been pushed to the walls. The despair of yet another move battled in her heart with the hope of a clean beginning.

This downpour was the great one Midwesterners awaited each spring, the one that washed the grit of winter into the sewers, then settled in to thaw the earth. Bess snubbed a cigarette in an ashtray she had just cleaned. From a sheet-draped end table, she plucked a steaming cup of coffee and held it before her with two hands. The steam of coffee, the foggy windows, the pouring rain: she savored this pause in a dreary week of unpacking, furniture lugging, wall painting.

When the yellow-striped Hudson rolled up, a bolt of anger shot into her heart. If granted god-like powers she would have blasted that car with lightning, incinerating its ego-mad owners. The sedan idled, huge raindrops ricocheting off its long, steaming hood. Out a back door popped Pat Reilly.

The Hudson roared off into the gray mist.

A minute later, Pat tapped timid at her propped-open door.

"Get in here," she said.

She eased the door shut. Pat's yellow rubber raincoat dripped on her gleaming wood floors. Bess dug a towel out of a cardboard box and threw it at him. It was fluffy, white, blue-striped with the words: HOTEL SAINT PAUL.

"Well, you'll be happy," said Pat, removing his raincoat, drying his thinning hair. "They're gone."

Bess, jaw clamped, contained her rage.

"Where's Eddie?" Pat asked.

"Out."

After an angry pause she added: "You couldn't resist, could you? You had to bring the movie stars by for one last reckless pass."

"Aw, gee, they're not so bad. He spends money, I'll tell you that."

"Good riddance ... the mouth on that girl. And Handsome Johnny can't pass a mirror without admiring his reflection."

"I need a favor."

"What a surprise. You're dripping. I'm trying to keep the floors nice. There's a damage deposit."

Pat unbuttoned his white dress shirt to reveal a sleeveless t-shirt that was almost as wet. He handed Bess the wet dress shirt.

"I'm the coat-check girl in my own home?"

"Actually, it's Harry needs the favor."

"And how is Harry? Funny I never hear from him."

"We've got a Van Meter problem."

"Van's another nut. Is it something in the water in Indiana?"

"Van's afraid to go back to his apartment."

"He ought to be."

"He's got heavy stuff back there. Bessie, the gang needs it."

"These people can't lay low. One minute they're hobnobbing in the nightclubs ..."

"One last favor, they'll be out of your hair."

Bess crossed her arms. She became aware that she was wearing her housecoat, a more revealing garment than she might have wanted.

"Excuse me," said Bess.

She dragged a cardboard box into the bathroom and locked herself in. She shed the housecoat to stand shivering in gray panties, rain beating at the frosted-glass window. She could not find a brassiere, but wasn't one of those big-breasted woman who absolutely needed one. She selected a rose-colored long-sleeved blouse, and a modest knee-length gray worsted skirt. The most important thing she needed to learn from Pat: Where was Harry? Unless she could contact Harry directly, she had scant hope of taking over the Green Lantern.

She stared into the medicine chest mirror. A bit vain yourself, Elizabeth. The red curly hair, a monthly appointment at the beauty parlor. Lipstick. Smudge of rouge, the hope of disguising a pale, lanky, mousy-haired woman slipping toward middle age. She compressed her lips. Her rival awaited in soggy clothes to be vanquished.

When she emerged, Pat was sitting on a cardboard box, smoking a Lucky, tapping ashes into his hand.

"Got an ashtray?" he asked.

"No I quit," said Bess.

"Since when?" said Pat.

She stood in the alcove, hands on hips. "Okay, what's your deal?"

"You need to fetch a tommy gun, two pistols and a vest."

"Belonging to Homer Van Meter, Dillinger gangster and

federal fugitive?"

"That's right. Say, you don't have coffee, do you?"

"Percolator's packed," lied Bess.

"Remember that apartment you arranged for Van Meter? Well, that's where the stuff is, but Van's in hiding now."

Bess laughed. "Oh *now* he's in hiding."

"He needs that tommy gun. They ain't easy to get. There's silver dollars in a paper bag on the kitchen table, grab that too. That's your fee."

"Why don't you do it?"

"I'm hot."

Bess sputtered.

"Nobody knows who you are, Bessie, please."

"You're hot? Don't make me laugh."

"Harry wants me to stay out of sight."

Bess loomed over him. "Let me talk to Harry. If he says so, I'll take your cleanup job. But I need to hear from Harry."

"I don't know where he is."

"But you talk to him!"

"He calls me on the safe phone."

"And you can't call him?"

Pat shook his head. He ducked into the kitchen, doused the cigarette in the sink.

"Bessie, come on. Nobody's following you."

"All right, I'll fetch their hardware but on one condition. I want Harry to call me direct."

"Do you even have a phone?"

"I will have, in the new place."

"Okay, when you get a phone, Harry calls."

"Reilly word of honor?"

Pat made the sign of the cross over himself. "Swear to God," he said. "I'll give Harry your number and ask him to call you."

"I want Dillinger's mob to stay away from Eddie. Clear?"

"Clear."

"The G-men are swarming all over town and it's time to lay low. Everybody. Lay low."

She fished a Raleigh out of her leopard purse.

"See I knew it," Pat said. "You can't quit. Nobody ever changes, not really. Once you start, you're a smoker for life." Pat lit her cigarette with his Statue of Liberty.

"Thank you," Bess said. "Where'd you get that lighter?"

"World's Fair."

She blew smoke. "How did a bat boy get mixed up with gangsters? You're no gangster, Patrick Reilly."

Pat lit another Lucky. "Trying to cut back, myself," he said. "You know Harry is a baseball fan. I used to see him and Gladys when I was with the Saints. The ballclub's manager introduced us. He recommended me. Harry asked me once: Can you get this ball autographed? I didn't know who he was."

"Oh come on, Pat, everybody knew."

"Honest to God! I got him the autograph, and he says, Murph says you're a good boy, stop down to the Green Lantern, I could use a guy like you."

"Well, isn't that a cozy story. Are you rehearsing it for the G-men?"

"I'm getting out of here."

"Do me a favor," said Bess. "Sneak out through the alley."

HOOVER DECLARES WAR ON GANGS HERE

Saint Paul Dispatch
April 3, 1934

BESS

It was raining when Eddie stumbled in, wet and drunk. Bess had packed their wardrobe, and escorted Eddie to the bedroom to show off her progress.

"That's my girl," he slurred. "Let me take you to dinner."

"We need to take a ride."

"To?"

"Lillian's," Bess said. "Then let's treat ourselves at the Grill Room."

"I gotta dress up?"

"So dress up. We're celebrating. The Indiana blowhards are gone."

"Yeah, I got the word."

Eddie stepped into the bathroom, opened the medicine cabinet, fumbled for shaving cream and razor. He shouted through the open doorway. "The new place is brighter."

"What?"

"The new apartment. Do you think it's brighter?"

"Hard to tell it's been so gray lately."

"It's bigger. Maybe that's it."

"It's a one bedroom, how is it bigger?"

Bess stood at the door watching him shave. He was a dark stubble sort. If he'd been a businessman, he'd need two shaves a day. Cave man, honestly, was part of his appeal. She was the brains of this outfit, he was the muscle. She fetched a pink button-down shirt and returned to the bathroom doorway.

Shaving-cream icebergs floated in the sink. Eddie wiped his straight razor with a hotel towel.

She said: "We have to fetch something at Lillian's."

He folded the razor, laid it on the sill of the pebbled glass window. The man never put away his weapons, his razor, his tools.

Bess said: "Lillian has got some of Van Meter's stuff."

"Oh." Eddie noticed he had nicked himself. "Goddamn it." He blotted that bloodstream with a tiny wad of toilet paper.

"I sent Lillian to Van's apartment to clean up. Van's stuff is at her house now. A couple of suitcases. Some of it is hardware."

"And...?"

"And nothing. We leave it in a locker at Union Depot and we're rid of that joker."

"Van's all right."

"Just the same."

"He's got balls. A good man to have on your side. He is not scared of a copper or a G-man either."

"Okay, handsome, let's ride."

Eddie's LaSalle, and their nice clothes, high-class furniture, and cash stashed around town, was owed to Eddie's talent for sniffing out vulnerable banks. The LaSalle was a particular point of pride, with leather seats, whitewall tires, defroster and radio. Sitting in it, Bess, a milkman's daughter, enjoyed a sense of privilege, maybe even luxury.

This sense was sharpened by their drive into Rondo. Here, in a neighborhood surrounded by Germans, Irish and Scandinavians, was a strip of Negro Saint Paul, consisting of storefronts and apartments, served by a streetcar line with the most erratic service in town. In Rondo lived nearly every dark-skinned human being in the city, from doctors to preachers to cutthroats, nurses to teachers to prostitutes. Barbecue shacks, liquor stores, grocers, barber shops, playgrounds, juke joints, churches, taverns and drugstores ran along the streetcar tracks. Bess had grown up in a big family in a poor, loud, lively neighborhood like this, only a white one, on the other side of town. Rondo reminded her of shivering winters huddled around a barely warm coal stove, of hand-me-down clothing and milk-and-cornbread suppers. She became a speakeasy flapper and rose above that scrabbling life. She discovered that drunken gangsters left extravagant tips. Anyone who believed money could not buy happiness had never endured a Minnesota winter on scant coal.

But only so much happiness. Bess often regretted taking the speakeasy path through life. They had a Catholic college for girls in this town, and Bess could never pass it without feeling ashamed of herself. The girls taking classes in there were no smarter than she was.

Eddie drove past the barbecue shack run by Lillian and her brother. It stood next to a shuttered newsstand, its windows steamed in the rain. A streetcar let off a family of three who, huddled, ran through the downpour. The storm had driven everyone else indoors. Eddie turned the LaSalle down a street of small homes and cruised past Lillian's house. The tulips lining Lillian's white picket fence had withstood the storm. He parked across the street and down an alley.

He drummed, fingers on steering wheel.

"Were we followed?"

Bess shook her head.

"Leave it running," he said. "I'll be right back."

Eddie slammed the door. He didn't like the radio playing while he drove so only now did Bess turn it on. A doctor's discussion of polio on KSTP caused her to tune its Minneapolis rival, WCCO. Yes! They were playing the Bennie Moten Orchestra, outrageous jazz, a cheerful counterpoint to the rain. Fat raindrops beaded the windshield, and the fog thickened. The rain beat so loud on the roof that Bess turned the radio to maximum. She huddled in her red corduroy jacket, feet tapping to the music. Saint Paul had some okay orchestras but this Kansas City sound, it was so alive.

Bess lit the last cigarette from a pack of Raleighs. She fished the coupon out, crumpled the pack, another fifteen cents wasted. Coupons, hell, she could buy twenty lamps with the money she'd save if she'd quit smoking.

With the back of her hand, Bess cleared the window fog. She saw Eddie stumble at the gate of Lillian's picket fence. He opened the gate, staggered, fell face forward, struggled to stand, took two steps, collapsed in the street.

She leaped out.

Men in trench-coats sprang on the fallen Eddie and one pointed a tommy gun at Bess.

"Don't shoot me! What are you doing?"

She ran to Eddie and saw with horror that he was bleeding, awful, from his head, his face distorted, ugly, his legs twitching, eyes rolling. How could he be shot? She hadn't heard a thing.

Bess dropped to her knees, cradled Eddie's bloody head. "Talk to me Eddie," she pleaded.

A neighbor lady appeared on her porch. Bess spread her arms and implored her: "My god! Help us! Somebody help us please?"

FEDS SAY DILLINGER WAS HERE

Saint Paul Daily News
April 4, 1934

The search for John Dillinger, notorious Indiana desperado, shifted back to Chicago today as one of his companions, critically wounded in an ambush by Federal agents Tuesday, lay near death at Ancker hospital.

Dillinger gangster Eddie Green confessed he was one of the men at the shootout Saturday at apartments on Lexington Parkway. Doctors have given him one chance in seven of surviving bullet wounds to the shoulder and head.

Green was wounded when he defied federal agents who accosted him in the home of a Negress, at 778 Rondo St. about 6 p.m. Tuesday. Green made a menacing move and was fired upon and shot. He arrived at this address in an automobile and had with him a woman who claimed to be his wife. Seeing her companion wounded, the woman called to a neighbor for help.

The woman was taken into custody, but has refused to make any statement concerning her identity or activities.

BESS

"Let's try again. Your name?"

"Bess."

"Bess or Beth?"

"Call me anything you want."

"Last name?"

"I want to see my husband."

"We may be able to bring that about," said the man in the fine gray suit. "Where did you say you were born?"

"In a manger. That's why my parents named me Beth. I was born in Beth-lehem under a bright shining star."

They sat facing each other, an oak desk between them, in a clean bright office overlooking Rice Park. Out there stood the Hotel Saint Paul and its swanky Grill Room, where Bess and Eddie would never arrive for dinner. Bess jammed a Chesterfield between her lips, stared out the window.

"I'd just quit smoking," she complained.

Inspector Clegg circled his desk and flick, lit her cigarette.

"The doctors assure us," Clegg said. "He has a chance."

Bess smoked with her free hand. The other was handcuffed to a green radiator that whistled at a chill evening.

"If you didn't know who he was, why did you shoot him? Why did you shoot my husband?"

Clegg's thick lips twitched.

"You cold, cold bastards." She sputtered tobacco flecks at the photo of J. Edgar Hoover.

"You should admit ..." Clegg said, "that the man you call your husband ... is John Dillinger. Then we will escort you across the street for a good night's sleep. In the morning ... we will see a judge about bail. Alternatively, you can wait here all night ... and we can resume this dialog in the morning."

"What's the charge?"

"Harboring a public enemy."

"That's a crime?"

Clegg pushed a clean glass ashtray at her. "Your husband admitted he's Dillinger."

"He's delirious. Because one of your men shot him and the doctors have pumped him full of drugs. He's not Dillinger."

"He looks like Dillinger."

"To hell he does."

"Suppose you tell me ..." said Clegg, sitting back, "exactly how you know what Dillinger looks like."

"I've seen newsreels. Look, maybe Eddie's trying to throw you guys off. I am not married to John Dillinger. Check Eddie's driver's license if you don't believe me."

"We did. And we gave the name Eddie Green to the newspapers. But criminals ..."

"He's not a criminal, he's an ironworker."

"... commonly use aliases. We still suspect he's Dillinger. Tell us more about your husband. How did you meet him?"

"I'm not talking in handcuffs."

"Suppose I take them off?"

"Still not talking."

"He shot at our agents ... this man you claim is not Dillinger."

"Baloney, Eddie never shot anybody."

"Oh yes, he's admitted it. He tried to kill two of our agents

… when they knocked on Dillinger's apartment door on the day before Easter."

"He's delirious. He was with me on Easter Saturday. All day. He didn't shoot any cops or anybody else."

"How well do you know Alvin Karpis?"

"As well as I know Franklin Roosevelt."

"How about Fred Barker and his brother Doc?"

"The only Doc I know is my physician."

"Does the name Harry Sawyer mean anything to you?"

"Tom Sawyer's brother?"

"I'd like to banter all evening," said Clegg. "But while we're trying to save your husband's life..."

"Save his life? You bastards shot him!"

"He forced our hand, unfortunately. Mrs. Dillinger, you have my word that our agency regrets these necessities."

"Oh really?"

"How about Tommy Carroll?"

"How about him?"

"When was the last time you saw him?"

"In my nightmares."

Clegg sat back. "I would like to take you to visit your husband ... he has been calling your name. I think it would be good for him to see you ... it would cheer him up, he is pretty seriously hurt ... but first, I need some basic information, so might we try again? Where were you born?"

"In a hospital."

"Any particular one?"

"It had beds and nurses."

"Where was your husband John Dillinger employed?"

"First National Bank."

Clegg grimaced. "And what was his position there?"

"He was in charge of withdrawals."

Clegg circled his desk, tapping a pencil on a leather

notebook.

Some man was out there, one-finger typing. Only a man, Bess judged, would type like that. Most of the agents seemed to have gone to dinner but this typist was tapping like a punch-drunk fighter.

"While we are here chatting," Clegg said, "your husband John Dillinger is in the hospital calling for you."

"Then take me to see him."

"I am afraid I cannot do that ... until I know who he is and who you are."

"He's Clark Gable, I'm Myrna Loy. We took a wrong turn out of Hollywood."

She smashed the cigarette on the radiator. She would have stomped it into their precious polished floor but the bastards had taken her shoes.

"Look, Inspector Clegg, I don't know John Dillinger, I never met John Dillinger, I don't personally believe the famous Dillinger has ever been anywhere near Saint Paul. I suggest you look for him in Chicago, where all the real crooks are."

"Maybe we will do that. Until then..."

He rose from behind his desk, picked up Bess's manacled wrist, and unlocked the handcuffs with a tiny key.

Bess rubbed her red-raw wrist. She looked up at the big G-man. She felt a flush of something warm, gratitude maybe, but that made no sense.

"Have a comfortable evening," Clegg drawled. "I will lock you in, but Agent Guerrero will have the key ... he will be in the next room until morning, should you have a sudden urge to communicate."

Bess had to pee pretty bad, but would wait. She wasn't going to give in to Clegg now.

"Is your husband Catholic? Should we call a priest?"

She shrugged, tried to keep alarm off her face. Did Eddie

need the last rites?

Bess watched as Inspector Clegg closed the door, then she turned and stared out the window at the city lights. Dark feelings surged inside her, but she couldn't get a handle on any of them. She had the odd vision of herself and Clegg as bride and groom, in formal black and white, at a flowered altar.

She shook that crazy vision off. She had to resist these G-men, for Eddie's sake. If he survived they would send him away for life as Dillinger's accomplice. But would he survive? Bess said a silent Hail Mary for Eddie. She didn't want him to die with bank robbery, a mortal sin, on his soul.

GREEN DYING, DILLINGER'S GANG BELIEVED SPLIT UP

Saint Paul Dispatch
April 9, 1934

FATHER MACK

Father Mack worked black rosary beads in his huge hands. He sat sweating on a bench, next to a clanking radiator, watching white-clad doctors, nurses and orderlies rush by. *Hail Mary, full of grace, the Lord is with thee...*

Agent Guerrero leaned against a wall. Protruding from his trousers pocket, a rolled-up Daily News. A nurse stopped to flirt. Guerrero whispered, she laughed.

Inspector Clegg appeared in the doorway. "Father?"

Father Mack entered to see Eddie Green writhing on sheets stained by blood and body fluid. Eddie moaned, legs jerking and twitching. He wore sweaty, rumpled white pajamas. Father Mack lay hands on Eddie's feverish forehead. He looked across the bed into Hugh Clegg's eyes. "The poor man is on fire."

"The doctors are trying, Father."

Father Mack set his black leather bag on a sculpted chair. He nodded at federal agents Short and Coulter. Despite the overheated atmosphere, the agents kept their suit coats buttoned tight.

Eddie, breathing with a rasp, muttered: "Bessie."

The agents exchanged glances.

"Where did you put the sweet rolls, Bessie?" cried Eddie. He tried to rise, fell back into a delirious sweat.

"Try again?" Coulter asked Clegg.

Clegg nodded.

Coulter walked into the hallway and returned with a red-haired nurse. The woman removed her white paper cap and approached the bedside.

"Here she is, Eddie," said Agent Short. "Bessie's here."

It was certainly not Bessie, and Father Mack scowled at both agent and nurse.

"Uff," said Eddie.

"Eddie," said Agent Short. "Bessie needs to know what you did with the money."

Eddie's eyes fluttered. There was no way to know whether his glazed eyes and fevered brain could recognize the red-haired woman at his bedside.

"Tell Harry he's running out of time," Eddie murmured.

Short said: "Tell Bessie where Dillinger is hiding, Eddie."

"Who?"

"Dillinger."

Eddie moaned.

"Come on, Eddie," said Short. "You know."

"He's in the garage underneath the bed," Eddie said.

"What garage?" asked Short.

Eddie licked his swollen, cracked lips.

Agent Short urged him: "Tell Bessie where Dillinger's garage is."

"Bessie," said Eddie and reached trembling for the nurse's hand. "Don't let them cut off my ears." Then he shouted in pain: "Oh, Lord!" A tremor rippled through him.

Short bent toward him. "Dillinger's garage. Where is it Eddie?"

"Keep looking," said Eddie.

"Where?"

"Under the goddamn bed," said Eddie.

"What city is it in?"

Eddie dropped the nurse's hand. "Call the fire department," muttered Eddie. "Hook and ladder. I'm way up here on the tenth floor."

Father Mack cornered Clegg at a white cloth screen.

"No way down!" shouted Eddie. "I'm gonna jump, I swear to God I'm gonna jump."

"You'll get nothing from a delirious man," Father Mack told Clegg.

"He is in and out, Father," said Clegg.

"Surely such tactics are unbecoming to the United States Government," said Father Mack.

Clegg said: "Perhaps you should hear his confession and depart, Father O'Sullivan."

Father Mack sized Clegg up. Big, soft as a banker, and Protestant. Would not last a round.

"Clear the room, then," Father Mack said, "and I'll administer the Sacraments."

The G-men stepped into the hallway at Clegg's urging, but Guerrero would not allow Father Mack to shut the door. So with his back turned to the agents, Father Mack donned his purple stole, pulled a small gold crucifix from his pocket, kissed it.

"Eugene Edward Green, child of our Merciful Lord, are you ready to make a Good Confession?"

Eddie snorted.

"Nod if you understand me, my son."

Eddie opened his eyes.

Father Mack blessed him with the sign of the Cross. *"In nomine patris, et filus, et spiritus sanctus."*

He put the gold crucifix in Eddie's clenched fist. A sideways glance revealed that someone in polished shoes had sneaked behind

the white curtain. Canon law allowed a priest to presume
Confession in cases of coma or delirium. To foil the snooping
G-man he absolved Eddie's sins in Latin:

"Dominus noster Jesus Christus te absolvat; et ego auctoritate ipsius te absolvo."

From his leather kit he brought a tiny gold container, the size
of a woman's compact. From it he extracted the Host wafer,
touched it to Eddie's tongue, broke off a sliver, and stuffed it into
Eddie' cheek.

A commotion in the hallway made Father Mack turn from
the suffering man. Out there a shouting match was developing
between G-men and Inspector Crumley. The obese detective,
jacket open, shoulder holster revealed, shook his finger in
Guerrero's face.

Guerrero closed the door, and in Eddie's room, the argument
among policeman was muffled. Poor Eddie's head had swollen and
was leaking clear fluid into the bandages. Father Mack stroked his
feverish forehead. "They have pierced my hands and feet," he
muttered. "They have numbered all my bones."

He filled a water glass from a white enamel pitcher. Wetting
his finger, he touched it to Eddie's parched lips. "If you have sins
to confess, Eddie, now is the time."

Eddie opened his eyes.

"Who are you?"

"Father O'Sullivan, agent of our all-forgiving Lord."

"Get me out of here, Father, this place is on fire."

"We hope to bring you home soon, Eddie."

Eddie gagged. His eyelids fluttered and a rasping noise rattled
his throat. Father Mack strode to the door, flung it open and
commanded Clegg:

"Fetch the doctor!"

Crumley stepped in. He shook Eddie's shoulder. "Where'd
you hide Harry's money?"

From the other side of the bed, Father Mack began to anoint, with holy olive oil from a tiny bottle, Eddie's eyes, ears, nostrils, fingers and feet, praying in Latin.

"You know it's in safe deposit, now," cajoled Crumley. "Give me the number."

Father Mack finished in English: "By the Sacred mysteries of man's redemption, may almighty God remit to you all penalties of the present life and of the life to come: may He open to you the gates of paradise and lead you to joys everlasting."

"Bess is outside," Crumley shouted into Eddie's ears. "She wants the number."

Eddie's eyes opened wide.

"Oh!" he said, and exhaled one final time.

EDDIE GREEN, GUN PAL
OF DILLINGER, DIES

DILLINGER GIRLFRIEND
FRECHETTE
NABBED IN CHICAGO

Saint Paul Dispatch
April 11, 1934

BESS

Bess, feeling weak and dizzy, stared into a hole in the ground that had received the remains of Eddie Green. Her lips trembled. She could either choke it all back or blubber like a terrified child. There were federal men watching so she bit and held. *I will come back and cry for you, hard-luck Eddie,* she promised his ghost. *But I told you, darling, Dillinger would bring us nothing but grief.*

Father Mack, scepter in his big hands, sprinkled holy water on the bronze casket. Eddie's brothers and sobbing mother, ignoring Bess as if she were a stray dog, threw flowers into the grave. Bess turned and linked arms with Inspector Hugh Clegg. With the heaviest steps of her life she forced herself to walk away from Eddie's grave. She told herself she was feeling weak because she had not eaten a hot meal all week, subsisting on ham sandwiches, apple pie and coffee delivered by federal office girls.

Inspector Clegg was dressed in funeral black, with the exception of starched white shirt, gray fedora, and dark blue tie. The jacket hung open, for Clegg might need quick access to his shoulder holster. Bess imagined that Eddie, looking down from Heaven, would be both horrified and amused that his burial was a police event. It was taking place in a tiny cemetery overlooking the

Mississippi. Four uniformed policemen patrolled the cemetery's borders on horseback. Around the grave, Saint Paul detectives outnumbered Eddie's relatives. Bulldog McMullen stood alert, as if gangsters with tommy guns might pop up behind the headstones. Inspector Crumley lumbered around in seersucker suit and Panama hat, as if vacationing in Palm Beach. Most of the G-men stuck close to their cars, which were packed with machine guns and bullet-proof vests. The cemetery gates were blocked by squad cars, and two cops with German shepherds sniffed around in the pine trees.

Only when she stepped away from the grave did the pall of Eddie's burial lift and permit Bess a shocking realization.

The cops were there to protect her.

She was a target now.

She walked toward the black police cars, terrified and weak-kneed. Alive, Eddie had been her insurance policy. The gangsters knew she could not talk without sending Eddie to Leavenworth. With Eddie in his grave, she had no reason to keep quiet.

They would get her, either the Barkers or the Dillinger gang. These gangsters had gunned down armed policemen and would have no trouble killing a tavern hostess. She leaned on the hood of a federal Ford and Clegg put a hand gentle on her back.

"Do you need a doctor?"

She shook her head.

"We brought one along."

"No," Bess whispered. "Please get me out of here."

She shook off that weak-kneed feeling and slipped into the back seat of the Ford. Beside her the dignified Clegg said softly: "I wish it could have been another way."

Father Mack got in and Bess was squeezed between big men representing the most powerful institutions in human history: the Roman Catholic Church and the United States Government. She shut her eyes, heard the clip clop of horses and the grinding start of police motorcycles. She flinched at the slamming of car doors.

"I doubt it will rain," said Father Mack.

Bess opened her eyes. Agent Short was behind the steering wheel. The tough cowboy agent Rufus Coulter, unlit cigarette in his lips, sat with a gun between his knees, barrel pointed up at the gray fabric roof.

"It looks to hold off," added Father Mack. He rolled down his window to let in soft April air. Behind her black veil, Bess began to leak tears. They seemed to well up directly from the lump in her throat.

They drove out the cemetery's road and her sense of alarm settled down to weary resignation. Her worst fear had not come true: she had imagined Lincoln showing up at the cemetery, seeking to protect her. She bit her lower lip. Feeling had returned to it, and pain, at least that was something.

Agent Short drove them to the streetcar-suburb of Mac-Groveland, and then up a long driveway and into a gray garage. The garage was detached from a bungalow painted the same battleship hue. Other agents pulled in behind to guard their exit from the garage. Father Mack and Inspector Clegg escorted her through the rooms of a cute, well-kept home, with polished oak floors and elegant furniture. All the shades were drawn, as if the agents feared a sniper.

When Bess pulled a pack of cigarettes out of her purse, Clegg said: "Out of respect for the owners, we will only smoke on the porch."

So Bess stepped onto that screen porch with Agent Short and Agent Guerrero as smoking companions. A breeze rustled just-budding trees and leaked through the screens. An upright piano and bench were jammed against the wall. She watched Cowboy Coulter and Father Mack climb into a federal car.

"Where are they going?" Bess asked.

"Lunch," said Guerrero. He was a handsome guy and could

hardly have been a year out of law school. "Believe me," he said, "you want Coulter to make your food runs. The guy's got a nose. He says he's never seen a town with such bland food. I said, what do you expect? It's all Irish and Norwegian here."

Bess was trying these new cigarettes, Kool. They did not come with coupons, unfortunately, but were minty and easier on the throat. Short lit her cigarette.

"So," said Bess, and blew smoke. "Are you the men who shot my husband?"

"No ma'am," said Short.

"I won't stand for this," said Guerrero, and glared at Bess as he walked into the living room.

Bess squared off with Short.

"Were you *with* the men who shot my husband?"

"Yes ma'am."

"You must be very proud of yourself, then. Big strong he-man."

Short stared through the screens at the street.

"Mrs. Green," he said in a confidential tone, "it might have been a terrible mistake, but that's not something I ... I'll deny saying it. We don't make mistakes at the Department of Justice, and when we do we don't admit it. I'm sorry for your personal loss, though, I can admit that."

"My *personal* loss," said Bess and blew smoke out the screen. "It has such a *government* sound."

She offered Short a cigarette and he accepted.

"Are you married, Agent Short?"

She lit his cigarette from a Green Lantern matchbook, its cover depicting a champagne bottle.

"Children?"

Short nodded.

In widow's black, she sat in a wooden-swing glider, removed hat and veil, dropped them onto a green-striped canvas chair.

"Too bad," she said, and shook her hair free. "Screwed up world."

Short sat on the piano bench. "I'll tell you one thing." He threw his fedora atop the piano. "Neither my son nor daughter is going anywhere near law enforcement."

"Why do you say that?"

Short reached for a glass ashtray.

"Honestly?"

"Honestly," said Bess.

"You can't blink but somebody tells you you did it wrong."

Inspector Clegg walked down the driveway and stood, hands on hips, surveying the street.

"I never said that," Short said. "We were talking about baseball, Mrs. Green. I understand you are a baseball fan. Cardinals or Cubs?"

"Oh, Cardinals, definitely."

"Leo Durocher, now there's a shortstop. He's the definition of a shortstop."

"I agree, Agent Short."

"Have you ever seen him play?"

"Yes, in Chicago, at Wrigley Field."

"Chicago?" said Short. "Ah. Haven't been to Chicago much, except passing through on a train."

Clegg drove away in a boxy green Buick. Guerrero poked his head out to the porch.

"Miserable son of a bitch," Guerrero muttered.

"Now now," said Short.

"I'd bust him man to man," said Guerrero.

"Edgar wouldn't like that."

Clegg's car turned the corner and out of sight.

Guerrero tilted his straw hat back on his head.

"Agent Guerrero," said Short, "believes he has detected a whiff of old-boy prejudice emanating from the East Coast establishment. Is that right, Guerrero?"

"What?" Guerrero said.

"Believe it or not," Short said, "there are white guys on Clegg's shit list, too."

Guerrero warned him: "Short, we're in the presence of a prisoner."

"I forgot," said Short. "Sometimes I feel like I'm the prisoner."

He lifted the piano lid and played casual chords.

"You play," said Bess. "Agent Short, I'm surprised."

"Just a few jazz chords. No baby is born with a machinegun in his hand, Mrs. Green."

He played the first few notes of Rhapsody in Blue.

"Clegg and Edgar Hoover are friends," Short said. "One mistake in this outfit, and you're chasing goat rustlers in Shreveport. I've already made my mistake. But I never said that."

"And what was that mistake?

He looked around. Agent Guerrero had exited the porch, and now stood out on the sidewalk.

"I had Dillinger in my sights and failed to bring him down." Short heaved a sigh. "What was your big mistake?"

"Mine, oh." Bess sat glum, head in her hands. "Where would I even begin?"

"I missed the War. So I thought, federal lawman, next best thing." Short stubbed out his cigarette, closed the lid over the keys. "Every young man wants to be a hero. Tell me, what was Dillinger like?"

"I never met John Dillinger."

"I thought we were being honest here."

Bess removed black high heels, rubbed her stockinged feet.

"I had an aunt who was a bootlegger," she said. "It was a two-girl operation. They may have been lovers, I don't know. That doesn't shock you, does it, Agent Short, from big bad Washington

D.C.? They operated a still. They wore dirty overalls and they were not afraid of men. They had the whole bootlegging operation in a garage, a home-built wonderland of boilers and pipes. I saw it before it burned down. I assumed it was a gang, rival bootleggers that burned them out. But I found out it was the Saint Paul Police, who torched them for not paying off. Correction. Not paying off *enough*."

Short nodded.

"That's when I decided whose side I was on. You're not going to tell that story to Inspector Clegg, are you? I don't want him knowing much about me."

"Clegg's all right. He can be a little rough on our Mexican friend there, but Clegg is a straight arrow. He's tight with Hoover, but he couldn't help me if he wanted to. Nobody can help me. I'm the guy who let Dillinger get away. I'm the scapegoat. I'll never live it down."

"Dillinger," said Bess. "He's as much fun as the Spanish flu."

"I thought you never met him."

"Hearsay," she said. "That's all it is."

"I thought you should know," Short said. "Some of the guys wanted to bring the Fireman in to work on you. Clegg said no."

"The Fireman?"

"He hoses people down," Short said.

"Oh," said Bess.

"Clegg figured he could win you over without, you know, tactics. We're civilized men, Mrs. Green, fighting an uncivilized mob, so ..."

Bess entertained the notion that Inspector Clegg actually liked her. Maybe was sweet on her. Had he protected her from harsh interrogation? Or were his agents toying with her, trying to make Clegg appear to be the Good Cop?

The blue Ford containing Agent Coulter and Father Mack pulled up and the two men emerged, carrying greasy white bags.

Father Mack mounted the front steps and said: "A Jewish deli open on their Sabbath. What do you think of that?"

"We're lucky," said Coulter. "That place smelled like a Jewish heaven, Father."

They all gathered at the dining room table. Father Mack removed beret and cassock to reveal sharp-pressed black trousers and a soft green shirt. Agent Guerrero grabbed a wrapped sandwich, announced that a percolator full of coffee awaited on the kitchen stove, then sat guard at the rear door. Agent Short took his sandwich to the screen porch.

Cowboy Coulter, Father Mack and Bess sat at the mahogany table, its lacy cloth already stained by their greasy lunch. There was no choice: everyone got pastrami on rye, sloppy with mustard, a sour pickle in wax paper, and cardboard tray of potato chips.

Father Mack blessed himself and prayed: "Jesus I ask your blessing upon this meal and all who partake."

"Amen."

"Splendid," said Father Mack.

Coulter, licking pastrami grease off his fingers, arose to remove his suit jacket. Underneath was vest, shirt, tie, gold badge pinned to the vest. A shoulder holster contained a black revolver.

He asked: "What do you think of Baer's chances, Father?"

Father Mack swallowed. "I've no interest in the fight game."

"I thought you were once a boxer, Father."

"And Jesus was a Jew until he saw the light."

"You don't read about boxing in the papers?"

"The game is fixed entirely," said Father Mack, crunching potato chips.

"Are you speaking from personal experience, Father?"

"Aye."

"Jeez," said Coulter. "I'm afraid to ask the next question."

"But you're a policeman and must ask. Proceed then."

"Did you ever take a dive, Father?"

Father Mack snorted. He set his sandwich down on its greasy bag.

"Have you ever taken a bribe, Mister Coulter? The question is insulting."

The lid over Father Mack's bad eye began to flutter. "The federal government," he steamed, "is but a bully, prosecuting this poor woman."

Coulter set his sandwich down, and seemed astonished at this turn in the conversation.

"Where in the name of God did you get your temerity?" the priest asked.

"Father," said Coulter.

"Father," said Bess, but she was secretly thrilled. Someone, at last, was taking her side.

"On the very day she put her husband into the ground ..."

Father Mack ignored the fact that Bess and Eddie were not husband and wife but had been living in Sin.

" ... you bring her back in handcuffs..."

"Nobody handcuffed me, Father."

"... aye but they might as well have, for a ninth straight day of imprisonment, prosecution and interrogation, all without legal representation. That would be an outrage in any country but Russia. Stalinist Russia! And here she is a fine, grieving Catholic housewife who's committed no crime except to take loving care of the husband you murdered."

"Just a goddamn minute," said Coulter.

"Murdered the man in cold blood, it even said so in the newspapers. To satisfy the bloodlust of your criminal in chief, J. Edgar Hoover. You murder her husband, then chain her to a radiator until the poor woman urinates upon herself, what kind of demons are ye?"

Coulter stood, wagged a finger in the giant priest's face. "There are harboring laws, Father. She harbored a criminal."

"Bah on your laws. Who convicted Eddie Green and of what crimes? The man was an upstanding Catholic. He would leave bags of groceries for the poor at the rectory."

"He would?" Bess said.

"And coats for the freezing children in winter."

"He did?" Bess said. "He never told me that."

"His money," Coulter said, "was stolen from banks, Father."

"Then stolen twice, because the banks first stole it from the poor."

"Okay, okay," said Bess, her hands held wide like a referee. "Eddie was no saint."

"Enough out of you!" roared the priest, glaring at Bess. "I've a mind to take you over my knee but you're too old for it entirely."

Father Mack snorted. He sank into his chair, dropped his big black curly head into his ham-sized hands. After a long deep breath he said: "By the mercy of God I've made a fool of myself. I don't know what gets into me."

He looked around, as if surprised to find himself dining with a G-man and his prisoner.

"The Devil got to me. And now I've spoiled our lunch."

"That's all right, Father."

"Will you forgive me, agent Coulter?"

"Certainly, Father."

"I beg your forgiveness, Mrs. Green."

Bess burst into tears.

Father Mack looked up to implore heaven: "McCarthy O'Sullivan, aren't you the awful priest, look at the embarrassment you've caused these suffering souls."

Coulter handed Bess a white silk handkerchief from his suit pocket.

Short stuck his head in from the porch. "Everything all right in here?"

"Yeah," Coulter waved him off. "All right. Been a tough day.

We're okay. Go back to your piano."

Coulter sat down to his lunch again. He said: "If Hoover found out Short played the piano on duty..."

"I should have mentioned, Father," said Bess, "I intend to plead guilty."

DILLINGER AND PAL
RAID INDIANA JAIL
TAKE GUNS,
SAFETY VESTS
FROM POLICE

Saint Paul Daily News
April 13, 1934

BESS

Bess had no hope of quitting smoking now. The goddamn cigarettes were going to kill her. She looked at her hand, low cards, no pairs. She dropped the cards face down on the table. She glanced at her four captors. They were winning. It was only pennies but they were taking every cent she had.

Over ten days of captivity, she had become strangely attracted to Hugh Clegg. She was ashamed of this feeling and did her best to hide it. It seemed disloyal to Eddie. If he wasn't already dead, it would kill him to know she was falling for a G-man. Could the dead read our thoughts from Heaven? Bess suspected they could.

Sitting beside the virile Mister Clegg was Coulter, the lean Arkansas cowboy, Guerrero, the exotic from California, and Short, the pale Washington bureaucrat. They all wore white shirts with loosened ties except for Clegg, who never removed his suit jacket. Emptied bottles of Coke stood like glass towers on a battlefield of playing cards, ashtrays, pennies, cigarette packs and plates smeared with scraps of pie.

Except for the Department of Justice office, it was dark at the federal courthouse. The only sound was relentless typing coming over the transom from another room.

"Your deal," grunted Coulter.

Bess shuffled cards. Her fingernails, once elegant red, were chipped and bitten down.

"Five card stud," Bess said.

"Most honest game there is," said Coulter.

Bess dealt cards. She took a sip from her Coke bottle, leaving red lipstick on the rim. Clegg had sent to Walgreens for lipstick and Pepto Bismol, small kindnesses that had caused Bess to favor him.

"Okay, I'm out." Coulter slapped his cards on the table. He walked to the big windows, stared at Rice Park. "Does it ever get warm in this town? Christ it's been a long winter."

"Mister Coulter," drawled Clegg, "we're in the presence of a lady."

Guerrero raked in the penny pot, his dark eyes lively. "That's how we play in Frisco. But for dollars."

Coulter, at the windows, lit a cigarette.

Short pushed back his chair. "I've got to get some sleep."

Clegg unbuttoned his suit jacket, dusted something off his shirt, fiddled with his gold circle tie clasp.

Bess lit a Kool. "All right," she said. "I'm busted out."

She didn't want the agents to notice her hands trembling, so after two quick puffs, she ditched the cigarette into the ashtray.

"We going to be here all night?" Coulter complained.

Clegg, like a kindly uncle, allowed a smile. "Don't mind Mister Coulter's impatience ... he's been in Saint Paul a long time ... you cannot blame a man for wanting to go home to his family."

Bess, in a flowered dress that was beginning to smell bad, sat on the radiator to which she'd once been chained.

Clegg walked to his desk, took out of its top drawer a gold cross on a gold chain, handed it to Bess.

"This was your husband's. He's in God's hands."

Bess was not going to cry in front of these G-men, although it felt like a golf ball was stuck in her throat. She bit her lips hard.

Clegg was trying to portray Eddie's death as a tragic mistake. Although Bess knew that was a lie, the gentlemanly treatment she had received from him had softened her. More and more she'd been thinking that, although G-men had pulled the trigger, it was Dillinger who had sent Eddie to the grave. She wrapped Eddie's cross and chain around her right hand.

"Mrs. Green, your son will never be publicly embarrassed."

"I appreciate that Mister Clegg, I appreciate your keeping my family name out of the newspapers."

"God willing ..." said Clegg, "you will have grandchildren ... and I know you have nieces and nephews ... and you must realize we cannot have a society of bank robbers, machine gunners, crooked policemen, thrill killers and kidnappers ... so tell us about Eddie. No harm can come to him now."

Bess felt something move inside her, as if someone had shifted a gear. She saw the kindness and intelligence in Clegg's eyes. Here was a G-man who knew mercy.

"He was a jug marker," Bess said. "That's all he was."

Behind her, G-men scrambled.

"Who did he mark them for?"

"Barker, Karpis, that mob."

"How about Lillian?" Clegg stood directly beneath the portrait of President Roosevelt. "We've gotten no help from your negress friend."

"Lillian is just a cleaning lady."

Agent Guerrero, sitting near the coatrack, pulled from his shirt pocket a tiny notebook and a golfer's pencil.

"So tell me about Eddie," Clegg said.

"Mister Clegg, Eddie would study banks. He was like an advance scout for the robbers. He had a talent for remaining anonymous. His picture was never in the newspaper until ..."

Bess looked down at that cross and chain wrapped around her hand.

"Until last week."

"What do you mean by *study*?"

"Oh, who worked in the bank, that kind of thing. Where the vault was, when the payrolls came in, where the police station was, the getaway routes."

"What gangs did he scout for? Specifically?"

"Barker and Karpis."

She noticed Guerrero writing furiously

"The whole gang," Bess said. "Freddie, the brother Doc, and the mother."

"The mother?" asked Clegg. "They rob banks with their mother?"

"No, no," Bess said. "Mother Barker doesn't rob the banks, she's just an old crank who travels with them. They ditch her and pull the jobs."

"Have you heard this?" Clegg asked his agents. "The mother is in the gang?

The agents, all three, muttered that they had not.

"You're certain?" Clegg asked Bess. "They go around with their mother?"

"Posing as a family, yes. Sweet old Ma Barker and her three boys. Karpis pretends to be the third son."

Clegg stared as if trying to engage her soul.

"After a couple of jobs, Eddie ditched the Barker gang. They were too crazy. They shot people for no reason. Doc especially. Doc hasn't drawn a sober breath since they got him out of prison. Doc is their executioner, but Freddie will kill you if Doc's too drunk to pull the trigger. They're vicious. That wasn't Eddie. He was a pro. Hurting people was stupid, he told them. The machine guns were for scaring people. Shoot up the town, everybody scatters, the robbers make their getaway."

She looked from agent to agent, hoping for a break in the wall of skepticism. "Eddie tried to tell them. When you shoot someone, cops bring the heat. Shoot a cop, the heat gets worse. Over in Minneapolis, a couple of winters ago, two dead cops, they arrested the wrong guys. It was the Barker gang that robbed that bank. Eddie had nothing to do with that. By then Eddie had broken off with the Barkers. He did not mark that Minneapolis job."

"Who did?"

"Some other guy, he's in Cuba now, I heard."

"The money in Eddie's safe deposit, it's not from the Minneapolis robbery?"

"No from the Hastings job. They weren't killing people down there. It was nice and clean."

"Mother Barker, what is her name?"

"Kate."

"What does she look like?"

"Short, heavy, kind of dumpy, old. Sometimes she likes to make her hair blonde but it always looks awful. Kind of a crooked mouth. Little tiny face. The Barkers are shrimps, all of them, they should've learned to ride horses and been jockeys. But that would be unfair to the horses, because the Barkers are as mean and dangerous as they are small. She wears nice clothes, Mother Barker, but very badly. It's a shame, the way she dresses."

"Karpis."

"Goes around with a dumb teenager, high school girl. Tiny thing, wears too much make up and thinks she's a gangster."

"Fred Barker."

"Vicious punk. Killer cold eyes. Hair trigger temper. Friendly as hell one minute, then flash, shoots you between the eyes."

"Doc Barker."

"Falling down drunk. Prison tattoos. Probably killed ten men and he's barely 30 years old. Hates women, you never see him with a girl. Bad card player, loses, gets all pissed off. Did I mention he drank?"

"Fred have a girl?"

"Paula. A junkie. She's got a smashed-in face from a car wreck. You can't miss that girl. A hundred pounds with stones in her pockets. Red or blonde hair, really pale, nuts about golf, but Fred doesn't play. Paula takes on a man at golf and would beat him, but she's drunk by third hole."

All three of Clegg's agents were writing in notepads.

"What else do you need Mister Clegg? South Saint Paul, put that down. Dead cop over there? Another job pulled off by the Barkers. It was Doc killed the cop with a tommy gun."

"Where are the Barkers now?"

"Chicago? Trying to launder ransom money? Just a guess."

"Wait. You're telling us that the Barker-Karpis gang committed all these bank robberies and the local kidnappings too?"

Bess nodded. "Mister Hamm was the first. The Barkers were delighted to see the Touhy gang go to trial for that one."

"Mister Guerrero," said Clegg. "Bring me the menu from the Grill Room, please."

Clegg stood. In all the hours she'd spent with him, Bess had never seen Clegg ill at ease, but now he fumbled, hands in the pockets of his pin-striped trousers, as if he didn't want to give away something.

Guerrero handed the menu to Clegg, who put it in Bess's hands. Bess only glanced at it. Lobster, oysters, steak.

"A chicken dinner would be nice," said Bess.

Clegg said: "A chicken dinner for everyone, Mister Guerrero."

Justice Department Memo

BESSIE SKINNER, alias Mrs. T.J. Randall, alias Mrs. Eddie Green, alias Mrs. Eugene Green, a ias Mrs. Ray Moore, alias Mrs. Rob Walsh ... has advised that she desires her real identity be kept strictly confidential in view of the fact that she is the mother of XXXXXX XXXXXXXXX and she does not desire any publicity which would in any way reflect unfavorably upon him or which would enable this son to identify her.

Inspector Hugh Clegg to J. Edgar Hoover
April 15, 1934

Justice Department Memo

... prior to the raid... at Sawyer's farm, an individual by the name of McMULLEN with the Saint Paul Police Department, tipped off HARRY SAWYER that the raid was about to be conducted.

Inspector Hugh Clegg to J. Edgar Hoover
April 15, 1934.

PATRICK

Pat enjoyed the ride up Rice Street. It was like driving back to pioneer times, past factories, taverns, apartment blocks, cafes, pool halls, grocery stores, bowling alleys and gas stations, and into the wide-open, black-earth prairie. He imagined covered wagons, Indians riding bareback.

It was the first sunny day after big storms. Tree branches littered the highways, and the storms had flushed the winter's snow.

"Nice, ain't it?" Pat said. "We could have a farm some day."

Dolly chewed Blackjack gum.

"You could show some spirit," Pat said. "Today, our lives change."

"How about my pancakes?"

"I'm driving you into the future."

"Oh are you?"

"We could keep pigs and chickens."

Dolly spit the gum into a tissue, tossed it out the window.

"Who's going to shovel the manure?"

Pat shook his head. "You're a hard boiled egg."

"And you're over easy with a busted yolk. Why would I want

to live in the cornball middle of nowhere? Look around! You ain't a farmer, Patrick. There's three seasons here: Ice, mud, and mosquitoes."

"Harry hires help, see? It's the help does the dirty work."

"Lord Patrick the First," said Dolly. "Count of, what the hell burg is this?"

"Shoreview."

"Lord Patrick of Shoreview."

Pat flipped her the finger.

"Oh, aren't you nice," said Dolly, and that was the last conversation until Harry's driveway. Pat swerved around a downed oak tree, a rotted old-timer with giant roots. Red-feathered chickens, pecking in the mud, squawked at his intrusion.

"Stay in the car and smoke your stinkweed, okay?"

"Thank you I will."

"You know what's next?"

"Breakfast?"

"No, next you're addicted to Yen Shee."

"Cut it out, Patrick."

"You'll be laying in that opium den on Fort Road, conked out of your mind."

"Leave me smoke in peace, will ya?"

Mud clogged Pat's brogans as he stutter-stepped toward the porch. A cowbell hung from a chain and Pat rang it.

Slender fingers parted curtains. A flash of blue eyes. The door opened a crack.

Opal frowned.

Pat whispered: "What are you doing here?"

"Cleaning up, supposedly."

"Aren't you going to let me in?"

"Harry's not here."

"Gladys?"

"Nope."

"Harry got a message to me," Pat said.

Opal unlatched the chain. "Come in." She shut the door behind Pat and chained it. "See what they did?"

Pat whistled. Some evil giant had turned the house upside down, then set it back, contents scattered. The kitchen cabinets were flung open, dishes, pots and pans heaped on the counters. Drawers had been pulled out and emptied of towels and silverware. Containers of flour, sugar, coffee and tea had been dumped onto the kitchen table. The icebox had been tilted over, lettuce, a milk bottle and a butter tub spilled to the floor. Charred wood and ash had been swept out of the cast iron stove onto the linoleum floor. Only the meat grinder remained in place, clamped to the counter.

Pat peered into the dining room, that too, ravaged by vandals.

"And I'm supposed," said Opal, "to clean it up before Gladys returns."

"Where is she?"

Opal shrugged. "She took the kid and drove away."

Pat shook out a Lucky, used his Statue of Liberty to light it.

"Look at me, I'm a nervous wreck," said Opal. "I don't know what to do. The G-men know my name now."

"Settle down," Pat said and fired up another Lucky for her.

"You know I don't smoke," she said.

"Start," he said.

She took an eye-batting puff on the cigarette. "I've got to get out in case the coppers return. My mother would die if my name got in the papers."

"The G-men are coming back?"

"They said: *Tell Harry we need to talk to him.*"

"You were here when they tossed the place?"

Opal nodded.

"Who were these G-men exactly?"

"They don't explain themselfs to girls."

She reached into her apron.

"Here." She handed Pat a business card.

H. H. Clegg, Inspector

Department of Justice

Division of Investigation

Washington D.C.

CApitol 4679

Pat decided not to point out that Opal had been visited by J. Edgar Hoover's personal errand boy. She was frightened already, and that news might cause her to piss herself. He slipped the card into his wallet.

"Don't worry," Pat said. "Tax cops. Nothing serious."

"Tax cops? Patrick, they're after Dillinger."

"Say, Harry left something for me downstairs. Were the cops down there?"

Opal, coughing on Lucky smoke, nodded.

"Shit," said Pat.

He opened the door to the cellar stairs and climbed down into the dark, dusty basement, feeling for the string that switched on a bare light bulb. What the light revealed made him feel better. The G-men hadn't tossed the whole basement. Maybe they'd been overwhelmed at the sight of all this crap. Boxes that the Sawyers had moved from their Saint Paul house lay in a circle around the asbestos-encased furnace. Most of those boxes contained bottles of bootleg liquor. A few had been busted open by the G-men but liquor wasn't what they were looking for.

Pat stepped into the coal bin, picked up a shovel, plowed coal away from one corner. Soon he uncovered a plank platform that lifted out to reveal a cemented-in safe. Its door was covered in a dusty sheet of thick oil cloth. This he tore off and worked the combination. Harry's genius mind had simplified it into multiples of four: 1-4-16-64.

In that safe lay nothing but a ring of keys.

It might have been a million bucks, the way Pat's shaky hands grabbed it. He ran upstairs to daylight.

Opal, on her knees, wielded broom and dustpan, sweeping stove ash from the linoleum.

Pat hugged her when she arose.

He whispered: "They got nothing on Harry, so they got nothing on you. Harry forgot to pay his taxes, that's all."

She felt warm and sexy against him.

Dolly blew the car horn, three angry blasts.

"I'll talk to Harry," Pat promised. "You'll be paid. You don't know nothing. If they take you in, cry and sob and put on the big act. They'll let you go. No cop can deal with a crying female. Okay?"

He ran for the Essex, opened the door on a cloud of marijuana smoke. This time, there would be no scolding. Let Dolly smoke!

He jangled the keys.

"I got 'em," Pat said. "We've got it made now."

"Then maybe I can get," Dolly said, "my pancakes at the Lowry."

JAIL TWO IN DILLINGER CASE

DOCTOR, NURSE CONFESS
THEY TREATED GUNMAN
WHO WAS SHOT
IN APARTMENT BATTLE

Saint Paul Daily News
April 18, 1934

PATRICK

In the hallway of the Hotel Saint Paul, Pat tapped on a door and shouted up through the transom:

"Room service!"

"To hell." Tom Filben opened the door and barked: "Get in here. How did you find me?"

"Easy," said Pat.

Filben closed the door. "I paid the bell boys to shut their mouths."

"I paid them to talk," Pat said, "so they collected twice."

"What are you so cheerful about?"

Pat dangled a ring of keys. "Somebody left these for me."

Filben backed away. On a linen-covered cart lay a half-eaten roast beef dinner, complete with gravy, potatoes and a bottle of red wine. Filben was dressed in a cream-colored suit, protected at the collar by a blue napkin.

"By Christ, Patrick, don't you know the chance you've taken coming up here?"

"I thought you'd want to know." Pat jangled the keys. "It's official. The Green Lantern is mine."

Filben glanced at congealing gravy.

"Just like the old days," said Pat. "Only better."

"Christ almighty, Patrick, do you know the Federals have got

Bess chained to a radiator underneath a photo of the scowling J. Edgar Hoover? Christ alone knows what she's telling them. Can't you get it through your thick Irish skull? The old days are gone! Don't you know I've just survived interrogation by Edgar Hoover's thugs? They're going to crack this town like an elephant stepping on a peanut. I didn't tell Hoover's men a thing. But every time they roust a level guy now, it'll be, oh, that weak-kneed Filben, he's the stool pigeon. Christ, I've already sent my wife out of town."

He stared out the windows at Rice Park. City crews sawed at fallen trees. On the steps of the federal building, men in dark hats and raincoats stood in conference.

"You're aware, I take it, that the doctor and nurse you arranged to treat your Indiana friend have been arrested. I'm thoroughly surprised they haven't thrown you in the dungeon."

"I've got friends," said Pat.

"Friends." Filben sputtered. "Patrick, I'm through in this town." He stared out that window. "California. Land of milk, honey and sunshine. I'll send you a postcard. You should go there sometime and see for yourself. On second thought," he turned to Pat. "Don't call, don't visit, forget you ever knew me."

"Tommy I'm here with a deal."

"The dealer is dead, the casino is burned to the ground. Wild beasts are snorting at the ashes."

"What are you talking about?"

"They know exactly what they're doing, the G-men. They call a fella in, keep him a few nights, it's like signing his death warrant. They let the gangsters do the rest."

"Nobody's looking for you Tommy, I would know."

Filben sighed.

"Patrick, you're not Harry. Don't try to be Harry because there will never be another Harry. You're a good-natured Irish cunt who ought to be running a pub in Limerick. Christ, there's a thought for you Patrick. Take the fast boat to Ireland, find the

O'Reilly clan. God bless the Irish, for all their faults, they will always take in one of their own. They'll begrudge it but they'll take you in. Start your life over in Ireland, and leave this accursed nation behind. We should have gone to Australia, all the millions of us wandering Irish, we would have taken over that entire nation by now. Christ Almighty, imagine Australia, a sunny Irish paradise, complete with jumping kangaroos."

"I was thinking of putting in more slot machines," said Pat.

"Forget slot machines. I'm out of slot machines in this country. My offer in Havana is still open, not that you have the sense to take it. I'm shifting my action to Cuba, by Christ, a good Catholic nation where they accept corruption as part of God's plan."

"You're going to run your Cuba operation from California?"

"Florida's out. Too many gangsters."

"California, though?"

"That's why I need a surrogate in Havana, Patrick. The deals are in place now. Cuba, there's a new sheriff in town, his name is Bautista, he's a good man for business, and there by Christ is not a single filthy G-man in all of Havana."

"I thought you had Powers in Havana?"

"Nobody's heard from Mick Powers in ages."

"So you're leaving Saint Paul."

"Christ, the thickness of an Irish skull."

Pat jangled the keys. "Aren't you going to congratulate me?"

"Would you congratulate a man who'd contracted polio? Patrick, this tavern will be your ruination. They will tap your phones and have G-men listening through the walls. And boy-o, when you arrive at Leavenworth, don't ask for Thomas Padraic Filben, because he won't be there."

He glanced at his meal tray. "Now may I get back to my repast before it turns ice cold? And allow me to say, Patrick, that I have thoroughly enjoyed our long association and sincerely hope our paths never cross again."

"Yeah, sure," said Pat. "Kind of early for a heavy dinner ain't it?"

Filben sat at the cart and spread his napkin. "The federal menu leaves much to be desired, a fact I pray you will never discover at first hand."

"You just passed on a great partnership," Pat said. He spat out the name: "Filben. You never were a level gangster. Everybody says so."

"May Bridget and all the holy saints of Ireland watch over you, Patrick. Now take my best wishes and skulk down the back stairs, will ye?"

U.S. SENATE TO SIFT CRIME HERE

A sweeping investigation of Saint Paul crime by a United States Senate committee was practically assured today ...

Saint Paul Daily News
April 21, 1934

PATRICK

Down on Fifth Street the Essex sat at rough idle, Dolly listening to the radio and running the heater. Pat slipped in behind the wheel. The car smelled like a Mexican whorehouse, all perfume, gasoline, and marijuana. Dolly chewed Blackjack ninety miles an hour.

"How long do I wait for breakfast, Albert Patrick? I'm starving. It's almost lunchtime."

"I just want to check in at the Lantern."

"Your tavern will be there after breakfast. That's all I ask in the mornings, Patrick, pancakes at the Lowry."

"Just let me walk in. It's mine now."

Dolly sputtered.

"Ours," said Pat.

"How about if I don't want it?"

"It's my dream, how could you not want it?"

"Oh, jeez, let me see. Harry's running scared, and G-men busted up his house. Eddie Green is dead, shot in the back by federal goons. J. Edgar's men have Bess locked in a dungeon. Pardon me, Albert Patrick Capone, if that ain't the life I crave."

"No imagination, that's your problem," said Pat. "Imagine us rich, imagine us in Florida all winter."

"Imagine pancakes, Patrick."

"One short detour," said Pat. "We're going to drive by."

"Let me out. I'll meet you in the cafe."

"You're my wife," said Pat. "This is our future. You're coming with me."

He rattled Harry's key ring at her. He worked the gears and zipped the Essex into traffic. Dolly gave a hungry look at the Lowry Café before they turned on Wabasha.

"Filben," Pat said, "is blowing town."

"Let him blow. I never trusted that glad-handing son of a bitch nohow."

"Where am I going to get my cars and plates if Filben blows town?"

"From a car dealer?"

"Filben knows how to hide the deals."

"Take my advice: Let somebody else play gangster boss. You've got a tavern to run."

"I want slot machines in the Blue Room," Pat said. "How do I do that without Filben?"

"Patrick," Dolly said, "I don't want to be a hostess."

"You too? You're bailing on me?"

"It stinks of cigars in there."

"We'll buy a fan."

"You come home at night stinking of gin and cigars so bad you can smell your own self. I don't want that life no more."

It drove Pat nuts that Dolly just didn't understand loyalty.

"What do you want?" he asked.

"Well, I wanted pancakes at the Lowry."

"You won't need to work once the tavern starts making money. You could stay home."

"Maybe I want to open a beauty parlor."

"You don't know nothing about beauty."

"I could learn."

"Beauty parlors stink too."

"I like the way a beauty parlor stinks."

Pat was shocked to see three police cars parked on Wabasha in front of the Green Lantern. Two green-uniformed goons were nailing lumber across the doors of his tavern.

Directing them was Inspector Crumley.

Pat yanked the emergency brake and leaped out.

"Hey!"

Crumley turned his fat head.

"What the hell are you doing?" Pat scrambled between police cars and shouldered a uniformed cop away from the tavern door.

A bulging arm locked around his neck. Said arm was clothed in a dark suit and ended in the swollen knuckles of the Bulldog. Pat was flung hard against a squad car.

"Back off," growled the Bulldog. "Police business."

Pat struggled to breathe. The Bulldog had him pinned to the car by the throat. The hammering, it was like the cops were driving nails into Pat's brain.

"Let him go," said Crumley. "He ain't trouble. Are you, Patrick?"

Goggle-eyed, Pat shook his head.

The Bulldog tried to knee him in the balls, missed, and bruised his thigh bone.

"Assaulting an officer," Bulldog growled as Pat limped away, tears in his eyes, something horrid burning in his throat. Crumley invited Pat into the narrow alley.

"What the hell, Jim?" croaked Pat.

"Just play nice, now," said Crumley.

"What'll it take?" said Pat. He reached for his money clip, it was sterling silver, framing a polished buffalo nickel. From it he extracted, in shaking hands, five twenties. He handed the bills to Crumley.

The inspector slipped them into his coat pocket.

"Thanks," Crumley said. "But that ain't it."

"I want to see Big Ryan," said Pat.

"Well he ain't taking social calls from bartenders. The heat's on. Lay low. This is all a show. It's for your benefit, don't worry. Protection, see? We nail you shut, keep away those Washington fellas."

"What do you mean?"

"Do you want your friends to shut you down or the G-men to shut you down?"

"I don't want nobody to shut me down."

The hammering stopped. Car doors slammed. Some driver on Wabasha honked in anger.

"I coulda told you and Harry," Crumley said, "not to bring that Indiana fella to town."

"I didn't bring him to town."

"Just cool out now, and wait for the blow-over."

"Yeah? When's that gonna be?"

"Patrick, you're welcome at my house any time."

"Would it do any good?"

"Mary would love to see you. Bring a coffee cake, you know the kind she likes."

"I ain't robbed any banks, I ain't killed any cops, J. Edgar Hoover don't know me from a newsboy."

He saw Bulldog leaning into the Essex.

"McMullen!" Pat shouted. "Get away from her."

He vaulted amid squad cars to get to the Bulldog. "Back off," Pat said. "Dolly ain't got nothing to do with this."

Dolly pushed open the car door. She emerged in modest yellow dress.

McMullen tipped his stained hat back, looked her over like a lion staring down a gazelle.

"I don't like the way you handle yourself," Dolly said to McMullen.

"No?"

"You strike me as a bully."

McMullen put his hands on his hips. "Jimbo," he said, "what's possession of marijuana?"

"Ten bucks," said Crumley.

"It ain't illegal," said Dolly.

"Twenty bucks, then," said McMullen. "We can always find something illegal on a dame like you."

Pat reached for his money clip.

"Fine suspended," Crumley said. "On account of the judge has a hard-on."

"You can't talk to my wife that way."

"We're friends, now," said Crumley.

"Our friends," said Dolly, "nailed our tavern shut?"

"Now," said Crumley, "don't you get into this, now."

Dolly said: "Where will you boys get spending money if you close all the taverns?"

"We're only closing this one," said Crumley.

"Big time investigation," said McMullen.

"We had to," said Crumley.

"J. Edgar Queer," said McMullen. "We're taking orders from a Washington faggot now."

"You'll be back pouring watered-down drinks before you know it," said Crumley.

"I never watered nothing," said Pat.

"Come on," Dolly said and took Pat's arm. "Never argue with an armed clown." She snarled at McMullen. "We're calling our lawyers."

"Now I'm scared," said McMullen. "Are you scared, Jim?"

"Naw. These Reillys are the nicest people," said Crumley. "I like 'em, don't you, Bulldog?"

"Love 'em to death," said McMullen.

PATRICK

Following pancakes at the Lowry, following an afternoon of cocktails, following fumbled lovemaking, following a nap, following a shared cigarette, Pat persuaded Dolly to accompany him to the tavern. He couldn't go alone. What kind of king has no queen?

It was sundown when they arrived. With the application of a tire iron and Irish muscle, Pat jimmied lumber off the Green Lantern's back door. Dolly sat skeptical in the Essex.

"You're breaking the law, Patrick. Call Melvin Purvis: Leavenworth 5 – 2 – 10. I hear he's got your number."

"Very funny. Are you just going to sit here?"

She shrugged. "Anything to drink in there?" She opened the car door. "Or did the cops steal it all?"

They entered a musty place, silent except for their footfalls. Pat threw a light switch, got a click in the dark.

"Bastards," he said.

High on a coatroom shelf were thick candles meant for special dinners, and Pat lit two with his Statue of Liberty. He and Dolly walked into the barroom, illuminated by candles.

Said candlelight revealed what looked like the aftermath of a riot, with upended bar stools, scattered broken bottles, and a cracked mirror. The cash register had been smashed, its cash drawer upside down in the steel sink. As broken glass crunched underneath their shoes, Pat and Dolly made a sharp turn into the office.

Pat set his candle on Harry's desk. Dolly set hers atop a steel file cabinet. The office, too, had been attacked by badge-wearing vandals. Paper was strewn everywhere. Dillinger's golf clubs lay bent on the floor. Harry's greatest catch, a mounted walleye, had been thrown to the carpet, crushed by jackboots.

"Those bastards make a mess," Dolly said. "Their mothers cleaned up after them, that's the problem."

Pat flung open a closet door. The cops had ripped out the secret phone but the safe was intact. He fumbled at its combination lock.

"Let me paint you a picture," Dolly said, "and it ain't Norman Rockwell."

Pat opened the safe door, almost had a heart attack of relief to see stacks of cash. He did not need to count it. Had the cops been able to open the safe, they would not have left a penny.

"Are you listening?" said Dolly.

"Yeah," said Pat, peering into a paper bag full of cash. "I'm listening."

"Bessie Green is talking chapter and verse to the G-men."

"Naw, she's standing up. They'll let her go. They got nothing on her."

"Bess doesn't like you, Patrick."

"We're old friends, you don't rat on old friends. Bessie knows what happens to stool pigeons."

"I don't want to be put in my casket by a cop, thank you. I want to be killed by something kinder, like cancer or heart disease. I'm hungry. Give me a Lucky."

Pat lit a Lucky in her lipsticked lips.

"I'm crazy about you, Dolly," he said. "Don't that mean something?"

"Yeah," said Dolly and blew smoke. "You and my mother. I open up my hope chest, and that's all I got."

"I know you care," Pat said. "Deep down."

"I ain't so crazy about love," said Dolly.

"Come on," Pat said. "Let's get a drink."

"I'd rather go next door for a sandwich. Don't you ever get hungry, Patrick?"

The two picked their way through the broken glass, set their candles on the bar and Pat discovered booze underneath the rail that the cops had missed. It was good stuff, too, not bootlegged but genuine Gordon's Gin. He candle searched for the sugar bowl and soda water and set about making the fizz. Hell, he could have been barkeep at a fancy place, like the Lowry or the Saint Paul. While the booze flowed, everybody loved a bartender. Even his crabby wife turned easy with a bubbling drink in front of her.

It wasn't no clip joint, your Honor, I always ran an honest tavern.

Dolly smoked, drank, stared at a poster. It depicted well-dressed people in a railroad bar car, traveling to some exciting destination, toasting the good life with bottles of Schmidt's.

"We should travel, Patrick. Like Florida or Yellowstone. I've never gone nowhere. World's Fair, jeesh, it's a train ride away but it might as well be in Moscow."

She smoked the Lucky to a nub.

"That mean old bastard," she said and wrapped her red-nailed hands around her drink. "Ah," she said.

Pat stooped behind the bar, feeling in the dim light, trying to rescue intact bottles of booze.

"Feel sorry for yourself," Dolly said, "and you'll have only yourself for company. That's what my old man used to say. Of course, that prick was the expert on self pity. But he did his Irish duty, I'll give him that. He used to slap the pay envelope on the kitchen table every Friday night, and Mom counted out his drinking allowance. Yup, times were good, during the War and right after.

Unless you were German, ha! Oh, but we Careys lived on thievery. My old man brought home something every night from the yards. Whole crate of cantaloupe, that'll give you the runs. Once before Christmas the dicks busted into a carload of baby dolls. Hell, the railroad cops stole more than the thieves. We had a closet full of Malt-O-Meal. We had a lifetime's supply of Dr. Lyon's Tooth Powder. We had ..."

Pat stood with a bottle of booze in each hand.

"Why do you stay with this life, Patrick? I want a simple answer."

Pat shrugged. "I'm gonna be the fella everybody comes to see."

"Oh come on."

Pat placed the bottles lovingly against the mirror on the devastated back-bar.

"Pat, this will never be the Green Lantern again. You understand that, right?"

Pat leaned over the bar. "Every town needs an arranger, okay? It's me now. Me! Big Ryan, he don't take no money direct. It's gotta go through channels. Harry was keeping money for Van Meter. A lot of money. It's from a Johnny D bank job. Van wants it back. I'm the one with the combination to the safe."

Dolly sighed. "Those boys are going to be killed, all of them."

"I gotta give Van Meter his money. I'm Harry's what do you call, appointed heir. If I don't get it back to Van…" He drew his forefinger across his throat. "All I'm doing is driving out there, throwing Van's cash out the window, and driving home."

"Driving where?"

"That's a secret."

"Take me with you."

Pat shook his head. "You don't trust me, do you?"

"Dillinger! It's like he's Babe Ruth and you're the bat boy.

You glow when you're around him."

"You don't know nothing, Dolly, that's your problem. Complete ignorance."

"Enlighten me, oh Swami."

"Look, when I get back to town, I'll have the rent and we can get us an apartment again. Look at us, our age, living with our mothers."

Some shuffling noise halted the conversation and a great, dark shadow appeared at the edges of the candlelight.

A rumbling voice said: "Look who's back in business."

Big Ryan stepped forward, police boots on crunching glass. He was a head taller than Pat or Dolly, and weighed more than both of them combined. He was built like a linebacker, but dressed like a banker, in exquisite brown pin-striped suit.

"I been wondering if you'd do us the honor," said Pat. "Have a seat, Chief."

Former chief Joseph Ryan tipped his fedora to Dolly, put his mammoth hands on the bar, glanced left and right at the devastation.

"Looks like Crumley's handiwork," said Big Ryan, and shrugged. "I'll buy the little woman a drink."

"I ain't little," said Dolly.

"They're running wild now," Ryan said. "Crumley and the whole detective division. I told them that would happen if they turned me out of the chief's office."

"What are you drinking, Chief?"

"Easy on the vermouth," said Ryan. "Dolly, you look like a million bucks."

"Yeah, well I feel like a nickel. Your boys busted up our place pretty good."

"Dolly, he just told you," Pat scolded. "They weren't his boys. Crumley don't have nothing to do with Chief Ryan."

Ryan shook his head, slow and sad.

"Dolly," Pat said, "powder your nose and let the men do business."

Dolly curled her lips harsh.

"That won't be necessary," Ryan said. He pulled a heavy wallet out of an inside coat pocket, extracted a $10 bill and said: "Let me buy the first round at the New Green Lantern."

"Couldn't take your money," said Pat.

Dolly rolled her eyes.

"I'm renaming the place after my patron saint," Pat said. "It'll be like every day's Saint Patrick's Day in here."

"Clever," said Ryan.

Pat mixed a whiff-of-vermouth martini for Ryan, and one for himself, and a sugary fizz for Dolly.

"So Harry's out of town," said Ryan.

"Parts unknown," said Pat.

"Loose ends," said Ryan. He raised his martini toward Pat and Dolly: "Here's to tying 'em up."

All clinked glasses. Ryan gulped martini. "So you're doing Harry's business now."

"Kind of," said Pat. "Nobody can fill Harry's shoes."

"Oh but they can try," said Ryan.

"Yeah," said Pat, uncertain.

"Pat, there's a fee that was never paid."

"Oh?" said Pat.

"Banking fee. Ten percent is $2500, the way I heard it."

"Jeesh, that's money," said Pat.

"Tall, skinny fella owes it."

Pat shrugged.

Ryan said: "Harry was good for it, but now it's gone bad, see?"

"I'll powder my nose," said Dolly. She snatched her purse and sashayed across the glass-strewn floor.

"Just so I know what we're talking about..." said Pat.

"Cash out of Mason City."

"Harry never came across?"

"You know those Dillinger fellas, Patrick."

"Not anymore, they blew town."

"If we allow excuses, the whole system goes off the rails. You don't want that, do you?"

"Hell no," said Pat.

"Somebody owes the system $2,500. It's the grease that keeps the big engine going. If Harry's on the lam ..." he spread his hands. "... we look for another fellow."

"I see," said Pat.

"You're Harry's best man so..."

"I am?"

"You got the keys to his office I hear."

"I don't have nothing to do with those Dillinger guys."

"That's not my problem. There were police services rendered to Dillinger's boys, Patrick, and those services need to be paid for. Forgiveness don't come into it. We're not priests. We don't forgive."

He tossed back his martini, stuffed the $10 bill into the pocket of Pat's shirt, and said: "See what you can do in a week."

He picked his fedora off the bar. "Your wife is a lovely woman to look at."

When Big Ryan was gone Dolly tiptoed to the bar.

"You were listening," said Pat.

"You're damn right. What is he talking about?"

"I don't know."

"Lovely woman to look at? Patrick do you remember the two girls who got acid thrown in their faces?"

"Oh come on, that wasn't Big Ryan. He's civilized."

"Then what's he talking about?"

"Protection money is owed."

"By who?"

"Van Meter didn't pay out of his share. See Van made a political contribution to Big Ryan last winter. So Van's thinking that covers him. But it don't cover him. Ten percent of his share out of Mason City and Sioux Falls, that's what covers him."

"What does this have to do with you, Patrick?"

"Nothing," said Pat. "Son of a bitch, how did he know? I just touched Van's money ten minutes ago, and this bastard shows up. He can smell money through the walls."

"What are you going to do?"

"How the hell do I know? I can't deliver Van a short bag. And Big Ryan's got to get his money."

"I told you, you're no gangster, Patrick. Stay out of this."

"I'm in, damn you."

"Patrick, they're playing you like a fiddle. Crumley busts you up and Big Ryan pretends to be sorry, then puts the squeeze on you. We'll end up murdered, Patrick, both of us."

"Nah," said Pat. "I got a brain, see? I got a brainy idea."

TWO CONFESS IN DILLINGER CASE

Positive evidence that it was "whistling" John Dillinger himself who blazed his way to freedom ... was in the hands of the federal government. Confessions were obtained from a Minneapolis doctor, Clayton May, and nurse, Gurniath Ladelle, who gave her name as Mrs. A. Salt.

FRECHETTE GIRL HERE MONDAY
DILLINGER'S GIRLFRIEND
GUARDED AGAINST RESCUE

While Evelyn Frechette sat alone in a Chicago cell awaiting removal to Saint Paul, Federal agents, fearing Dillinger might try to free Miss Frechette, took special precautions.

"The trouble is that no one can tell what mad things Dillinger might attempt to do. He is likely to try something that no one else on Earth would dare..." said one federal agent.

Saint Paul Daily News
April 22, 1934

PATRICK

Dillinger was in a rotten mood.

He stared at the trees through a window framed in knotty pine. Beyond ugly barren trees was an icy lake and dull gray sky. On the far shore of the lake: dark, chilly pine forest. It looked cold, lonesome and blue.

Pat felt sorry for the guy. Johnny lost his manhood the day the Feds captured Billie Frechette in a Chicago tavern. Dillinger had no choice but to drive away like a coward. Now Billie was a prisoner of that asshole Melvin Purvis.

Pat was not fond of Billie, but every level gangster needed a woman. By rights, Billie would be here, ordering drinks, cursing like a longshoreman, demanding clean sheets and towels from the management. This room would smell of Billie's perfume, and not men's stinky feet.

"Gets dark early in these woods," muttered Johnny.

He shrugged off his gray suit jacket, picked a detective magazine from the night table, and sat on the bed to read in the gloomy light. He flipped pages, and that was the only sound he made for quite a while.

He wasn't a farm boy gone bad anymore, he was John Dillinger, the world's most famous criminal. It said so right in the magazine.

He tossed the magazine aside.

"How the hell did this happen?" he asked, and stuck an Old Gold between his lips.

Pat lit Dillinger's cigarette with his Statue of Liberty, and fired up a Lucky for himself. He coughed smoke. "Maybe I'll switch," he ventured. "They say Old Golds are easier on the throat."

Dillinger didn't answer. Pat began to squirm in his chair, feeling like the man who wasn't there.

A tommy gun lay over Dillinger's suitcase, like he was a ballplayer, and that was his bat. Pat had traveled with ballplayers plenty on the trains. In the minors, players carried their own bats, balls and gloves from town to town. In the same way, gangsters carried their weapons, bags of cash and bullet proof vests. Pat didn't see much difference between a baseball team and a gang of bank robbers, except that the gangsters had more money.

Pat crouched like a catcher in front of the fireplace, which the owner had heaped with logs. He picked up Startling Detective Adventures and just as he was about to crumple its pages for kindling, he asked Dillinger:

"Hey, you seen this one?"

No answer from Johnny.

"Jimmy on the cover?" said Pat.

Dillinger grunted.

"Lousy drawing of Jimmy," said Pat.

The magazine showed a snarling gangster with a cigarette clenched in his teeth, and cradling a tommy gun. The headline said:

BABY FACE NELSON, BANKERS' NIGHTMARE

Pat crumpled inky pages, stuffed them under the logs, lit them, and yet another gangster story burned to ash. He dusted off his hands, stepped over to the card table and unzipped his leather carry bag.

"Are you okay, Johnny?"

From his bag he extracted a carton of Old Golds and a no-label bottle of bourbon. He walked these up to Dillinger's bed and said, "I brought you the good stuff, Harry's special bourbon."

"Yeah, set it over there," said Dillinger. He lay down on the bed, his back turned to Pat staring at dark pine paneling.

"It's sundown," Dillinger said. "Listen to the crows. There's G-men in the woods."

"Well I just drove through those woods," said Pat. "There ain't any G-men because there ain't any cars. They sure as hell can't walk here from Chicago."

Pat finished off his cigarette at the window. He blew a smoke cloud into the glass and coughed. It was a lousy season to be up here, too late for ice fishing, too early for a boat.

"Guess I'll go downstairs," Pat said. "You need anything, John?"

Dillinger farted.

"I guess that's it," said Pat.

Down in the big dark dining room the girls sat at the bar. The boys played poker at a round table. The poker table was a mess of money, cards, chips, hats, booze bottles, ashtrays, beer glasses. Chair backs were hung with expensive suit jackets, but there wasn't a weapon in sight.

A great mound of poker chips lay in front of the littlest guy, Jimmy, known to the world as Baby Face Nelson. Red Hamilton was so drunk he was nearly asleep. Tommy Carroll was lighting one cigarette from the butt end of another. Homer Van Meter was inspecting the depths of his wallet.

Pat pushed a chair over to join the game but Van Meter pointed at him, hostile.

"Hey little prick, I need to see you."

Pat pointed to his chest. "Me?"

"Sounds like trouble," said Jimmy.

"Deal asshole," Red told Tommy.

"Yeah you," said Van Meter. He rose and rudely grabbed Pat by the lapels of his best suit.

"Say, hands off," said Pat.

"Yeah," said Van Meter.

They walked through the front door and onto the parking lot. It was a mud lot, with telephone poles laid down to keep the cars from rolling into the stone foundation. Johnny was right, the crows were making a lot of noise, and now dogs were barking behind the cabins.

"Where's the rest?" said Van Meter and snapped his long fingers.

"What do you mean?" said Pat.

"Don't play dumb," said Van Meter. His tie was loose, he was sweating into his wrinkled blue shirt.

"I didn't count it," said Pat. "I never count it. Harry put your name on the bag and stapled it."

"He stapled it."

"Yeah."

"He fucking stapled it."

"A paper bag, so what?"

"There was eighteen in there."

"So?"

"Couple of grand missing." He snapped his fingers again.

"I don't know what Harry did with every single dime."

Van Meter threw his head back as if making an appeal to heaven. "We're not talking about a dime, are we?"

"I'll ask around," said Pat.

"I'm sure you will, punk," said Van Meter. He shoved Pat, two rude hands to the chest. "If you gotta drive back to Saint Paul, so be it. Have the dough next time I see you."

He gripped the brass door handle and snarled: "You hear me?"

Pat, rattled, watched the door close on Van Meter. He sat lonesome on a log. It was already getting cold in these damn north woods.

I didn't keep no money for myself, Your Honor. I took $2500 out of Van Meter's bag and saved it for a certain detective, that's all.

He felt in his suit jacket pocket for his last Lucky, crumpled the pack and tossed it in an oily puddle. The gangsters and their fancy cars, they had him surrounded. From Pat's point of view down on the log, all those high class cars were running him over.

Drunken laughter leaked out of the barroom as Pat walked around the lodge and down the wooden steps to the lake. Underneath pine trees, winter's snow was fighting off spring. Pat was sorry he'd come now. He'd thought the boys were going to treat him like they treated Harry, but no. More of this errand boy shit.

Pat wandered the cold lakeshore, ice here and there among the rocks. He wondered if he should have stayed with the ball club, a Saints bat boy forever.

Two coward mutts slinked around the corner and began to bark at him.

Hell, everybody liked him on the Saints. Fetch this, fetch that, but nobody roughed him up or threatened to kill him. They had a good time. Those players, their real game was drinking and girls. Still, they loved a ballgame. No feeling like a game-winning hit, unless maybe it was getting laid. Pat, painful to think about it, could recall his three pro at-bats in great detail, the whizzing fastballs, way faster than anything he had seen on the sandlot, and the foul tips, his stinging hands, and the umpire screeching *yer cut.*

Over the lake Pat watched sea gulls, a thousand miles from the ocean, lost creatures, innocent things who didn't know how to get back home to the sea. Wisconsin sea gulls, a sad breed. Maybe they flew in from Lake Superior, Pat wouldn't know, he'd never seen that fabled inland sea. Hell it was only a train ride to Duluth, everybody said it was a pretty city perched up over the lake, but he'd never taken that train. He wasn't a traveler, more of a home boy. Downtown Saint Paul, he knew every concrete inch.

Pat shoved his hands into his pockets to keep them warm. He couldn't go in and play cards after Van Meter's humiliation. He didn't have the money for their game anyway. Couldn't stay out here in the chill. Didn't want to go back to Johnny's room and what, read a year-old Field and Stream?

So Pat walked toward the lodge, jeez, these Germans, worse than the Irish, all this dark stuff, what did they have against sunlight? When he slipped through the lodge's back door he headed to where the girls gathered, at the bar.

Jimmy's wife Helen looked like a cheerleader, but knit like a grandma. Red's chubby girl Cherry sat at the bar, head down like a drunk. Van's girl Mickie, the dark Italian, was telling a story from her whore-dancing days in Chicago.

Tommy Carroll's girl, Jean, glared at Pat.

"What are you doing here?" Jean spat. Obviously Pat did not measure up as a gangster, in Jean's mind.

Jean was a fake blonde, a freak really, with a delicate body and enormous breasts. Jean wore a brassier that pushed those breasts out like a diving platform.

"I came to see if you ladies needed anything," said Pat.

"Already with the Irish bullshit," said Mickie. She was dressed ridiculous: a green pants-and-jacket outfit with leather riding boots. Van Meter had promised to take her horseback riding. Mickie hadn't figured out that Van Meter was the joker in the gangster's deck.

"Where's the bartender?" Pat asked.

"At dinner," said Jimmy's Helen. She was knitting a purple scarf for one of her babies. "Did you miss the fish fry?"

"That's all right," Pat said. "Not hungry. Hey, I'm a bartender, any ladies like a fancy drink? Everybody likes my sloe gin fizz."

Pat slipped behind the bar. He sneaked a glance at the poker game. Tommy Carroll, of dark stubble and scarred face, raked chips toward himself. Looming above him was the head of a moose. From across the table, dangerous little Jimmy glared.

"Helen?" Pat said. "Fizz?"

"Sure."

"Jean?"

"Yeah ... okay."

"No charge, ladies," said Pat. "Drinks are on the house. How about Lady Godiva, will she be drinking?"

"I'm Lady Godiva now?" asked Mickie.

"The horse riding outfit," said Pat.

"She was naked, dummy," said Mickie.

"The horse was naked?" said Jean.

"Lady Godiva!" said Mickie. "She was naked." Suddenly Mickie didn't seem so sure. She turned toward Jean. "Wasn't she?"

"Let's all get drunk enough to puke," said Jean.

"That's cheerful," muttered Helen, staring into her busy knitting hands.

"Yeah and he ain't too cheerful, neither," Pat said.

"Who we talking about?" asked Jean.

"The man upstairs."

"Oh him," said Jean. "Who gives a shit?"

"I don't know how to put it," said Pat. "He's glum."

"That's a real word in the dictionary?" said Mickie. "Glum?"

"Morose," said Helen. "I would say he's morose."

"Where'd you go to school?" said Mickie. "Yale? Maybe he's just depressed. Now that's a word I understand."

"It's his little Injun," said Jean.

"His squaw," said Mickie.

"Every chief needs a squaw," observed Jean.

Pat served each woman a gin fizz in a frosted glass.

"Now look," said Helen, "any of us could get put in handcuffs."

"True," said Mickie with a drunken nod.

"Ah," Jean waved it off.

"Wonder where Billie is now?" said Helen. "Poor kid."

"Shitting a brick in Chicago," said Jean.

Helen whispered: "He'll bust her out. I know him. And I'm not letting Jimmy go with him."

She rested her half-knit scarf and silvery needles on the bar and drank from her icy fizz.

"Cherry?" she said.

Cherry picked her head up. Underneath it was a book.

"Cherry?" Pat said, and rattled the ice cubes in the drink he had served her.

"She's sick," said Helen. "Stomach."

"Oh," said Pat.

"Appendix operation," said Helen. "It didn't go so good."

"Oh," said Pat. "So Cherry, you reading books now?"

"She's always reading books," said Helen.

"The Ol' Swimming Hole," said Pat reading off the title. "James Whitcomb Reilly."

"Yeah," muttered Cherry, "the Hoosier poet, Reilly. But he ain't no relative of yours."

"Bicarb of soda," said Pat. "That'll fix you up."

"God no," moaned Cherry.

"She's been like this all day," said Helen. "Poor thing. Red ought to get her to a doctor."

"Red?" said Jean. "He don't give a shit. He goes where Johnny goes. The traveling twins, that's what I call 'em. Always on the road together. Why do they even need girlfriends?"

Pat opened a bottle of Hamm's for himself.

"Say," he said. "It's going to be a swell summer."

"If it ever gets here," said Mickie.

Pat leaned against the back bar, resting one arm on a giant cash register built of wood and brass.

"Keep your hands out of the till, Reilly," said Jean. Then to Helen she said: "I never seen such a born thief."

"Aw, don't insult him," said Helen. "He's all right. You're all right aren't you Patrick? Jeez, Jean, he made you a drink."

"I was having a good time down in Louis' place," complained Mickie. "There's no music here."

"I heard Louis kicked you out," said Jean, "permanent. For being a paid whore."

Mickie glared at Jean and lit a cigarette.

Cherry moaned.

Helen picked up her knitting.

Pat lifted his beer bottle. "To Little Bohemia!" he said. "And a fun weekend."

"I don't know," said Mickie. "This place looks a little ... disgusting ... to me. All these fucking dead deers on the wall. Why do they got to kill a deer for?"

The women drank a toast and Mickie said: "Creepy. Don't you find it creepy, honey?"

"Mmmmm," said Helen.

"This place reminds me," said Mickie, "of the dark woods in a fairy tale. You know, Hansel and Gretel.

"And you're the witch," said Jean.

"Oh fuck you," said Mickie, "you've been on the rag all day." She crushed her cigarette in a tin ashtray that was overwhelmed with butts.

"We're supposed to be on vacation," said Jean.

"Who?"

"Me and Tommy."

"So vacate already," said Mickie.

"Big he-man confab," said Jean and rolled her eyes.

"How are you ladies enjoying your drinks?" asked Pat.

"Very tasty," said Helen.

Mickie held her glass up in salute.

"A little light on the gin," said Jean and puckered her lips.

Cherry moaned.

"Patrick," said Helen, and slipped her knitting into a wicker handbag. "Can I talk to you, honey?"

U.S. SENATE SETS ASIDE $25,000 FOR SAINT PAUL CRIME PROBE

St. Paul Dispatch
April 21, 1934

PATRICK

It was a glum Saturday or maybe you could say morose. All day the sky was a nasty gray shield against sunshine.

Johnny, he had to be imagining his girlfriend, slapped around by G-men. He stood on the cold lakeshore, hands in the pockets of his gray tweed trousers. Despite the windy chill, he wore no jacket, only a long sleeve white dress shirt and a gray vest. A gentleman was not properly dressed without a hat, but Johnny had left his back in the room. His view across the lake: dark cottages, empty boat docks, icy scrim. Even the flagpoles flew no colors. It was like the chill gray world was waiting, stubborn for a spring that would never arrive.

Pat sat on the gray wooden steps that led from the lodge down to the lake. He inhaled the aroma of pine trees. He sipped steaming coffee from a white mug, thin blue line at the rim.

"I know they don't treat you level," said Johnny, "but you've got to understand. You want to be tough on the outside no matter what ... " he thumped his chest ... "you feel in here. You learn that in prison. That's a level guy's finishing school, and you haven't been there yet. What are tough guys supposed to think when they see you behind the bar, making pink drinks for ladies? See, a level guy would never do that. They're looking for a man who'll stand up to the cops. You know, Pat? You know?"

Pat, cup to his face, felt a quiver of self-pity crossing his lips.

It started with his mother and went through everybody he knew, even his idol Harry, everybody treating him like a boy, not a man. For a long time he'd blamed that on being five-five in thick heels. But hell, Jimmy was two inches shorter, and nobody dared treat him like a boy. The whole thing left Pat feeling his instincts were wrong, because his instincts had told him, go behind the bar, keep the ladies happy.

Johnny sat beside him. "You figure on bad luck," he said. "Sometimes there's not a damn thing you can do. I hate that feeling, helpless."

Pat felt disappointed that Johnny had changed the subject to his own troubles. He slurped coffee.

"And sometimes," Johnny said, "you just have to know the right people."

"Yeah," said Pat.

"And you..." he touched Pat's chest with his finger, "know the right people in Saint Paul."

Acid coffee backed up in Pat's throat. Radio music started up in the barroom. Johnny looked over his shoulder.

"Party before breakfast, that's my gang," said Dillinger, like he was proud. "But why is it my gang? Jimmy the gun nut, Van the cheapskate, and Tommy, his dick twice the size of his brain. That's the famous Dillinger gang. Why is it my gang? Why not put the heat on Jimmy? He wants to be the boss anyway."

Dillinger reached under the steps, packed a snowball, pitched it onto the lake, where it skidded over the ice.

"Here's what I need," he said. "Two tommies, two vests. A clean car. Get me a three-day pass from your cop friend, Big Ryan."

"I'll see if I..."

"Don't see, do," said Johnny. "A basement apartment, basement you hear? I want a trench I can fight out of. I'll give Piquette a chance to get Billie off. But if she's found guilty, I'll break her out. It's how far between the federal courthouse and the jail?"

"Two blocks," said Pat. "They might ... they might have her in an armored car."

"But first they've got to get her into that car."

"They'll pull into the jail's garage and shut the door behind them."

"So it's the courthouse steps. That's our chance. Me and Van Meter. Jimmy's out, he's got kids you know, he's taking his family to the coast. Not Tommy, he's drinking too much. Me and Van. Vests and tommies. Be over in thirty seconds."

Dillinger looked Pat square in the eyes. "Where'd you get that coffee?"

"You want a cup?"

"All of a sudden," said Dillinger, "I do."

Pat wandered back toward the kitchen. Okay, he didn't mind so much being an errand boy for Johnny, since Johnny wasn't a bully like Van Meter or Tommy.

A couple of fat ladies were peeling potatoes in the kitchen. Pat waved them a good morning and held a clean white mug under the coffee urn. Kaiser roll would be nice, but they hadn't laid any breakfast out.

Pat's hands were shaking. From one lousy cup of coffee?

He opened the icebox because Johnny liked his milk and sugar. He fumbled the big glass milk bottle. The kitchen ladies didn't notice. Pat was no janitor. The spilled milk, the cats would lick it up. He sweetened and lightened Johnny's coffee.

Well, Pat figured, if he was the fixer who arranged Billie's rescue, he'd go down in history. That would end his goddamn boyhood and start his life as a man. Level gangsters would drive up from Chicago to meet him, just like Capone's boys used to come up to kiss Harry's ass.

That was how it all worked, by secret arrangements. Nobody

in gangland believed the crap that got written up in the newspapers. It was all fixed. It was like the movies, where there was somebody in a back room banging out the script. And that was him now, Patrick Reilly, writing the script for the movie *Billie's Rescue*.

He felt the glow of glory, could taste it here in this cold kitchen. Billie was to be tried in the federal courthouse in Saint Paul, and with Harry gone, a mild-seeming fella name of Reilly was the grand arranger now.

He poured his own coffee, steaming, black.

The fix had to work through Big Ryan. Hadn't he called Pat the heir apparent?

Cup of coffee in each hand, Pat nudged open the kitchen door and walked down the concrete path. Johnny sat on the dock, legs swinging over icy water.

"Thanks, kid," he said and took the coffee.

Kid. That was the part Pat wanted to get rid of. He imagined Billy the Kid, how he must have hated that name. Just like Jimmy hated when the newspapers called him Baby Face. No gangster dared call him Baby Face, not even behind his back.

"We'll need a getaway driver, a lady" said Johnny. "They'll never suspect a lady. Too bad Bessie's locked up. We'll switch cars three, maybe four blocks away."

"On the far side of the river," said Pat. "I know just the place.

"Me and Billie down in the back seat, a lady driver who won't talk."

"I know one," said Pat, thinking of Dolly.

"Van takes his own car."

"We need three cars?"

"I can count," said Dillinger.

"This is going to cost."

"That's the trouble with the outlaw trade." Dillinger sipped coffee, grimaced. "The expenses." He dipped into his shirt pocket for a pack of Old Golds, shook one out. Pat restrained himself. He was going to quit lighting peoples' cigarettes.

"Need a hideout afterwards," said Johnny. "Deep woods. No neighbors."

He puffed smoke but the lake breeze blew it back into his face. He coughed.

"Big Ryan," said Pat. "He ain't the chief of police no more, he's only a detective, but he pretty much runs the town. I don't know what his price is, but he's got a fishing lodge, way up north, no roads, you get there by boat. My friend Filben owns this lodge, according to the paperwork. It's a couple of paddle strokes from Canada."

"Canada," said Dillinger.

"Gonna be expensive," said Pat, "because you need two boats. Either that or drag one across the land. What's that called, portage, right? See, that's why it's a great hideout. Feds coming, Filben's game warden gives you an hour's notice. Even if the Feds got wise to you, you'd be trout fishing in Canada when they arrived."

"Billie grew up in the Wisconsin cold," said Dillinger. "She can take the cold."

Pat blew waves into his hot black coffee. "It's a lot. The weapons, the vests, three cars, two boats, female driver, payoff to Big Ryan. Probably ten thousand dollars."

Dillinger whistled. "What do you think I am, a kidnapper?"

"I know it's a lot."

"Look, I can get it, and more. Anything left over, get some cash to my old man. After I'm gone."

"I can do that."

"Tell him he'll get a post card someday. In French."

"I didn't know you spoke French, Johnny."

"Billie's French."

"I thought she was Injun."

"She don't like to be called that," Johnny said.

He puffed Old Gold, sipped cafe au lait. He dug into his vest pocket, produced a small velvet case and drew out something glittery. He dangled it over the lake: a white gold chain with a diamond-and-gold crucifix.

"For Billie," he said

"Nice," said Pat.

"When I get her free," said Dillinger.

2 SLAIN AS DILLINGER ESCAPES TRAP

St. Paul Dispatch
April 23, 1934

PATRICK

"We must be getting close," Pat said, hands tight on the steering wheel of his speeding Essex.

"You been saying that for a half hour," Opal complained.

The Terraplane's headlights beamed feeble into a dark wet night. Rain pelted the windshield, fought off by the erratic pulse of a single wiper. Pat's view was dark road, window fog and streaky rainwater. The road was gravel-mud, built for logging trucks.

He took one hand off the steering wheel to light a Lucky. The flame of his Statue of Liberty lighter illuminated red knuckles, dirty fingernails, a gold pinky ring.

"Watch out for deer," Opal said.

Bringing Opal along was Pat's showoff idea. At the request of Jimmy's Helen, Pat had driven a moaning Cherry to her doctor in Saint Paul. Pat felt miserable, an errand boy, back and forth like one of Filben's yo-yos. For five hours he had put up with Cherry's whimpering at every bump in the road.

Once he'd dropped Cherry at the doctor's, he drove to the Green Lantern. He removed from the tavern safe $2500 that Harry had kept out of Van Meter's bag. It was Harry's commission, to split with the cops, small bills, mostly fives. Did the cops even know about this? Or was Harry going to keep it for himself? Pat didn't know, but right now Van Meter needed to be paid or else.

Wanting to chow down before the long drive back, he'd called Opal, then met her at Martinucci's for dinner. Over spaghetti and wine, he'd done something a little stupid maybe. He'd boasted about his friendship with a guy whose name was in the papers every day, a fella whose name started with a D.

Opal begged to go along. Mister D was like a movie star these days, Clark Gable with a tommy gun.

Pat had figured it would boost his image, a return to Little Bohemia with a cutie on his arm. A gangster was nothing without a girl to admire him.

"Now we're close, right?" Opal said as they drove through the dark rain. "Now can I open it?" She held that gym bag full of cash in her lap.

"Okay," said Pat. "But remember, you never seen what's inside."

She zippered it open.

"It smells funny," she said.

"It was buried on Harry's farm."

Opal dipped both hands into the bag and riffled a bundle of cash. She suddenly zipped the bag shut. "Oh my God, my fingerprints."

"No radio stations up here," Pat complained.

"Patrick, I can't be caught with hot money."

"Money's money. Ain't you heard?"

"Turn on the radio," said Opal.

"I just said, there ain't no radio up here."

He slowed the Essex.

"Here we go."

He turned down a dark gravel driveway through pine trees. Dogs barked. His headlights banked off two cars parked crossway, blocking the road.

"Oh for Christ's sake," said Pat.

Pat left the engine running and slipped out into a miserable foggy drizzle.

Men in suits appeared on either side of those blocking cars. One of them had his hand raised to deflect the Essex's headlights. The other man held a rifle. Both were shouting.

Whatever they were shouting did not come through as loud as the word that popped into Pat's brain: *Deputies.*

Pat vaulted up the running board and into the driver's seat. Opal ducked into her seat. Pat jammed the gearshift into reverse.

The windshield exploded and showered them both with glass. It sounded like some mad cowboy was lashing the air with a bullwhip and thunk thunk, two zingers pierced the thick steel of his auto. Pat drove full panic reverse, skidding backward onto Route 51.

The Essex flew into a ditch, its headlights illuminating the treetops.

Pat floored the gas pedal, spun his wheels, furious, tires spinning, smoking, rocking in the cold muddy ditch. He leaped out and put his shoulder to the car's trunk. "Drive!" he shouted to Opal. "Move over and drive us out!"

Opal squirmed behind the wheel and the Essex stalled. She fired it up again and Pat, inhaling tailpipe smoke, pushed with the mightiest effort of his life. The Essex spun out of the ditch and onto the highway, splattering Pat with mud.

Pat hauled himself into the driver's seat. Opal moved over and flung the gym bag out the window and into the ditch. A bullet punctured the car's right rear tire with a horrible ping and whoosh.

"Go, Go, Go," screamed Opal.

Pat leaped out to retrieve the gym bag.

Opal slid behind the steering wheel. She hit the gas so hard the tires only spun and smoked. Pat, precious gym bag in his grip, leaped onto the running board. The car went crabwise, nothing but smoking strips of rubber between the right rear wheel and the road. Opal half drove, half skidded into a turn.

"Stop, damn you," Pat gasped. "Let me in!"

Opal, demonic look on her face, just kept driving.

Pat clung to the window post as the car wobbled along, smelling of smoking rubber and overheated steel. He dropped the gym bag onto the seat.

"You trying to kill me?" Pat shouted.

Opal braked to a swerving stop. She revved the engine insane as Pat ran around, flung open the door, and shoved her into the passenger's seat.

Now Pat floored the accelerator.

"We're caught. We're dead," said Opal. "This tub ain't going to make it another mile."

"This tub's gonna get us back to Saint Paul," Pat said.

"Oh my Jesus," said Opal. "I'm not okay."

"What do you mean not okay?"

"I mean I'm bleeding."

"You're shot?"

"They got me in the underarm, look at that."

She held a bloody finger up to the shattered windshield, and there in the backlight of the headlamps, displayed a smear of blood.

"Goddamn cops. Ow. It hurts."

Thump thump the Essex struggled along. Pat was afraid that, on top of everything else, they were leaking gas.

"Oh, I don't have enough trouble," Opal whined. "Good Jesus they almost killed us."

"They're not following us?"

"There's nobody back there. Slow down. Don't kill us now."

Whatever rubber had clung to the wounded wheel had peeled off. The Essex now made a steel grinding sound and left in its wake a shower of sparks.

Pat tried switching the lights off but it was too dark and wet to drive blind. An old pickup truck passed them honking, as if to tell them they were driving on three tires and were too dumb to notice.

"Maybe just deputies back there," ventured Pat.

"Shoot to kill," said Opal. "It's G-men. They got your friends trapped." She knelt in the seat and stared through the rear window. "Oh my God, they'll shoot them all."

Pat only then realized he was bleeding, cuts from the busted windshield. It had a hole so big you could throw a softball through it. Cold rain blew stinging into his face.

He wiped blood off his neck with his shirt sleeve.

"I'm hit bad," he claimed.

"Me too," cried Opal.

Driving that wreck through the dark woods, Pat swore off the Dillinger Gang. The Eagle Laundry, safe, steamy, forty-five cents an hour with a paid lunch, that was his future.

Tears were leaking down Opal's cheeks, and they made Pat realize that yes, all the boys would be slaughtered, and maybe the girls too, by the lousy murdering Federals. He made the sign of the cross over himself and prayed for his friends.

I didn't see nobody at Little Bohemia, Your Honor, I just went out there to catch a fish. Yes, Your Honor I go fishing by myself all the time.

Pat began preparing an alibi. He'd spent the whole weekend in Chicago, see, it was closing week at Hawthorne, a groom he knew had the inside line on some longshots. That's when you wanted to be at Hawthorne, on closing week, the wiseguys looking to recoup their losses, with their favorite jockeys pulling stunts. Look! He could show off his gambling profit easy.

His mind busy fabricating an alibi, Pat ignored the bizarre thumping from the rear of his car for the fifteen miles of slower and slower progress until they reached Minoqua, the turnoff for the Twin Cities.

Minoqua: a lakeside crossroads of moccasin shops, fudge

shops, ice cream parlors, taverns and lunch counters. Busy in summer, deserted in spring. Only the taverns were open this late. The taverns and one lousy Esso station where the guy was shutting the lights off.

Pat pulled in at the pump. Hands shaking around his Statue of Liberty, he lit a Lucky. From the gym bag he extracted a fistful of bills.

"You threw this away?" he scolded Opal. "That's how guys get killed. This ain't our cash, you know."

He limped out of the Essex and approached the red-and-white gas station office. The pavement was all greasy puddles but the rain had eased to windy sputter.

"I can let you have a little gas, but we're closing," said the attendant. "You shouldn't smoke."

"Near the gas pumps?"

"You shouldn't smoke, period. Not good for your lungs."

He was a neat-dressed little guy, white shirt and bow tie, as if he hadn't done a bit of dirty work in his life. His blond hair was parted in the middle, but his face was flat, maybe a bit of Indian hiding there. Despite his spiffy outfit, he had dirty grease monkey hands. He was a loser and Pat hated him.

The grease monkey whistled. "What the hell happened to your car?"

"Hit a deer," said Pat.

"With your windshield?"

"Yeah," said Pat. "A leaper. Drove into a ditch trying to avoid it."

"Buck or doe?"

"Buck," said Pat.

"Well," joked the grease monkey, "you've got your buck this year."

"Listen," said Pat, "I need a new tire for the back there."

"Well," said the fella, "It's almost ten, I was gonna go home, you know."

"I can make it worth your time," said Pat. He held out five bucks. "How's that to get 'er started?"

The man stared at the fiver.

"Plus, of course, whatever the tire costs."

The fella looked up the dark road.

"I was going to go drinking with my girl, you know."

"Ten dollars then," said Pat. "Buy her dinner."

"Deal, buddy," the man said. "You got your girl in there? She can wait in the office."

As the man drove the wounded Essex to the lube pit, Pat and Opal shivered in the shadows, intently watching the sparse traffic. No way would they wait in the half-lit office. If a cop car turned in now, they were ready to run through the swamps.

Why, Pat wondered, did no G-men chase them? What kind of fight would Johnny and the boys put up? The walls of that lodge were log-thick, maybe they were holding off the G-men. They sure had enough ammo to go all night.

The grease monkey dragged a big red jack over to the Essex and slipped it under the right rear wheel.

"You sure somebody wasn't shooting at you?" he called. "These look like bullet holes to me."

"Just fix the tire, please," muttered Opal.

"Yeah, hunters," called Pat. "That's what panicked the deer."

"Hunters, at night? This time of year?"

"Yeah," said Pat and tried to laugh. "Poachers, I guess."

"Only people from Chicago," said the fella, "would do something like that."

"Yeah," said Pat.

"So," he said with a glance at the license plates, "you're from Minnesota."

"Yeah," said Pat.

"Minnesota people are okay. They're not like Chicago

people."

He jacked up the wounded wheel.

"Man, you chewed this rim up."

"We can pay," said Pat. "We got the money."

DILLINGER, EIGHT GANGSTERS ESCAPE TRAP IN WISCONSIN; 3 DIE IN ALL-NIGHT BATTLE

Saint Paul Daily News
April 23, 1934

MIDWEST DUST STORM RAGES UNABATED

Winds 47 mph, falling trees, airplanes grounded, dust in atmosphere one or two miles deep. Laundries booming, ballgames canceled.

Saint Paul Dispatch
May, 1934

BESS

On a ferocious hot day, in a whirling dust storm, Bess was a prisoner of luxury in the Lowry Hotel. She was locked in a room on Floor Eight, guest without a key. A connecting door led to an identical hotel room containing federal policemen on rotating duty. Bess had never seen the inside of a jail. G-men delivered room-service meals, the latest magazines, a novel by her favorite author, Edna Ferber, playing cards, clothing, and bottles of Coca-Cola, she being granted one over ice every evening.

But not even the mighty federal government could bring relief from the punishing heat. A monster dust storm had been raging for days, and the hotel windows were jammed shut, the cracks stuffed with wet towels. It was only May, but the room temperature neared 100. A pathetic electric fan atop the dresser provided the only breeze. Bess stood for hours sweating in its artificial wind, regretting all the mistakes of her life, and staring out the window into the smothering dust cloud.

Down in Rice Park, the carriage horses had their heads wrapped in burlap bags. Autos drove with headlights blazing at noon. Streetcars were swallowed by a beige fog. Pedestrians wrapped their heads in kerchiefs against hot winds that whipped through the downtown canyons. Up on the hill, the Cathedral of Saint Paul appeared and disappeared at the whim of the storm.

The G-men would divulge no news from the hot dusty world. The lone exception concerned the shootout with the Dillinger gang at a resort called Little Bohemia. The G-men, voices shaking with anger, informed her that the Dillinger gang had killed one of their agents in the woods of Wisconsin.

Bess set an iced glass on the window ledge and poured Coca-Cola into it. She popped open a bag of potato chips and crunched through them, tasting only burnt salt. She was dressed in a black one-piece cabana outfit that in happier times would have covered her bathing suit. Her red hair was growing darker roots. She stared glumly in the direction of her apartment, where the bastard landlord would any day now auction her furniture.

Inspector Clegg appeared in the pass door, tapping lightly, a gentleman asking permission to enter.

Clegg sat in a striped chair. He alone among the G-men retained jacket and tie no matter the heat.

"They told me," said Bess. "I was sorry to hear that."

"You're not as sorry as Dillinger's men will be."

Bess turned to the white enamel sink, washed her hands in cold water. She used the Lowry's yellow towel to dry them.

Clegg said: "Mister Purvis is quite angry."

"I imagine so," said Bess.

"Baum was his good friend, and he leaves young children. Purvis feels responsible."

"Dillinger's no friend of mine," Bess said. "If he hadn't barged into town, Eddie would be alive today."

"Mrs. Green, we have honored our deal to conceal your family name from the newspapers and spare your son public embarrassment. Now we ask you to honor your part."

"But I have told you everything."

Coulter appeared in the doorway, wearing a sweat-stained, short-sleeve white shirt. "If we let you out, you won't last two days."

"She knows that," Clegg snapped, as if irritated with Coulter. Whether this dialogue had been rehearsed, Bess could not tell.

"If Doc Barker don't get her," Coulter said, "Dillinger will." He took a bite of a ham sandwich. Now Bess decided they were play-acting, for Coulter had ignored his superior's rebuke.

"Where does Dillinger drink?" Coulter asked. He mopped his brow with a red bandana.

"I don't know Chicago," Bess said.

"What makes you think he's in Chicago?" Coulter asked.

"Hunch," said Bess.

Coulter nodded. "Female intuition." He bit into the sandwich, a spot of mustard falling onto his shirt.

"We assure you," said Clegg, "that your son is safe. He is with your sister. We have an agent watching him."

It seemed the icy glass in her hand was sending a chill through her overheated body.

"The sooner we catch Dillinger," said Coulter, "the safer everybody will be."

Bess sat on the bed, facing Coulter and Clegg, close enough to get a whiff of Clegg's cologne.

Bess realized that the Barker Gang and the Dillinger Gang had strong reasons to kill her. The code of the underworld, however, had always held family members safe from retribution. But would desperate gangsters, fearing the electric chair, make an exception in her case?

"I want my son moved out of town."

"We might be able to do that," said Coulter. "What do you think, inspector?"

Clegg shrugged.

"I have relatives in Des Moines," Bess said.

Coulter finished his sandwich and licked his fingers.

"Please," said Bess.

"I was imagining a better future for Lincoln," Clegg said, and toyed with his gold watch chain. "Some of our agents, Catholic men, have spoken with your confessor. Father Mack has lobbied for Lincoln's acceptance into St. Thomas ... despite deficiencies in his high school grades."

Bess nodded.

"However," said Clegg, "his acceptance is not yet assured and ... I doubt the Brothers would welcome the protracted attention of the Department of Justice."

"All we need," added Coulter, "is that rat bastard Dillinger."

"But we do not need," Clegg said, "the profanity."

"Sorry chief," said Coulter.

"One of our men has been slain," said Clegg, "and we want Dillinger very badly now."

"So tell us," said Coulter. "Where is Dillinger?"

"I don't know, he never calls me anymore."

"Sarcasm will not shield you, Bess," Clegg said.

"I've told you a hundred times," said Bess. "He likes ballgames, movies and nightclubs. He never stays in any apartment for long. I'm sure he's got a new girl now that you've locked up Billie. He may be shadowing Billie here in Saint Paul. It wouldn't surprise me if he and Jimmy and Van tried to bust her out of prison. He's like that. He's a romantic. Gallant. The chivalry of busting Billie out, that would appeal to him."

"Does he have a weakness for drink?" asked Clegg.

"Not really."

Coulter asked: "Does he have a weakness for women?"

"I suspect he does."

"What about Tommy Carroll?" asked Coulter.

"He's around Saint Paul somewhere. He's a wife-beating bum. Check the hospitals. His wife will turn up with a black eye, I guarantee you."

"Van Meter."

"Check the bowling alleys and pool halls."

"Baby Face Nelson," asked Coulter.

"Jimmy and his wife? Look for teenage sweethearts. Romeo and Juliet with a tommy gun. He loves her, and she's mad about him. They've got two little kids they've left with a relative in California. So if I were you I'd check California."

"It's a big state," said Coulter.

"Somewhere outside San Francisco. Vallejo, maybe? I don't know much about California."

From an inside coat pocket, Clegg produced a photo of Jimmy Williams, aka Lester Gillis, aka Baby Face Nelson.

Coulter took over the interrogation.

"That's him?"

"That's Jimmy."

"How about Red Hamilton?"

"Him I never met."

"Where's Harry Sawyer?"

"I don't know, but wherever he is, he's not far from a bottle."

"So you told us the Barkers go around with an old lady."

"She's their mother. Freddie and Doc's mother."

"This is her?"

Coulter allowed Bess to study a picture of an ugly woman standing near a Christmas tree, a doll at her feet.

"That's her. Look, all these gangs operated under the protection of Big Ryan. If you really want to clean up this town, it's Joe Ryan, the police chief, you need him in handcuffs."

"Mister Hoover," said Clegg in deep bass tones, "doesn't want a Saint Paul cop. He wants Dillinger."

"How do we get Dillinger?" barked Coulter.

Bess answered, but only in her head: Follow Pat Reilly.

"I'm sorry gentlemen," Bess said. "Will you excuse me?"

She rose wobbly, and walked in bare feet to the bathroom.

Even the floor tiles seemed to radiate heat. She shut the door and felt overwhelmed, an abandoned soul in a stuffy Hell.

She opened the mirrored door of the white tin medicine cabinet. It was empty but for a card of bobby pins and a pink bottle of Pepto Bismol. The G-men would not even allow her to keep aspirin. She closed the door and stared at the ghost in the mirror. That ghost used to be Bessie Hines, before any man had gotten hold of her name. That ghost used to be Bessie the joyriding teenager, the tavern party girl, the gangster wife who counted bundles of cash and sneaked them into safe deposit.

She watched her trembling hands reach for the Pepto Bismol. She drank all of the miserable liquid. The dregs dribbled pink and disgusting out of her quivering lips. She fell to her knees and vomited into the toilet. One, two, three spasms and a choking sputter. It felt like her head would burst, eyes popping out. She rocked back on her haunches.

"Bess?" Clegg said and knocked. "Are you all right?"

"Just the heat," answered Bess, and heard his footsteps retreat.

She wiped the bowl clean with toilet paper, stood at the sink rinsing her mouth, then brushed her teeth. She replaced the toothbrush in its white porcelain holder. That toothbrush seemed like an executed woman, hung by the throat.

"Snitch," she whispered to the mirror. "Lowest form of life."

She tugged wet towels away from a tiny frosted glass window and worked it open. She wasn't sure if she just wanted to look out or maybe squeeze through and jump. In flew whirling dust. An Ash Wednesday saying ran through her mind: Dust thou art and to dust shall return.

She was gripped by a crazy hope that down there in the city she would somehow see Lincoln. She had this feeling for Lincoln now, that he was a piece of her, although a strange piece, unknowable, a terrible barrier between them, despite her intense feeling, her desire to inhabit his soul, feel his feelings and see with his eyes.

But the older her son got the more he seemed a stranger. When he looked at her with teenage contempt it chilled her with despair.

Dust blinding her, she worked the window shut.

Clegg tapped again.

"Mrs. Green."

"I'm all right."

She ran cool water into the bathtub. She stripped off her clothes. One thing she knew, Inspector Hugh Clegg would not burst in on a naked woman.

Cool water throbbed out of the faucet. She sat in the tub and scooped water on her head, like a baptism. Red dusty streams fell from her hair, down her chest and off her breasts.

A bar of Ivory soap in her hands, she massaged her face.

She could help Lincoln and betray Pat Reilly.

Or she could shield Pat Reilly at the cost of Lincoln's future. If the G-men wanted to, they could leak her true name to the press, perhaps endangering her son, certainly humiliating him and destroying his one slim chance to get into college.

Clegg's words seemed to echo in the burbling water. *Do you want your son to grow up in a nation of machine-gunners and thrill killers?*

"Mr. Clegg? Open the door just a crack please."

When Clegg wedged open the door, she sunk deeper into the bathwater . She heard him drag a chair across the floor. She glanced over her shoulder and saw that he had pushed that chair to the bathroom door and was sitting in it backward. They were back-to-back now, Bess chin deep in dirty water.

"The man you want is Pat Reilly, Harry Sawyer's errand boy."

"He's come to our attention," Clegg said.

"Whenever the big time mobsters came to town," she said,

"Pat arranged for their cars, delivered loans from Harry, hooked them up with the local girls, got them guns, brought them to doctors and nurses. Pat ran any errand they needed. If Dillinger returns to Saint Paul, he'll look up Pat Reilly."

"And where can we find Pat Reilly?"

Bess gulped, her throat tight.

"He lives with his mother on Sherburne Street."

"No longer."

"The family owns the Eagle Laundry, check there. His wife's name is Dolores. Some call her Dolly, last name Carey, she lives with her mother over near Swede Hollow Park. Supposedly they're getting a divorce, but Dolly's a soft touch who will always take him in."

Coulter, behind Clegg, asked: "Where else?"

Bess could see neither of them. It was the only way she could keep talking, with the G-men out of sight. She focused on her pale knees rising above the bath water.

"The Green Lantern tavern," she said.

"It's shut down," said Coulter.

"The pool hall. In the Hamm building. You can't miss him, Pat will be losing to every hustler in town. Plus there's a horse wire in the back room. Pat looks like a news boy, but don't be fooled. He knows every gangster on your list."

"Including Dillinger?"

"Especially Dillinger."

The bathroom door shut with a gentle click.

A moment later, she heard the outer door close, the lock turned. Bess dunked herself. Could she open her mouth and drown? Did she have the courage?

She arose dripping, and drained the murky water. There was almost no need to dry herself in the horrible heat, but she attended her body with a luxurious yellow bath towel. Wrapped in hotel robe of the same color, she peered out the bathroom door.

The agents were gone.

She stepped in front of that whirling black fan and tugged her robe open for the cooling breeze. She searched her purse for cigarettes, in the hope that maybe a Kool had fallen to the bottom somewhere. The one she found was broken. She backed away from the fan's artificial breeze, lit the cigarette, stared out the window.

Unable to see much in the dust storm, Bess had a sudden insight into the G-men. They were seeking revenge, not justice. They were bent on avenging the death, at Little Bohemia, of their fellow agent Carter Baum. The G-men had become a murderous gang, fixated on the destruction of Dillinger.

She felt ashamed of herself for ratting on the hapless Pat Reilly. "Run Patrick," she whispered. "Run for your life."

She raised her arms so that the fan might cool more of her, her hands up like a gangster surrendering. She stared out the dusty windows at a world that was getting darker all the time.

"Lincoln, wherever you are, your terrible mother has betrayed the underworld to save you."

JUSTICE DEPARTMENT MEMO

Mr. Clegg said he thought that Pat Reilly is the man to get, that frankly they had been informed that if they drugged him or hit him in the head with something ... that he would give them more information than anybody else possesses in the Twin Cities.

— Special Agent Sam Cowley

ALBERT REILLY IS INDICTED

Albert W. Reilly, alias Pat Reilly, former mascot of the Saint Paul American Association baseball team, has been named in a secret indictment charging him with conspiracy to harbor Dillinger in Saint Paul ... Reilly's indictment was revealed as Department of Justice agents sent hundreds of circulars throughout the country with his picture.

Saint Paul Daily News
May 3, 1934

BETH GREEN PLEADS GUILTY TO CONSPIRACY FOR HARBORING DILLINGER; DEFER SENTENCE

In a surprise move by the federal government today, Beth Green, "wife" of Eddie Green, slain by federal agents here recently during their hunt for John Dillinger, the Indiana Houdini, was arraigned in federal court today and pleaded guilty to charges of conspiracy in harboring Dillinger.

Mrs. Green and Dillinger's "moll" Evelyn Frechetti, are charged with harboring Dillinger at a Lexington Avenue apartment shortly before he shot his way out of a federal trap with a machine gun ....

St. Paul Daily News
May 5, 1934

FATHER MACK

The flame of a pink candle flickered in the wind. Said candle was fixed into a gold-plated holder on a pure white tablecloth, a tiny flame between rugged Father McCarthy O'Sullivan, age 44, and pretty Opal Milligan, age 21.

Father had dressed casually in an open-neck green golf shirt and black trousers. Opal's dark purple blouse dipped in a deep V that revealed neither brassiere nor cleavage. It did display her soft shoulders and slender arms. Their table was on the Hollyhocks' porch, under awning for the mild evening. From the sunset-tinted lawn wafted the aroma of emergent grass and the moldy Mississippi, which flowed relentless, as it had under ice all winter, as it had flowed since the very invention of winter.

Opal, slurping her Tom Collins, excused herself for a trip to the ladies' room and Father Mack watched her go, weakened by the Devil's Temptation, offering a prayer for purity to the Blessed Virgin, the busiest of all saints.

Jack Peifer sat in the chair Opal vacated.

"Bless me Father for I have sinned."

"I've heard that line before," said Father Mack.

"I think you might be tempted yourself, Father, with hot stuff there." Jack shouted at his head waiter. "Sam, fresh oysters for this table."

Jack said out of the side of his mouth. "They're rumored to give a man special powers."

"I already possess special powers," said Father Mack.

"I'll see you about that someday," Peifer said. "What do you think about Baer-Carnera, Father? How would you bet that? Give me the word from on high."

"I'm for the underdog, whoever he is."

"See me before the fight. I can get you the best odds in town."

"Ah, but the game is fixed."

"Is it, Father? I'll be damned."

"You very likely will be. Speaking of odds, what are the chances, then, of discovering the whereabouts of Patrick Reilly?"

Peifer sputtered. "He's not welcome here. I don't want G-men shooting up my place. Although who knows? It might help my reputation. Half my customers come here hoping to see Dillinger walk through the door."

Jack ran a hand through his greasy hair and lit a cigarette. Father Mack noted that, once the sharpest of dressers, Jack had gotten sloppy. Bit of a pot belly, jacket wrinkled, wide garish tie loose at a flushed, stubbly neck. A man soaked in drink rarely fits his clothes.

"Sooner or later, all the gangsters come here," said Jack. "It must be something about the warm hospitality. Or maybe they come to gawk at my wife." He tapped ashes into a glass four-cornered ashtray. "Pat will be back. He can't survive outside Saint Paul. You know I started out as a turkey farmer, and I still am a turkey farmer, in a way. These gangsters are my flock and they all come back at sunset."

Smoke rose from his cigarette, danced in the breeze.

"To play our game, Father, you've got to have the calculating mind of a bank president, the courage of a prize fighter, the hard heart of a bail bondsman. Pat Reilly doesn't have any of those things. With strict training, he might have made a decent waiter. God help him when the G-men get hold of him, he'll squeal like a pig in the slaughterhouse. And what do you want him for?"

"I want to save his soul."

Peifer laughed. "And what does little Trixie have to do with saving his soul?"

Huge moths, flying up from the great river, beat at the screens, lusting for candle light.

"That's all right father," Jack said, "a man is a man, ordained or not. I can get you a room upstairs for ten bucks. Hell, make it five, clerical discount. Use the back stairs."

Father Mack glared at him.

"Excuse me Father," Peifer said. "Didn't mean to insult you. I'm a little drunk. Occupational hazard."

He looked over his shoulder.

"That's why I trust Sam. Doesn't drink to excess, doesn't smoke, doesn't gossip, doesn't steal. The goddamn Japanese, father, ain't they something? They'll take over the world someday. And this one's a Catholic. Can you believe that, Father, a Catholic Jap?" He drank from his silver flask. "Here's to the Japanese. A disciplined people, Father. Unlike say, your average American turkey."

Opal, on high heels, negotiated the transition from nightclub carpet to porch floorboard.

"Oh, here's Trixie," Jack said. "Well, I'd better be off, father, love hates a witness."

He smashed his cigarette into the ashtray and nodded to Opal.

She set both hands on the table and leaned in toward Father Mack. When Peifer was out of hearing she whispered:

"He's on the way."

They left the nightclub porch and waited in Father Mack's

plain black Plymouth underneath a budding tree. Under the spell of Opal's perfume, the priest held his hands tight to the steering wheel.

Opal worried a perfumed pink handkerchief. Night clubbers arrived and departed, their headlights glaring off the windshield.

"It's very posh isn't it father?"

"I suppose."

"I could never get a job in such a posh place. Jack Peifer doesn't trust women. See, all the waiters are men."

"So it seems," said Father Mack.

"I'm not thinking about myself, Father, but a girl needs a job too."

She crossed her legs and Father Mack tried not to notice.

"Can I show you something, Father?"

Opal dug into her purse, popped open a tiny box and handed it to him. In the faint light he saw it contained a ring, some dull stone flanked by two diamond specks.

"It's a promise ring, father. I had it appraised for $45. It's the nicest present a fella ever gave me. He musta stole it somewhere."

That pink twisted handkerchief lay on the lap of her purple dress. A burst of laughter and piano music came from the nightclub.

"But I'm giving it back."

She sighed. "I tried dancing in a roomful of men, Father. I needed the money. They laughed. They hooted. They screamed for me to take my clothes off. But I'm a Catholic, Father."

Father Mack patted her hand.

"So I give up on dancing and ask for work at the Bell Telephone and what do you think they told me? You're too young. You ever worked a switchboard, little girl? Excuse me Father but how can you get experience when Bell owns all switchboards?"

"Indeed."

"I was in girl trouble once, father. I was only sixteen. My

mother sent me away to one of those terrible places. At night us girls were crying in our beds, you could hear the sobbing even with cotton in your ears. In there I met a girl who said go see Harry Sawyer. He hires girls gone wrong all the time.

"I was hoping for something special, Father, but Harry gave me a job cleaning his houses. He has two houses. And his wife is a holy terror. So I quit him, and now all I got is a part-time cafe job, a half-divorced boyfriend wanted by J. Edgar Hoover and a promise ring."

"Probably a stolen one at that," said Father Mack.

Opal sighed. "I could make five hundred dollars cash tomorrow. All I do is walk into the federal building and talk."

"You mustn't do that," said Father Mack.

"Why not? I'm riding into a lousy sunset father and I'm only twenty-one years old."

"Child, think of Judas and his thirty pieces of silver. What good did his money do him? He went out and hanged himself directly when he realized his sin. If you take their filthy lucre it will be spent in a few days, but you'll carry the shame of the turncoat to the grave."

"But it's America that's looking for him. Don't you believe in President Roosevelt, Father? Don't you believe he's trying to get the whole country out of this mess?"

"It makes no difference to the fate of this great nation whether poor Patrick is persecuted."

A switch was thrown in Father Mack's brain: Opal transformed from sexy siren to sniveling, greedy child.

"Jesus himself was a criminal, executed by authority of the Roman Empire. Beware of power and those who wield it child. Because they will one day wield it against you."

"You're scaring me father."

"And well I might. Dillinger is a danger to certain well-fed bankers. But a man like J. Edgar Hoover is a danger to all."

"I don't get it, Father."

"You will. Once Hoover's agents have extracted the information they want, they will discard you like trash. The shameless persecution of the women they arrested in the Wisconsin woods shows how much regard they have for innocent bystanders. And the poor workmen Hoover's agents shot out there, they were innocent all."

Opal sniffled.

"The government is a necessary evil, but it is still evil. Government men it was, who shot poor Eddie Green in the back, Eddie a fine Catholic, Eddie who never sent a man to the early grave and who was generous in his gifts to the poor. They gunned the man down giving him no chance whatsoever, and only by the grace of God did they not murder poor Bess his wife too. Who's to say they won't gun down our Patrick?"

The ends of Opal's lips pointed in the direction of Hell.

"You said the men laughed at your dancing, but the fellows with gold badges will laugh at you too. Daughter of the humble Irish classes, housemaid, waitress, moll of gangsters, they will hold you in contempt."

Opal began crying.

"Be loyal to your own downtrodden people. We are the only ones who will ever love you. It's your own humble people who will be there to soften the blow when your dreams crash to earth."

Opal sobbed

"Ourselves alone," said Father Mack. "As it was in the beginning, is now and ever shall be, world without end, Amen. Those are the truest words, my child, in our holy religion."

Father Mack took a deep calming breath, touched Opal's face, tender, as if comforting a heartbroken daughter. She dabbed her tears with her lacey handkerchief, commandeering the Plymouth's mirror.

"I'm spoiling my youth, father," she said.

A car rolled up the driveway and parked window-to-window with Father Mack.

Pat Reilly, in the dim glow of reflected headlights, leaned out. "Looking for me, Father?"

Opal burst out of the Plymouth and slipped in beside Pat, blubbering kisses.

"Thanks, Father," Pat managed to say amid Opal's attentions.

"A word with you," said Father Mack, but Pat drove into the Devil's dark night, one taillight missing.

DILLINGER A NICE BOY, SAYS RECENT HOST AT LODGE

Emil Wanatka, owner of Little Bohemia resort, describes Dillinger men as polite, women as helpful, sober.

Saint Paul Daily News
May 8, 1934

FATHER MACK

Father Mack watched the chrome ball rattle into slot 17. Across the roulette table, a woman screamed. The dealer pushed two stacks of blue chips at her. She dropped her burning cigarette to the green felt table, where it was snatched up by the croupier's quick fingers.

She wore a shimmering gold dress that highlighted her thin shoulders. A peroxide blonde in denial of age, she leaned heavy on the lipstick and booze. She ran her hands, all greed, through the chips. Only when she turned to kiss her husband did Father Mack realize who she was: the wife of a justice of the state Supreme Court.

Her husband, tall, hawkish, silver-haired, exquisitely dressed, was accompanied by a shorter, darker figure, whom Father Mack recognized as the most infamous criminal defense attorney in either Minneapolis or Saint Paul. Jack Peifer led the attorney, the Justice and his wife to the bar, where he bought them a drink. Then he twisted through the crowd toward Father Mack. With a tilt of his head, Jack beckoned Father Mack to the back office.

"Roulette," Jack said, closing the door. "Is a merciless game. The only chance to win is to quit when you're ahead." He shrugged. "You do want the big fish to go home winners once in a while."

His words were slurred. Jack was succumbing to that disease which so often conquers nightclub owners.

Jack's lazy Rottweiler rattled her chain, sniffed, and rolled onto her side.

"Sam said you wanted to see me. What can I do for you, Father?"

Father Mack, in black cassock, patrolled Jack's office, scanning the photos on the walls. They depicted prizefighters, golfers, tennis, hockey and baseball players. Father Mack stopped at a cartoon depicting Lefty Gomez, stretched out in his windup like a huge spider, baseball in hand.

"I'd rather be lucky than good," Father Mack said, and tapped the glass that covered the cartoon. "Now there's a fellow."

"Ah," said Peifer. He poured whiskey deep into a round fat glass. "So you wanted to talk philosophy."

He pushed a glass and the bottle across his desk at the priest.

"I'm a dropout father. Life got too complicated for me in the eighth grade. Once I learned to count money, I had no need for further education. And to tell you the truth I never got along with the nuns. They had a habit, no pun intended, of making dire predictions about my future. But I haven't done so badly, have I?"

Father Mack sat down across from him.

"I've a distribution problem," Father Mack said.

"Oh?" Jack creaked back in his oak chair. His pink shirt was offset by a black tie. His fingers were heavy with rings, a gold watch was strapped to one wrist and a silver bracelet dangled from the other. Mister Peifer was quite the man for jewelry, and such men were not as sure of themselves as they put on.

Father Mack reached inside his cassock and removed a wad of $20 bills, which he laid at the edge of Peifer's desk. "I'm after giving this to a certain female."

"Ah," said Jack.

"A bit at a time."

Peifer nodded. "I understand, Father. You're a man underneath the robes."

"Ten dollars the week."

Peifer scratched his belly through his pink shirt and yawned. "Chicken feed, Father."

"It's as much as the poor girl makes for a week's hard labor. Her and the mother live on the dole."

Peifer shrugged. "I suppose one of my boys can take care of that, Father. They'll want their fee, though."

"And how much might that be?"

"Twenty five percent."

Father Mack whistled.

"Let's see," Jack said, counting the bills, "that would get you thirty seven weeks of payoff. But I'd advise against it."

"Would you?"

"Sure, I'm not making a dime on it, but you see, Father, hush money doesn't work. What happens when it runs out?"

"When it runs out, the difficulties will have gone away."

Peifer scratched his nose. "So nine months of payments, do I calculate that right with my eighth grade math?"

"We're not speaking of that class of problem."

"Oh no?"

Father Mack snorted. Why, the two of them in the ring, corpulent Jack wouldn't last a moment. But here in the back office of his casino, Jack was champ and Father Mack just another sparring partner.

"She is a waitress by the name of Opal Milligan."

"I remember," said Peifer. "You two had cocktails on the porch. Candlelight cocktails, as I recall."

"Aye."

"Now she's threatening to go to the Archbishop."

"Nothing like that."

"You know, Father, there are ways to take care of this problem that would cost a hell of a lot less."

"And those are?"

Father Mack was suddenly aware of that poor chained dog, staring at him with big brown pleading eyes.

"Father, back at Saint Aloysius, the nuns used to crack us across the knuckles with a ruler. And why did they do that? To enforce discipline on unruly children. In the case of this girl, a crack across the knuckles would only set you back one hundred dollars. I know fellas who enjoy that sort of thing."

"Absolutely not. I'll have nothing to do with it. I merely need money distributed discreetly to this child."

"Okay, Father, suit yourself."

"I will."

"I've never told a priest he's a fool, and I'm not going to start now. But take it from me, Father, this nightclub is my church, and I know my parishioners. When it comes to money, enough is never enough. Take that greedy judge's wife I steered away from the roulette wheel. You'd think she'd take her pile of cash and go home. But I guarantee you that instead of being grateful for her luck, she'll soon be back at the table trying to win more and more and more. Some people can never get enough. I don't know what kind of sin that is in your Church, Father, but in my casino, greed is the original sin."

"So you will do me the favor."

Peifer shrugged, lit a cigarette, shook out the match.

"Say, Violet and I, we're thinking of," he blew smoke, "marriage."

When this brought no response, Peifer said: "A Cathedral wedding. She'd look pretty good walking down the aisle." He shook his finger at Father Mack. "She's got knockout girlfriends."

"Is your intended a Catholic?"

"Grew up Lutheran, she's a hell-bound heathen now. I know the Archbishop is stingy with Cathedral weddings for non-Catholics, but, say, what's his favorite cause? Legion of Decency? Sodality of the Blessed Virgin?"

"Have you approached him directly?"

"I haven't been to church in a while. To tell you God's truth, the Archbishop and I haven't been best of pals."

Jack rocked back in his oak chair.

"Harry's been his man in this town," Jack said. "And I never understood that, Father, because Harry is a dirty rotten Jew."

With a red handkerchief he wiped sweat-and-hair-oil from his brow. "Be that as it may, Father, no hard feelings. Harry's gone. My game's the only one in town now."

"Watch your tongue, Mister Peifer. You'll not drag the Church into your business."

Peifer blew smoke. "Oh, your Church is already in. And it wasn't me done the dragging. See Tommy Filben, master of the sleight of hand. He's the one connected Harry to your man in the funny hat."

Father Mack, in red-faced anger, loomed over Peifer's desk.

"The Bishop's Miter is not a funny hat. And the Church gives no blessing to criminals. Now do we have a business deal or do we not?"

"I hate to say I don't trust a priest, Father, but I've learned not to trust anyone. You get my wife that Cathedral wedding, and then we'll talk."

Father Mack snatched his cash from Peifer's desk and stormed for the door.

Jack called after him: "Harry poisoned the Archbishop against me!"

Down the grand staircase Father Mack bounded. He rushed through the dining room with its overdressed candle-lit diners and white-clothed tabletops. Down the porch stairs he ran and slipped into his Plymouth, where he sat breathing like a race horse after the finish line. He pushed the starter button, got only a clicking sound, got out of the car, flung open the hood, jiggled every wire he could see, and then was able to start the car. He drove the river road to the Chancery and backed into his privileged spot near the garden door. Across Summit Avenue he strode in a soft summer twilight, entering the Cathedral from the side door.

In the Cathedral gloom he approached the altar of his patron, St. Joseph the Protector. He blessed himself. He lit a candle with a taper. From the pocket of his cassock he withdrew one $20 bill and slipped it into the candle rack's coin slot.

Poor St. Joseph, the most neglected of saints. All the adulation given to Mary, while Joseph's back-breaking labor went unrewarded. Why, Jesus himself ignored the man.

Father Mack dropped to his knees on the padded kneeler. Saint Joseph, he prayed, look upon your humble servants and grant us patience, grace and wisdom in our trials, Amen.

He arose from his knees and hustled out the main doors. There on the broad steps he beheld the twinkling lights of a corrupt and dangerous city.

Wisdom? Perhaps wisdom was too much to ask, even from the stepfather of Our Lord.

FRECHETTI GUARDS DOUBLED, FEAR RESCUE ATTEMPT

Saint Paul Daily News

May 17, 1934

FATHER MACK

Father Mack had surrendered many freedoms to serve his Holy Mother the Church, and even more to maintain his position at the Chancery. His daytime duties were light. But he was required to report to the Chancery library at 10 p.m. every evening, unfailing. From 10 until daylight he was to doze in a plush chair, at the foot of the stairs to the Archbishop's quarters, within reach of a shillelagh.

The Archbishop was growing feeble and paranoid. In the past year two prominent Saint Paul men had been kidnapped, and His Excellency had turned Father Mack into a de facto bodyguard.

For that reason Father Mack had been helpless when Pat had driven Opal away from Peifer's nightclub. He'd had only minutes until his night duties began.

But daylight brought freedom.

As Mrs. Bold served His Excellency his unvarying breakfast of sliced bananas, a half-grapefruit, and Shredded Wheat, Father Mack carried two bags of golf clubs to his plain black Plymouth. He coasted out of the lot, jump-starting the engine with a gravity assist from Cathedral Hill.

Down to the slums he drove. Scruffy margins of dying lawn

surrounded the shoddy brick building Pat had chosen as refuge. Father Mack let the clutch out easy and the Plymouth crept down a dirt driveway toward a wide ramshackle garage. Parked there was Pat's Essex. One rear taillight was missing entirely. As Father Mack walked around the Essex, he deduced that the light had been shot off. That conclusion was buttressed by a blown-out windshield and bullet holes in hood and doors.

Like Doubting Thomas, Father Mack poked a thick finger into one of the bullet holes. It was sharp-edged, the green paint chipped to bare steel.

He looked toward Pat's apartment to see the shades drawn tight.

He returned to his Plymouth and waited, engine idling. He pondered the problem of his unreliable starter. It was something in the wiring, said the second garage man, who like the first, replaced the starter but failed to find a remedy.

Father Mack's long legs, stuffed in that little coupe, began to cramp. The huge hands that had knocked men to the canvas, that had blessed penitent sinners, that had anointed the dying and applied ashes to ten thousand foreheads, thumped helpless on the black steering wheel. He retrieved his rosary from its golden pouch. Our Father, Hail Mary, Glory Be. Around and around without end, the sacred circle, as traced by the sun and the moon, in homage to their Creator, the Original Catholic.

A noise from above interrupted his meditation. That noise was made by Opal, sneaking down the wooden fire escape. She slunk down the alley, wearing the rumpled clothes of a sinful evening. She crossed Marshall Street and awaited the streetcar, a tavern floozy among respectable shop girls and insurance clerks. When the streetcar rolled away with Opal aboard, Father Mack slipped out of his Plymouth, cassock flowing, and pounded up the stairs to awaken Saint Patrick the Fugitive.

Who first appeared as a suspicious eye in the keyhole. Who

then opened the door toss-haired, reeking of beer and cigarettes, in sleeveless undershirt, floppy trousers, barefoot.

Father Mack pushed in. "Put some respectable clothes on yourself and come with me."

Pat worked a cigarette out of a pack of Luckies, his hands shaking. "How did you find me?"

"Quickly, man, pack a bag with toiletries and a change of clothing."

Pat turned for his bedroom and Father Mack sat on a slumping couch. From a beer-stained coffee table he retrieved a True Detective magazine, featuring the Dillinger gang on the cover. This cartoon Dillinger was a leering thug, tommy gun in hand, cigarette in mouth, buxom blonde at his side, showing ripped blouse and provocative shoulder.

He wondered whether Dillinger's soul could be saved. He called in to Patrick: "Is Dillinger Catholic?"

"I don't think so, Father," said Pat. "He's from Indiana."

Pat appeared at the bedroom door. "Far be it from me, Father, but where are we going?"

Father Mack peered out the blinds. "There's not a moment to waste my boy. If I can find you, so can the government men."

Pat, hangover clumsy, bumped a chair, shouted in pain.

"Bring what money you have."

"It's all over town, father. I learned from Harry. Keep it spread out."

"Grab what you can and we'll send someone for the rest," Father Mack said.

"That's how Eddie Green got killed," Pat said. "Going back for something."

"Hurry, in the name of Jesus, we may have but minutes."

Father Mack held the door open and followed Pat down the rear fire escape and into the Plymouth, its engine idling and spewing smoke, Pat breathing like an Olympic sprinter, wearing a cheap rain jacket and bookie's cap.

Just as they entered the Plymouth, the skies began sputtering rain. Father Mack said: "The nerve of you, driving a car filled with bullet holes."

"I only drove it at night, Father. Hey, the cops are my friends."

"Are they?"

"Well, most of 'em."

"God have mercy on the ignorant," muttered Father Mack. He drove along the streetcar tracks until reaching the Mississippi, then turned down the river road. When they passed the just-completed Alt mansion, black cars of policemen clogged the driveway, a response to gangster threats on the family.

"They're great friends of the Archbishop, and a fine Catholic family," observed Father Mack. "I don't suppose you were involved in that disgraceful kidnapping."

"Under the seal of confession, father?"

"Under the seal."

"It was Harry who snatched Rick Alt."

"Harry Sawyer?"

"The G-men don't know, and they ain't never going to find out from me. Ricky Alt cheated Harry. So Harry set up the snatch with Freddie Barker and Karpis."

"And what did you have to do with the kidnapping?"

"Practically nothing, Father."

"Another question. Opal. The ring you gave her, did she give it back?"

"Could we stop for a drink, father?"

"It would be wiser to do so out of town. Did she give you the ring back?"

"Yeah, she broke up with me, how did you know? She told you, didn't she? She told you I gave her the ring and she didn't feel right going with an almost-divorced man."

"The priest," he said, "is a keeper of all secrets, holy and unholy."

"Don't it make you wonder, Father, if there's any loyalty left in the world?" Pat rubbed his stubbly face. "I'm ashamed Father, that I broke my marriage vows."

"And not for the first time, I venture."

"But so has Dolly. She spreads her... ah," Pat waved off that complaint.

"God tolerates saints but He loves sinners, Patrick, that is one of the mysteries."

As they passed the Hollyhocks nightclub, Father Mack glanced at that occasion of sin, quiet now, one of its Japanese minions hauling trash out the side door.

"In the woods of Wisconsin, Patrick. Did you do any shooting yourself?"

"No Father. I don't even own a gun anymore."

"And that is the truth on your immortal soul?

"Yes father.

Pat glanced into the back seat.

"Golf clubs, Father? I don't play."

"It's to fool nosy policemen should we be stopped."

Over the concrete bridge they drove, past the great stone Fort Snelling. "Built to frighten the poor Indians, and at that it succeeded," Father Mack observed. "But as a training ground, it proved useless in the War Against the Hun. Equestrian training indeed. There'll be no horses in the next war."

"Where are we going, Father?"

"If we're stopped we claim to have a golf date in Mankato."

"I don't know anyone in Mankato, Father."

"My point precisely. Tell me about this Dillinger fellow."

"Oh, I don't know, he's an ordinary sap. He's kind of blue now, since they jailed his girlfriend. He ain't a big-time killer, Father, like they say. He's got a mean streak like anybody who's been in prison, but mostly he's a good time Charley. He'd just as soon be at a ballgame eating peanuts and drinking beer if they'd leave him alone."

"And this Baby Face?"

"Jimmy. Nobody calls him Baby Face like in the newspapers. He's the one to watch out for Father, although if you met him in a pool hall, he's just a regular guy. Loves cars, loves to talk about cars."

"Is Baby Face a Catholic?"

"His wife prays a lot."

"Patrick, in a few weeks at most the federal men will capture this Dillinger fellow and then Mister Hoover will forget you ever existed. They will hold a big show trial announcing that crime doesn't pay, although we know very well that it pays handsomely. Now that Dillinger's gang has killed a federal agent, Mister Hoover's future depends on capturing him, and capture him they will. In the meantime you are to be a caretaker in Mankato."

"We didn't shoot nobody in those woods, Father. The government boys did all the shooting. Assholes. They shot each other and now they're blaming us in the newspapers. A caretaker?"

"For the good sisters. You're to stay out of taverns, pool halls and horse parlors."

"A caretaker!"

"They hire an outdoorsman every spring."

"Father, I ain't no woodsman."

"Can you mow a lawn? Use a rake? It's a simple job and by fall Hoover and Dillinger will have resolved their heavyweight match and you will be home in your beloved Saint Paul. They'll never think to look for you in a nunnery. But you're to stay away from that waitress.

"Opal?"

"Under no circumstances are you to contact her. She is a danger to you, Patrick."

Father Mack slowed the car at a bumpy patch of concrete where crews had laid a new road to the airport. As he was driving around the hazard, Father Mack was startled by a siren. Glancing into the rearview mirror, he pulled to the side of the road.

Pat looked over his shoulder.

"Holy shit," he said and sank in the seat.

Father Mack kept the Plymouth running, figuring he had a fair chance of outracing that police jalopy. Let them try to arrest the Archdiocesan Provost, let them just try.

From the squad car emerged the lumbering elephant James Crumley and his sidekick Bulldog McMullen. Crumley wore a rumpled seersucker suit, McMullen was suited in pale grey, topped by a stained fedora.

"Good morning, Father," chirped the Bulldog. He moved aside for his superior in both weight and rank.

"Well, well," said Crumley, his fat hands on the window ledge. "Headed out of town?" The effort of striding ten yards left Crumley panting.

Father Mack trained his good eye on Crumley. "You're a bit out of jurisdiction, aren't you? The bawdy houses and taverns are back that way."

"Federal men are looking for this little guy," said the Bulldog. "How are you this morning, Patrick?"

Pat lit a cigarette with his Statue of Liberty, and coughed.

"We were watching the airport road," the Bulldog said. "Fella named Dillinger, you might have heard of him. He travels on airplanes, has friends in Saint Paul, that's what I hear."

McMullen tipped his fedora. His breath smelled faint of whiskey.

"William," said Father Mack, "I haven't seen you in church since the Pope wore knickers."

"Had a nasty cough all winter, Father. Hate to cough in church. Disturbs the old ladies."

"I hear whiskey helps a cough," said Father Mack.

"Father," huffed Crumley, "you're keeping company with rogues now."

"As did Our Lord."

"Well you know," said Crumley, "Inspector Clegg would love to talk to this Irishman right here."

"I don't see anyone in that seat, do you? I see a couple of earnest detectives hoping to get a priest's blessing on a fine spring morning. A priest who has heard their confessions."

Bulldog slapped the Plymouth's fender.

"Whaddaya say, Jim?"

Crumley shrugged. "I don't give a damn about Clegg or any federal man," he said. "They don't put nothing in my pocket."

Bulldog said: "Now you're thinking holy thoughts, Jim. We don't want to pester a man of the cloth. Have a good morning Father and don't pick up any hitchhikers."

Crumley waved a fey goodbye.

Father Mack jammed the Plymouth into first gear.

Pat sighed. "Are they following us, Father?"

"If they'd wanted to arrest you they missed their chance."

"Mankato," said Pat. He blew Lucky smoke out the window. "How long to I have to stay in hiding, Father?"

1200 JOBLESS
DEMONSTATE ON SITE
OF OLD COURTHOUSE

As the entire night shift of the police department stood by armed with night sticks and tear gas bombs, 1200 unemployed workers gathered at the old Courthouse site, 4th and Wabasha, in a demonstration for unemployment relief measures ... Inspired by the Communist Party, the workers at one time attempted a march on the 4th street entrance to the Courthouse but found their way blocked by a squad of police ... the workers favor the unemployment relief bill now in Congress, which includes no discrimination against single, foreign, or Negro workers ...

Saint Paul Daily News
April 20, 1934

FATHER MACK

The train station was strangely quiet for a Saturday morning but then, many travelers would be delayed by all the mad union strikers. Father Mack hustled Bess's son Lincoln toward the Empire Builder, its great black locomotive steaming and huffing with stalled energy. He could feel the heat of that locomotive's mighty boiler as Lincoln, gym bag in hand, baseball mitt tucked under his arm, mounted the Pullman car's steps.

"You will awaken in mountains such as you have never seen," Father Mack said.

Lincoln after a cold stare, disappeared into the passenger car.

Father Mack, guarding against last-minute escapes, stood at the coffee bar until the Empire Builder churned out, and then walked through the glorious depot and into the spring sunshine.

There in front of the depot Father Mack had to recalculate his morning. He could make no further progress downtown driving the Plymouth. The strikers were assembling in front of the Federal Building for their march on the Capitol. The trolleys were backed up all the way to the Loop. Honking, angry drivers clogged the streets.

Sometimes as he passed a stalled, cursing driver, the honking stopped and the occupants chirped out an angelic "Good morning, Father." Father Mack detested this behavior. It was every priest's

Hell that Catholics believe they own you, and have the right to stop you, tell you a sentimental story, ask your blessing, or confess there on the street corner. This was the fruit of a Catholic education!

So Father Mack took to the alleyways whenever possible. As he approached Rice Park he began to weave through a crowd of union men, mixed in with corporate spies, shop girls, lurkers, bums, prostitutes, private eyes, waitresses, idle drunks, government clerks, excited children and city policemen. On a platform in the center of the park, a rough man was shouting into a bullhorn, not a word of which could be understood. Cops on horses, cops in paddy wagons, surrounded the noisy, agitated crowd. A phalanx of uniformed cops and plainclothes federal agents defended the Federal Building.

Father Mack's mind reeled back on a tour of the hellish past, where Ireland, having wrested itself from England, melted into a boiling chaos. The madness of Irishman vs. Irishman had driven him out of the Republican Army and into the priesthood. It all came back to him now like a sudden, violent illness, the blood-lust Republicans, the night raids of the Black and Tans, Ireland broken down into clans and secret societies, all with endless suspicions, rivalries and hatreds. In Cork City, the mud-streaked madmen bombed a police station, killing their own cousins along with the Constabulary. The morning after that cowardly bombing, McCarthy O'Sullivan determined to escape the Devil in Ireland, only to have The Evil One reappear this summer on the streets of Saint Paul.

He looked up at the third floor of the Hotel Saint Paul and there, at a balcony window, he saw a big shadowy figure. He counted off the windows and yes, that would be the office of Big Ryan. The shadow appeared only briefly at the window, as if checking on the mob scene below.

In this rough and angry crowd the black shirt and white Roman collar won him deference. It got him waved past the shotgun-armed Pinkerton thugs who blocked the entrance to the Hotel Saint Paul. Now he strode through the lobby and up the fire stairs to the third floor offices of the Saint Paul Protective Association. He steeled himself to confront the *Arcana imperii*.

He knocked on the glass pebbled door. His knock echoed in the empty hallway. He knocked again. No movement within. He shouted: "It's Father O'Sullivan!"

Not a creak answered, not a rustle. As he was poised to knock a third time, the elevator bell dinged. Up the dim hallway, electronic doors slid open and there appeared two dark figures, one of them massive, blocking the sunlight from the end of the hall. They registered in Father Mack's brain as men in suits and then resolved to James Crumley and Bulldog McMullen. Crumley in the tight-fitting seersucker suit, McMullen with suit-coat thrown open, as if he might reach for his weapon.

"Well now," said Crumley, gasping for breath, "just the man we were looking for."

"Afternoon, Father," said McMullen, and then checked his diamond watch. "Or is it still morning? Is it morning Jim?"

"It's morning somewhere," said Crumley. "Maybe in Omaha. Is that where you hid Pat Reilly, Father, in Omaha?"

"Nobody'd think to look in Nebraska," observed McMullen.

"I've come to see Detective Ryan," said Father Mack.

"You have a better chance of seeing the Pope," said McMullen. "Ain't that right, Jim?"

"Ryan's out," said Crumley.

"We got another big fella wants to see you," said the Bulldog. "Tell him, Jim."

Crumley wiped his sweating face with a blue bandana.

"It's urgent, ain't it Jim?"

"You need a police escort," said Crumley.

"Sirens and all," said the Bulldog.

Father Mack followed them to a police sedan. McMullen kept

his promise, blasting out of the hotel's parking garage, siren wailing to part the horses and cars and people in the big swirling crowd. The squad car did a slow loud crawl until it reached the Seven Corners, and after that zoomed up to the Cathedral.

"What do you think of Cavalcade now, Father?" the Bulldog asked. "I know you backed him in the Derby." He stared at Father Mack through the rearview mirror.

"Hey, off-track horse betting ain't legal, now," said Crumley.

Siren silenced, McMullen pulled the squad car under the flowering arbor of the Chancery.

"It's your boss wants to see you," said McMullen, turning to face Father Mack in the back seat. "The Archbishop's the boss of the Church, right Jim?"

"You'd better believe it." Crumley opened the door, stepped out of the squad car, and dusted off his suit.

"He's one step below the Pope, right Jim?"

"Two steps if I remember my Catechism. You're leaving out Cardinals. Right Father?"

Father Mack stepped out of the squad car and measured Crumley. "What is this about?"

"Let's take a walk, Father," said Crumley.

They left McMullen at the squad car and ambled through a maze of hedges toward the Chancery garden. "Nobody does nothing in this town," huffed Crumley, "that we don't know about it." He fluffed his bandana.

"We have a man at the train station, now. A five dollar bill buys a lot of information in this town."

Father Mack set his jaw.

"We saw you put the kid on the train."

One punch! But that would end his priesthood, even if the man deserved it. Father Mack tightened the clamp on his manly impulses.

"We're doing you a favor," said Crumley. "Your boss has

been informed."

Father Mack grabbed Crumley's blue silk tie. "You'll hang someday," he said. "I'll see to it."

After a shove at Crumley's chest, Father Mack crossed the manicured lawn, past the flowerbeds, to the Archbishop's favorite spot. Here was a bench in the shade of a blooming fragrant lilac bush, a hilltop site overlooking the city and the Mississippi.

Even from this holy hilltop, it was evident the city was in turmoil. The sound of sirens echoed off limestone cliffs. Traffic choked every road, streetcars jammed the Seven Corners.

Crumley withdrew through the hedges and in a moment, the Chancery door was opened by Detective Big Joe Ryan. Taking his arm was the frail, black-robed Archbishop.

Big Ryan steadied the Archbishop as they shuffled down the flagstone walk. His Excellency flashed a weak smile, Detective Ryan a grimace. Father Mack reached for the Archbishop's elbow, but was waved off.

"No, no thank you, that's perfectly all right, Father," said the Archbishop, and lowered himself to the bench. He patted Father Mack's arm. Ryan wiped his own forehead with a monogrammed white handkerchief.

Then Ryan turned his back to them, walked off a pace, as if his deepest interest was taking in the city view.

"I understand that you put a young man on the train to save him from the gangsters," His Excellency said. "He is bound for Gonzaga?"

"Yes, Excellency, that is true."

"Well done. You're a good man in the trenches, McCarthy. That's why you're Provost.

"Thank you, Excellency."

"Our people have done well here," said the Archbishop.

"They have indeed."

"*Salus populi, suprema lex esto.* Do I need to speak English,

Father? Or will the language of the Church suffice?"

"What instructions do you have for me, Excellency?"

Big Ryan whirled. "Where's Pat Reilly?"

Father Mack looked to the Archbishop. His Excellency's face betrayed no emotion.

"I cannot say," said Father Mack.

"You cannot or you will not?" asked the Archbishop.

"I'm afraid he's in danger," said Father Mack.

Big Ryan, sweaty face just inches from Father Mack's, growled: "You're damn right, he's in danger."

Mrs. Bold stepped out of the kitchen door, realized she was intruding, and ducked back in like a frightened mouse.

"I want to know right now," Big Ryan demanded.

"I'll not break the Seal of Confession," Father Mack said.

Ryan's face turned red with anger. He snorted and looked to the Archbishop.

His Excellency shrugged.

"He told you in Confession where he was?" Ryan demanded.

The Archbishop set his frail hand on black gabardine at Father Mack's knee. "It would be best for our people," he said, "if Reilly never again appeared in this town."

Father Mack stared into the cold blue eyes of his superior. "I must ask Your Excellency for a clarification."

Ryan scoffed, shoved his hands into his trouser pockets.

"It would be terribly disruptive," said the Archbishop, "if this Reilly fellow were to fall into the hands of federal agents. You will save the man's life if you can keep him in hiding."

"I think I understand, Your Excellency."

"*In domo Patris mei mansiones multae sunt.*"

The Archbishop looked directly at Big Ryan and said: "In the house of my Father, there are many mansions. One of Our Lord's more puzzling utterances, isn't it? How can a mere house contain mansions?"

Big Ryan shrugged.

The Archbishop sat back against the bench, his liver-spotted hands resting in his lap, trembling against black cassock.

"A privileged view, wouldn't you agree Father?"

"Beg pardon?"

"Quite the view from here," said the Archbishop.

FATHER MACK

Father Mack suspected, even as he was dialing Mankato, that this would be a futile phone call. Mother Superior informed him that Patrick Reilly had appeared but once at the Sisters of Good Counsel. Patrick had been shown the gardener's shed, been given instructions, received a modest advance, and then disappeared. A nun's bicycle had since been missing.

Father Mack slammed the telephone down.

Even now Reilly had probably wormed his way back to Saint Paul, having sold the bicycle for drink and bus fare. Father Mack picked up, from the corner of his room, the shillelagh he had brought from Ireland. Shillelagh priests, that's what they called them in Ireland, sadists in black who struck boys and girls on the street for misbehavior. Father Mack had always despised the shillelagh priest but just the once he'd like to administer a beating to the little bartender who had put him in a fix.

Using the shillelagh like a cane, Father Mack leaned on it and stared at a table that was covered in lace and framed photographs. His mother with a basket of strawberries. His father smoking a pipe. The stone ruins of his grandfather's house, at the end of a rural lane, where fourteen children had been raised in two rooms. Amid those pictures stood a dark wooden crucifix, Our Lord joining the human race in its agony. Although he had been a Catholic even in the womb, only now did he accept the meaning of his own religion. Sooner or later all of us are nailed to the cross, and now it was the turn of McCarthy O'Sullivan of Ballydehob, Ireland.

He unbuttoned his cassock and pulled it over his head, revealing a white T-shirt over a muscular chest. From his closet he selected a bright green polo shirt. At the sink he brushed his teeth, his reflection black curly hair, one eye blue and one shuttered, gleaming teeth that never needed a dentist. He set off, shillelagh in hand, down the stairs, through the library and out to his plain black Plymouth.

Saving his starter, he rolled the automobile to ignition, and drove across town to Swede Hollow. *Many mansions,* he mused. *My Father's house has many mansions.* What exactly did the Archbishop mean by that?

At the ramshackle home of Nora Carey, he left his engine running and crossed the street. Nora sat on her porch rocking, and arose at his approach. She, in wrinkled blue house smock, invited him in for tea, but Father Mack, one hand on the stair rail, one polished shoe on the lower step, cut her short.

"Do you know the whereabouts of Patrick, then?"

"I ... I haven't heard from him at all, Father. I'd heard he left town."

"You've received no letters, no phone calls, not a trace of the man?"

"No, Father."

"And this is the truth before God?"

She put her hand over her heart.

"I'll need to speak to your daughter."

"She's not here, Father."

"Where is she then?"

"Oh, Father, I'm so ashamed."

"Where!" Father Mack demanded.

"Try the hotels, Father."

"Patrick is to contact me immediately. By telephone, by messenger, but under no circumstances is he to appear at the Chancery. Do you understand?"

When Nora answered with a frightened nod he turned away.

"Won't you come in for tea, Father?" she shouted after him.

Back downtown he drove and into the garage at the Hotel Saint Paul. In the dark-paneled, clubby Grill Room he waited for his eyes to adjust to the dim light that the wealthy and sinful preferred. None of the daytime drinkers was Dolly Carey. He turned for the plush lobby, intending to query the bellman, when out of the woman's rest room pushed Dolly, in shiny gold dress, stiff blond hair, big black purse over her shoulder.

"Father," she blurted.

He led her outside to the garden.

"I must find Patrick immediately," he said.

"Beats me, Father, I don't know where he is."

"When was the last time he called you?"

She shrugged. "Couple weeks ago?" She dug a crushed pack of Chesterfields out of the junkyard in her purse. "He ain't the most reliable fellow," she said, and lit the cigarette. "I'm never surprised when he disappears." She blew smoke. "But we're through, Father, as a married couple, that's it."

"He will call you."

"Oh, I can't wait."

Her breath smelled of liquor, her makeup was smeared, her nails bright red.

"There are people looking for him."

"Yeah," said Dolly, "and one is named J. Edgar Hoover."

"There are darker forces wishing to do him harm. He cannot return to this city."

She tapped cigarette ashes into a pot in which grew a tiny, fragile tree.

"He brought it on himself, Father. He wanted to pal around with Dillinger, and this is where it got him."

Father Mack stood. "He is to call me immediately. He is to stay far away from Saint Paul."

"Sure, Father," said Dolly, and brushed her hair back.

Father Mack left her in the hotel garden and hustled across Rice Park, so recently the site of a labor riot, and peaceful now, with office workers enjoying a moment in the sun and jobless men wasting yet another day. He passed the library and descended the steps to the County Jail, built on a cliff overlooking the Mississippi. It seemed to Father Mack that they had sited this jail deliberately, to torment the prisoners with a view of the free-flowing river.

The deputies, Catholics most of them, buzzed open every door for him but he was stopped by Federal Agent Guerrero, who occupied a schoolboy's desk in the hallway. It seemed the local deputies had set up the federal agent for humiliation, keeping him out of their offices and at a child's desk.

Guerrero was reading a newspaper which featured an outsized headline:

GET DILLINGER, UNCLE SAM'S CRY IN WORLD'S GREATEST MANHUNT

"I'm to see Bess," announced Father Mack.

"Yeah, sure, Father," Guerrero said, and looked over the newspaper. "But I'm supposed to listen in."

"Not to Confession."

"Especially to Confession."

"Not to the sacramental kind."

Guerrero gave a dispirited wave. "I never saw you, Father."

A deputy let Father Mack into Bess's cell, which consisted of one wall of steel bars and three of white brick. The G-men had extracted from Bess all crucial information, and were no longer willing to waste manpower guarding her hotel room. So she had been booked into the Ramsey County Jail, but isolated for her own safety, at the end of the block, and the cells across and next door contained no prisoners.

Bess sat on a clean white mattress fixed to a steel bunk bed. She wore a blue denim prison shift and slippers. She'd been repairing a flowery blouse with needle and thread. Her red hair had been cut short to above her ears. Without makeup her skin was pale and freckled.

"Father!"

The cell door clanged shut behind him.

Father Mack sat on steel stool that was bolted to the floor. That, a tiny steel desk, and a toilet completed the furnishings.

"Lincoln is safe," he said.

Hands trembling, Bess dropped her sewing into her lap.

"He will be under the tutelage of Father McGinty, a Jesuit I know well. Classes begin in September, and he'll have every chance to make the ball team."

Bess arose and gripped the bars of her cell, looking out the window at the Mississippi.

"I dreamed it, Father. I dreamed of this day."

When she turned to the priest, tears rimmed her eyes.

"A college man," she said.

"I need something from you," Father Mack said. "Patrick Reilly."

Bess backed down to her seat on the mattress, hunched forward, engaged the priest with her startling green eyes.

"How can I help you with Patrick Reilly?"

"Bess," he said at hardly more than a whisper, "there are

forces in this town that would murder Patrick to silence him."

Father Mack stepped to the cell bars to spy on Agent Guerrero, who was at his desk working a crossword puzzle. Father Mack returned to his stool, leaned forward and took Bess's hands.

"Patrick must be kept clear of the Federal men."

Bess's chapped lips quivered. "Oh."

"Under any circumstances. This is in utmost confidence between us."

Bess looked down as if studying the concrete floor.

"So you're in this business, too, Father."

Father Mack arose from the stool, jammed himself into a white brick corner, as if getting as far from Bess as possible in this cramped cell. He folded his arms over his chest.

"I'm a priest, not a fool. I've no trust in the police. I need someone who can find Patrick."

"It's Jack Peifer you need. He's gone into hiding, I hear."

From her shift she took a pack of Camels. "I'll never quit smoking in here, Father." She lit a cigarette, shook out the match and said: "Jack has underworld spies everywhere. Since Harry blew town, your only hope is Jack."

Bile rose into Father Mack's throat. He thrust one arm through the bars to signal the deputy.

"Your son," said Father Mack, "his parting words at the train station, were to say how he adored his mother."

Bess blew smoke. "Father, I thought it was a sin to tell a lie."

"Now we've reached the depths of despair, have we not?"

"He loathes me, Father. His jailbird mother."

"It's from the darkest depths we rise, purged of sin."

He kissed her hands, then made the Sign of the Cross over her.

BETH TO PRISON

Beth Green, sentenced to 15 months in the women's reformatory in Aldertton, W. Va., was taken to prison today by a deputy U.S. marshal and a matron.

Mrs. Green, wife of Eddie Green, slain gangster, will have the right to apply for parole within five months

St. Paul Daily News

May 25, 1934

FATHER MACK

Rather than take arms against his own people in a vicious civil war, McCarthy O'Sullivan had entered the priesthood and ultimately left Ireland. He had escaped Satan twice, once in the seminary and once on a ship sailing away from the doomed Irish Free State. But from his American dilemma there seemed no escape.

So his mood was agitated as he drove his dark Plymouth along the Mississippi and turned into the grand driveway of the Hollyhocks Inn. He let his auto roll to the wide-open doors of an enormous garage. Sam Tanaka, inside that garage, worked at the open hood of a cream-and-brown Hupmobile. Sam turned, wrench in hand, as Father Mack's car stopped in the shadow of the garage.

Sam, in driver's cap, white sleeveless shirt, gray tweed trousers, stepped over a scattering of tools.

"I'll see your boss," said Father Mack.

"He's out of town, Father, gone fishing."

"With whom and where?"

"Tommy Filben's cabin, way up north. The lake Tommy owns with Big Ryan and the Archbishop."

"Owns it with the Archbishop? Owns a *lake*?"

"You didn't know that? Maybe not on paper ..."

Father Mack retreated to his Plymouth. He sped down Fort
Road, past Seven Corners and through downtown traffic. During
that drive he worked out just how blind a fool he'd been. So his
Excellency had mixed in with wealthy gangsters. That was why he
so feared kidnapping. The Alt, Bremer and Hamm families, too,
had been mixed in with gangsters before their kidnappings.

Maybe that's what the Archbishop meant by many mansions.

Father Mack parked behind the shuttered Green Lantern
tavern. He accepted, as he stepped from his auto, that he was
finished as Provost. No matter the Archbishop's sins, or even
crimes, he, Father Mack, would be marked as a rebel, in an
organization that valued loyalty above all. His next assignment
might be a mission to the mosquito-bitten natives of the Amazon.

He pushed through glassy doors into McCormack's Town
Talk. He was driven by a demon: nothing, not death, not torture,
terrifies the Irishman like fear of betrayal. He cornered Lillian in
the dank hall between restroom and kitchen.

"Where is the child waitress?"

Lillian, steak platter in one hand, gave the priest a look of
hostility that softened to indifference.

"Called in sick."

She slipped past the priest. "She gets away with a lot around
here."

Father Mack, ignoring diners' greetings, set upon the Cop
Corner. There huddled Crumley and the Bulldog. McMullen stood
out of respect for the Roman collar and Crumley made a feint at
rising.

Father Mack sat in an orange stainless-steel-and-plastic chair
facing them both.

"Our young Miss Milligan," said Father Mack, but suddenly
found himself out of breath.

McMullen poured whiskey from a flask into his coffee cup.
Crumley paused in his sweaty, self-appointed task of consuming a

mountain of potato salad. He shouted to Lillian: "Potato salad for the Father.

"Delicious," he told Father Mack. "Loaded with bacon, now."

McMullen drank from his cup, his hat tipped back, his suit-coat open slovenly.

Father Mack said in a voice only the detectives could hear: "We must keep the girl away from federal agents."

The detectives exchanged a glance.

"Oh," said Crumley, "we've made tramps disappear before."

"Leave it to us, Father," said McMullen. "It can be arranged, believe me."

"No harm must come to the child."

McMullen said: "What do you think we are, Father, Protestants? We don't hurt nobody, do we Jim?"

Crumley, chewing potato salad, only shook his head.

"We can stick that girl so deep in the hole," McMullen said, "you won't find her with a searchlight. Over at juvenile, right Jim? Nosy newspapermen aren't allowed to know juvenile arrests. Nobody will ever find her."

Crumley swallowed and said: "Book her under a good name now."

"Annie Oakley," said McMullen.

"We used that one," said Crumley.

"What are we using now, Smith?"

"With an e on the end, now. That's how we keep track of them."

"Opal Smithe," said McMullen.

"You know we get by on a hundred a month, now. City claims it's going broke, cutting our pay."

"Slashing it to hell," said McMullen. "It's a shame, public servants."

McMullen drained his whiskey cup. "I guess the Inspector

wants to know what's in it for us poor cops."

"Forgiveness for all your sins," said Father Mack.

"I can get that in any confessional, Father," McMullen said.

"Am I being offered a guarantee?" asked Father Mack. "You can put this young woman in a safe place where federal agents will not find her?

"Yup," said Crumley.

"And, before God, you'll not harm the girl?"

"Oh, we're delicate, aren't we Jim?

"Like ballet dancers," muttered Crumley.

"Ballet dancers with badges," said McMullen.

"You'll track her down this afternoon, then."

"Now, Father," said Crumley, wiping his lips with a paper napkin, "you know my wife Mary, she's got arthur-ritis in the knees. And it's hard on her, lugging ice to the icebox every day."

"It's a terrible struggle," said the Bulldog. "A certified medical condition."

"I heard of these electric iceboxes, now," said Crumley. "I seen one down in the window at Meyer Electric. Works off an electric plug, don't need no iceman."

"Would be a wonderful gift for a hard-praying Catholic woman," said McMullen.

"I don't want nothing for myself, Father," Crumley said. "You know that."

McMullen said: "Delivery is what, Jim, an extra three dollars?"

"Throw that in," said Crumley.

Lillian delivered to Father Mack a clear glass plate loaded with potato salad. Crumley reached with his fork to spear chunks of potato. "You should visit my back porch Saturday night," he said. "We always got a card game going."

"Very friendly game," added McMullen.

"Seen the Archbishop there sometimes, back in the old

days," said Crumley.

"It's been a while since he come over," said McMullen. "But the Arch can keep a poker face, all right."

"And now," said Crumley, "with an electric icebox, we'll be able to cool all the beer you bring over."

McMullen asked: "Is it okay for a priest to bring beer, Jim?"

"Hey," said Crumley, "you know, everything's legal now."

Father Mack drove madly up Cathedral Hill, and pulled into his spot at the Chancery. He flew into the kitchen and startled Mrs. Bold, who was doing a jigsaw puzzle at the kitchen table. Father Mack regretted his rushed and dramatic entrance: the poor woman got little enough time off from the Archbishop's stern gaze.

She stood away from the jigsaw puzzle as if it were spilled poison. Father Mack put an arm around the woman's solid shoulders and squeezed.

"I need a favor from you," Father Mack asked, "and likely it will be my last. I want you to plan a trip for me. Let it be a one-man journey leaving as soon as possible."

He led Mrs. Bold to the great dusty globe, where the sun streamed in around red velvet curtains. "The train through Chicago to New York. And then the steamer for Liverpool or LeHavre, whichever departure comes first."

His finger moved on the globe from New York to Europe. "The next link is the ferry to Dun Laoghaire, and then a train connection to Cork. From there I will arrange for someone with an automobile to pick our traveler up and bring him here, to the village of Ballydehob."

His fingertip covered all of Ireland.

"There a man can stay a lifetime and no souls outside the village will know."

"And when would you like to return, Father?"

"I'm not the one," said Father Mack, "who'll be traveling."

He gave her a long penetrating look. "The traveler's name is Albert Patrick Reilly Junior."

No flicker of recognition passed her face. The woman was, apparently, innocent of gangster connections.

"God bless you, Mrs. Bold," Father Mack said.

DILLINGER'S GIRL GOING TO PRISON

SUES FOR $500 FUR COAT LEFT BEHIND IN GUN BATTLE APARTMENT

St. Paul Dispatch
June 2, 1934.

PATRICK

Pat sat forlorn at the bus station, flipping the pages of the Saint Paul Dispatch. Mankato! The Saint Paul newspapers arrived late in this rube town, and cost a nickel. Still there wasn't nothing in this rag to read. Another nickel gone! Mankato was bleeding him. He kicked the leather valise at his feet. That black bag, which once carried cash to famous crooks and dangerous cops, now contained only stinky clothing.

He left the bag under the wooden bench, almost daring one of his fellow bums to steal it, and walked to the pay phone. He lifted his wallet out of his jacket pocket. Two fives, a twenty, a bunch of singles, $44 altogether. He had lost some playing pool and a little more on the horses. He was renting a camping trailer at the edge of town, and the rent was due. If he paid it, he would be broke, pedaling around by bicycle, like a little boy. Not that he could afford a twenty-five cent phone call, but he had to talk to Dolly.

He dropped two dimes and a nickel, an outrageous price for a call 90 miles upriver.

"Long distance operator, please. Thank you sweetheart. Yes, Saint Paul, Minnesota, Payne 4212. Person to person, thank you."

"Hello?"

The operator said: "Person to person for Dolly Reilly please."

"Who's calling?" demanded his mother-in-law.

Pat stuttered.

"Your name sir?" asked the operator.

"Patrick Reilly!" his mother-in-law shrieked. "The police are looking for you."

Pat flashed for the operator, begged her for a refund, got no justice, staggered back to that hard wooden bench. It felt sweaty hot, suffocating in that fuming stinking depot, big ceiling fans on strike like the rest of this goddamn country. Bums, ugly girls and traveling salesmen sweated under those idle fans. Patrick could fully imagine his future as a vagrant. He was almost convinced he would never make money playing the horses, out here in Rube Town, cut off from any backside tips.

His budget called for coffee or a roll but not both so he bought a buttered roll from a bald-headed rube at the counter and ate it, stale and rancid. What was the difference between him and the stinky vagrant on the next bench? Forty-some dollars and a pocketful of change. There was no hope of finding Harry, wherever he was. Florida? Reno? Fat Fuck Crumley, the nerve of that prick shutting the Green Lantern, which had shoveled so much cash into his own pockets. Damn it he missed Harry, employer, mentor, friend, wise man, fountain of cash.

Plus he just plain loved the man.

Pat finished eating the roll, dusted the crumbs to the floor, and called person to person for Opal.

"She's out," Opal's mother shouted into the phone, but at least Pat got his coins back.

One last desperate call to Payne 4212. Maybe, Pat hoped, Dolly and Nora were arguing right now because Nora had bounced his call.

"Hello?" Dolly barked. "Yes operator. No! Mother, I'll handle it. Hello? Patrick? Patrick are you crazy, calling here? Don't you know who is listening?"

"Give me that phone," he could hear Nora demand.

"Patrick I don't know where you are but you'd better not come back here."

"I'm calling the police," Nora shouted into the phone.

"Mother how are you going to call the police when I've got the phone?"

Nora moaned and Dolly said: "Patrick, the police are listening. They've searched the house twice. Don't you know the G-men are looking for you?"

"Don't you tell them nothing."

"Look, Patrick, tell the federal men what you know. They want Harry. They want the Barker Gang. And most of all, they want Dillinger."

"I don't know nothing," said Pat.

"Oh bullshit. Can't you tell the truth for once? Why do you have to stand up for all these gangsters? If you told the police what you know, they'd let you off easy.

"Mother!" Dolly shouted.

Then into the phone, Dolly said: "Oh my God, she grabbed her purse and now she's ... I've got to go Patrick. If you don't want to talk to the cops, stay away. Final word. I care for you, Patrick, don't get hurt."

He stood dumbfounded, holding the phone.

Pat crossed the street, sidestepping the muddy trolley tracks, heading toward a narrow dark tavern. It had no particular name. Legal taverns were so new, half of them didn't have names yet. A hand-lettered sign in a dirty window said:

3.2 beer

Of course, they served stronger stuff, Pat could smell the gin just walking in, which meant they paid off. So even in dopey

Mankato, it was all arranged.

At one time, this dark cave had been Tommy Carroll's speakeasy. But you know, Tommy had them headaches. And his wife was overly fond of yen shee. She was the cashier, a disaster. Heroin and cash registers don't mix. So Tommy Carroll went broke, traded the barkeep's apron for a bulletproof vest, and joined the Dillinger gang.

Pat huddled in the corner where a shaft of unwelcome light sifted through the grime of the front window. He ordered a beer. When the barkeep went off, Pat raised a glass to Tommy, because you should always drink to the dead, it helps lubricate them out of Purgatory. Dirty filthy Iowa cops that gunned him down. Pat had known many level crooks — Harry, Karpis, Freddy Barker — but every cop he'd ever met had been a dirty double-crossing son of a bitch.

Oh, already the future was letting him down. It would be free beer and hot dogs if Tommy still owned this joint, plus a tip on a horse at Sportsman's Park, gangster gossip, and maybe an errand to run for money.

Here in this clip joint you had to watch the bartender didn't shortchange you. Pat slid one nickel across the wet bar for another glass of flat beer.

He picked up yesterday's Pioneer Press, lying damp on the bar. All you could read in this dull light were the headlines: Dillinger this, Dillinger that, Dillinger, Dillinger Dillinger. He was like the Angel of Death, this guy. As Tommy had found out, you ran with Dillinger, the cops used that as an excuse to shoot you down.

Dillinger? Sure, I met him, Your Honor, but I begged him to turn himself in.

Pat felt his way deeper into the dark tavern until he reached the payphone, bolted to the wall just outside of the piss-stinking men's room.

He called the Town Talk, station-to-station.

"Opal? Do you know who this is?"

"Long distance?"

"No it's me, Pat."

"I know. Long distance? Where are you?"

"Can I come see you?"

"I don't know. I can't talk long, I'm at work."

"I know, I called you at work. I want you to meet me when you get off."

"After lunch. Two thirty."

"Take the bus to Fort Snelling and walk over the bridge. I've got something for you. I'll be waiting."

He walked blind into the sunlight and sauntered along Riverfront Drive, like a fellow on an amiable errand. He cast secret glances at every parked car. The only way he could steal a car was to find one whose rube owner left the keys in it. Sometimes it seemed to Pat that he was cursed, a man of no talents. Tommy Carroll, and lots of other guys, could start any car in less than a minute. Back in his pickpocket days, Pat had only been the bumper, never the dip. He had known a hundred gangsters but none had ever invited him on a bank job, not even as wheelman. He'd dreamed of playing pro ball, but couldn't hit or field, so the Saints had made a him a mascot. Even at the family laundry, he'd only been a substitute truck driver. All his life he'd been trying to live down being Junior, Albert Junior. Call me Pat, will ya? Okay, but all that changed was his name.

As much as he wanted to steal a swell-looking Buick or Packard, the one car left with dangling keys was a rusty, dark blue Chevy. Pat hopped in, turned the key, drove away. By the time the lazy Mankato cops put these plate numbers on the teletype, this jalopy would be abandoned in the Twin Cities.

In two hours Pat reached the outskirts of Saint Paul,

stopping just across from Fort Snelling, on a cliff overlooking two mighty rivers. Patrick parked in Mendota Cemetery, just a few paces from where they'd buried Eddie Green. He watched the bridge. It was a million tons of concrete and four long lanes of asphalt. Not even J. Edgar's men would be able to tail Opal across it without being spotted.

Your Honor, I was only visiting the grave of a recently deceased friend.

That was Opal walking alone, a tiny figure dressed in gray, holding a pillbox hat to her head as a vicious wind ripped down the Mississippi. Pat watched intently. No other pedestrian was on the bridge. Traffic was light, and any car following Opal would have been easy to spot. When she finally reached Mendota Road, Pat sped out the cemetery gates, let her into the stolen Chevy and zoomed frantic for the cornfields.

Opal said: "Nobody followed me, okay? Jeesh!"

Pat, watching the mirror, pulled over at a filling station, underneath the shade of a lone oak tree, alongside a picnic bench. Opal, in gray cafeteria uniform, its white Peter Pan collar grease spattered, looked withered by the hot afternoon and her long walk.

"You could buy a girl a drink," she said.

Pat wandered over to the gas station. Yes, good strategy, buy two Cokes and check the radiator and the greasy rubes will not wonder why we stopped. He folded open the hood, and with a rag, twisted off the radiator cap. Whoosh, a burst of steam. "A little overheated," he called over to the grease monkey.

In the dirty office he stopped in front of a red steel tub of Coca Cola, iced down. Pat had scorched his hand opening the radiator and now let it linger in the icy tub. He pulled out two bottles, put a dime on the ledge of a filthy cash register, opened the bottles with the gizmo imbedded in the side of the ice bucket. He walked back to Opal at the picnic bench. She'd taken off her hat and loosened the top buttons on her blouse.

He set an icy, sweating gift before her.

"How you been?"

Opal shrugged.

"Getting along with your mother?"

"Hell no." She sipped. "Refreshing," she said. "Thank you."

"Aren't you going to ask me where I've been? What I've been up to?"

"Nope."

"I won some money playing the horses," he said.

"Oh really."

"Yeah, and I want to come back to town."

"I seen your name in the papers."

"I was in Chicago for a while, you know, at the World's Fair, and all."

"Oh really? I suppose you saw Sally Rand giving a fan dance."

"You ought to try that. You want to be a dancer, don't you?"

"But fan dancing is lewd, Patrick."

"Aw," said Pat.

"But I bet Chicago was fun."

"Yeah, you get tired of it after awhile. So now what I need ... say, have you seen Father Mack lately?"

Opal pursed her lips. "Nope."

Pat offered her a Lucky. "I'm trying to quit. Too expensive."

He lit his own. "I'm offering you a free smoke."

"It's addictive," she said.

"What I need from you," Pat blew smoke, "is to rent me an apartment. Not in Saint Paul, too hot, but Minneapolis, close to the action downtown."

"What kind of apartment?"

"Whatever you can get for this." He slipped a few bills from his wallet, handed them to Opal, and she counted them.

"More like a rooming house," she said.

"Hey rents are dropping."

"I'll see what I can do."

"Then you can come over."

"I can hardly wait." She studied the gas station. "I'll bet that bathroom is filthy." She locked Pat's money in her purse. "When do you want it?"

"Now."

"Anything else?"

"There'll be a tip in it for you, when I get settled."

"Whoopee," said Opal.

"What's the matter with you?"

"Look, I'm tired." She stood and stretched. "And I've got to be back for the dinner shift. Are you going to drive me all the way in?"

"I don't know," said Pat.

"Because if I got to use the bus I should leave now."

He jerked his thumb toward the car. "Got to cool the jalopy off."

"Well that bridge is awful long, get me back to the bus stop at least."

"You could quit that job when we get going."

"I thought you were married?"

"Divorced."

"I'm a Catholic, remember. My mother's got pictures of Jesus all over the house."

"Quit that stupid night shift at least."

"And live on what?"

"I have my ways," said Pat.

"Race track winnings, oh please."

Pat walked to the filling station, and returned with a watering can of galvanized steel. He was kind of ashamed of himself for lying to Opal, when his real goal was to win back Dolly. He could see a future: Rip the boards off the Green Lantern's doors, the party begins again, minus Bess-the-rat, who rots in prison. Harry was too smart for the G-men, and sooner or later would get back into the Saint Paul game. Pat had a sneaking suspicion that someday Houdini Dillinger might escape and return, like magic, thumbing his nose at Hoover.

Opal? No future with Opal. Opal was too ... she complained a lot, for a young kid. Plus she didn't have you know, the big thing a level gangster needs, the loyalty. The ... the ... commitment, that was the word. Opal figured the gangster life was all about nightclubs and big cars and jewelry. She didn't understand the brotherhood part. Us against them. We're the level guys. The cops are crooked. Bunch of shakedown artists is all they were.

He poured cold water into the Chevy's radiator and sneaked a glance at Opal as she sat frumpy and frowning at the picnic table. She was kind of a gold digger, Pat judged. Yep, the more you spent on Opal, the more she liked you. Now Dolly, the woman he'd wisely chosen to marry, she wasn't like that at all. You took Dolly out to the ballrooms on Saturday night, so she could see her old crowd, and you bought her buttermilk pancakes at the Lowry on Sunday, and you were all set. Opal was cute, but Dolly, she was his woman eternal.

DEPARTMENT OF JUSTICE MEMO

June 30, 1934

On the afternoon of June 26, 1934 OPAL MILLIGAN, a former girlfriend of PAT REILLY, called the Saint Paul division office and advised that she had previously been interviewed by Inspector Clegg, who requested her to advise them when she receives any information relative to the location of PAT REILLY.

On Friday June 22 she went with REILLY to a Minneapolis address and rented an apartment under the name MRS. BOB JOYCE. She stayed with him until the evening of June 25. Agents Notesteen, Brennan and Melvin drove her there, making her point out the apartment.

At 6:30 a.m., June 27, Agents Brennan, Melvin, Notesteen, Walsh, Anderson, Coulter and Nicholson asked Minneapolis police to meet them with a squad car at the corner of Chicago and Franklin.

Police, including two Minneapolis officers, began surrounding the house and Coulter went in and got the janitor's key. He opened the door but the chain lock was fastened. Several calls were made to the occupant to unfasten the chain. He shortly came to the door, released the chain, and permitted the agents to enter.

He admitted he was PAT REILLY and was requested to dress, and a search of the apartment revealed he had no guns or anything of value therein. His person was searched and it was found that he had on his person one $1 bill, one $5 bill, a nickel, a lucky piece, a pair of horn-rimmed glasses, and a comb.

NAB DILLINGER HENCHMAN

Swooping down on a Minneapolis apartment, a squad of heavily armed Department of Justice agents early today jailed Albert W. Reilly, henchman of John Dillinger, fugitive Indiana desperado. The capture took place in an apartment house at 620 E. Franklin Ave. Taken completely by surprise, Reilly, also known as Pat Reilly, surrendered without a struggle. He was in bed when federal agents rapped on his door.

St. Paul Daily News
June 27, 1934

PATRICK

Inspector Hugh Clegg stood with his back to the door. In his office now was exactly one hardwood chair for visitors.

Pat sat in it backward.

"Okay, so," Pat said. "you want to know how to catch Dillinger."

Inspector Clegg nodded. He was dressed dark, like he'd be attending a November funeral. But it was already a sweaty summer day in that office, the ceiling fan turning like a whirling joke, the lone window, big as a barn door, let in nothing but hot dust.

"I've already told you guys..." Pat said.

Clegg held up a hand for silence.

"I despise falsehoods," said Clegg. "Ask for me when you're prepared to tell the truth."

And then he walked out.

At the click of the door Pat stood and looked out the window at Rice Park. Was that Dolly over there on a bench, dressed in red, sitting alone near the taxi stand? He waved but before he could get the woman's attention in walked a small man with jug ears.

He was solid, a man in his 30s, nearly bald. His black trousers were cinched tight by a belt. They belonged to an expensive suit that had been shed down to white t-shirt. The man's arms were thick like he'd been a hick farmer working a pitchfork all day. He clutched a small bulging white paper bag in his hand.

Pat turned from the window. He had not seen this G-man before and figured this was the guy, the Fireman, he had heard whispers about.

"Can I smoke?" Pat asked.

"Nope," said the Fireman.

The Fireman sat on Clegg's desk. From the white bag he extracted one shelled peanut, cracked it, popped the nut into his mouth, and let the shell flutter to the polished floor.

"Mister Clegg ain't going to like that," Pat suggested.

"Like what?"

"Shells on the floor."

"Who's Mister Clegg?"

"Are you kidding? Your boss."

"I don't answer to any boss," said the Fireman, and crushed another peanut in his meaty hand.

"Can I see your badge?" asked Pat.

"Nope," said the Fireman. He spit out a fleck of peanut shell. "Where did you bury John Dillinger?"

"He ain't dead."

"So you know John Dillinger."

"Not really."

"Then how do you know he's not dead?"

The Fireman crushed another peanut.

"Look," Pat said, "I'm trying to help you guys, is all."

"First you told us he's dead..."

"No, I said it was Tommy Carroll claimed he was dead."

"Then you tell us he's not dead." The Fireman spilled peanuts on Clegg's desk and studied them as if the were spelling out a secret message. Without looking at Pat he said: "Sit down."

His lips curled nasty.

Pat backed into the heavy oak witness chair.

"Remove your shoes."

"I want to see my lawyer. McMeekin."

The Fireman pursed his lips.

"You don't need a lawyer. You might need a doctor. You might need an undertaker. But you don't need a lawyer."

Pat kicked off his moldy summer loafers.

"And your socks."

Pat bent double to strip off his white cotton baseball socks.

"They stink, get 'em out of here."

"What?"

"They stink go put them in the corner."

Pat began to rise but The Fireman foot-shoved him back into the chair.

"Who told you to get up?"

"You did."

"Get up, then."

"Are you going to push me down?"

"Get up."

The Fireman knocked Pat into the chair with a punch to the chest.

"You play square with me," he snarled, "I'll play square with you. Your feet stink."

"Yeah, well I'm sweating."

Ballplayers never rubbed the spot where they'd been hit by a pitch and Pat decided it was best now to pretend he didn't hurt. "You didn't give me a chance to shower."

The Fireman stepped on Pat's bare foot and shifted his weight until Pat cried in pain. Then he backed off and sat on the desk, picked up a peanut, rolled it in his hand as if he were considering something.

"I don't like you," he said.

"I ain't all that fond of you," said Pat.

"You're causing my country pain, so my country is going to cause you pain."

Pat couldn't help it, he grabbed his bare foot and massaged.

"You think it hurts now? We have just begun. Where is John Dillinger right," he pounded the desk, "now?"

Peanuts rolled off the desk and onto Clegg's shiny floor.

Pat sighed.

"Have you had breakfast?" asked his interrogator.

Pat didn't answer.

"I'm going to order from across the street," the Fireman said. "Let's see, sausage and eggs and home fried potatoes. How do you like your eggs?"

"Soft scrambled," muttered Pat.

"Me too. I hear the food is pig slop in Leavenworth."

Pat swallowed, dry.

"You could be there twenty years," said the Fireman. "Let's see, that's about ... ah... twenty-five-thousand pig slop meals."

Pat said: "I want McMeekin, my lawyer."

The Fireman laughed. He stepped to the window, looked down onto Fifth Street, and said: "I think I see your lawyer now, down in the park. Oh, wait, that's a bum. He's begging for change."

Pat closed his eyes.

The Fireman kicked him in the shins. "Don't go to sleep on me, one of our men died at Little Bohemia. We're not joking here, Reilly, this is not a comedy act."

"I don't even own a gun," Pat lied. "I didn't shoot anybody. I never even shot a squirrel."

The Fireman spit out the window.

"I ain't dumb enough to shoot a cop" Pat said. "Look, I'm just a guy. I ain't got no money, no job, no fancy education, all I got is friends."

"You mean the Dillinger Gang."

Pat sighed.

"Describe your first meeting with Dillinger."

Pat pressed his lips.

"Lie on the floor."

"What?"

"Get down on the floor and curl up like a baby."

"Why?" Pat said, but slipped out of the chair, lay on his side on the polished wood floor, and curled up.

The Fireman nudged Pat's ribs with his shoe tip. Looming over Pat, he said: "Where did you first meet Dillinger?"

Pat, breathing heavy, said: "He came to my tavern. He ordered a beer. I don't know. Beer ain't illegal anymore."

"What kind of beer did he drink?"

"Schmidt's is all we serve."

"What day was this?"

"I don't know, like, two weeks before St. Patrick's Day."

"Who was with him?"

"Nobody."

"The Indian dame?"

"Yeah."

"Baby Face?"

"No."

"Red Hamilton?"

"No."

"Van Meter?"

"No."

"Tommy Carroll?"

"No."

"Karpis?"

"No."

"Get up," said the Fireman.

Pat, shaky, slid into the chair.

"Thank you for telling me the truth," said the Fireman. "You're Catholic, right? Me too. We both know it's a sin to lie." He ate a peanut. "So, you met John Dillinger in early March at the Green Lantern tavern. His only companion was Billy Frechette. He drank a Schmidt's beer. And then what did he do?"

"He left."

"Get down on the floor. Liar!" The Fireman kicked his shin. "Now."

"Don't kick me," Pat pleaded.

"Drop your drawers," said the Fireman.

"Aw, come on."

"Let's see that shriveled dick."

"Hey, man, that ain't right, I thought you were Catholic."

"Trousers off, or I'll rip 'em off."

Pat, lying on the floor, slipped his trousers down around his ankles, and curled up, hands protecting his scrotum.

The Fireman laughed. "Just what I thought. Not much in the balls department."

In Pat's new view, the floor that had looked so shiny was actually covered with a fine dust. His eyes focused on the rusty iron legs of the radiator, and the strip of light leading to the steno room, where the clicking and clacking had gone silent. Pat felt ominous sick when he realized the steno girls had been sent away on break.

"What did Dillinger do after you met him? Why did he come to your tavern?"

"He gave me a bag of golf clubs to hold for him."

"Golf clubs."

"Yeah."

"What was in the bag besides golf clubs?"

"Well, there was a rifle."

"So you looked into the bag."

"Yeah after he left."

"What did you do with the bag?"

"I put it in my office."

"There were sticks of dynamite in the bag, too, right?"

"I didn't see any."

The Fireman bombed Pat with a shelled peanut.

"You don't lie too good, Reilly."

"I didn't see no dynamite. If it was in there it was at the bottom of the bag."

"So let's get this straight. You're John Dillinger's accomplice. Knowing he was Dillinger, you agreed to store weapons and dynamite for him."

Pat coughed, his lungs begging for nicotine.

"It's a shame," said the Fireman. "Because now we're talking federal prison for sure."

"I ain't saying nothing then."

"Knowing John Dillinger was a wanted man, you failed to notify authorities."

"Oh come on," Pat said. "The authorities around here, they're all crooks."

"Not your Federal Government," said the Fireman. He shook his head. "We're not crooks. You could have come talked to us. Sit up. Raise your trousers. You're a disgrace, Reilly."

Pat restored his twisted boxer shorts and dusty wrinkled trousers to the dignified position. He was zipping up when the Fireman bombed his chest with a peanut.

"That's what you're giving me," said the Fireman, "Peanuts. Here."

Pat slumped into the chair and the Fireman lobbed another peanut. It hit the radiator and fell to the floor.

The Fireman shook his head. "We'll note that for the record. Prisoner was offered a meal, and threw it to the floor."

He looked at his watch. Bit his lower lip.

"Okay," he said, and glared at Pat. "Don't squirm, I hate when my prisoners squirm."

Pat sat up straight.

"Squirming makes me feel bad. And when prisoners squirm, next thing you know, they want a favor. Like can I smoke. Or can I use the bathroom. And then when they realize this is just the beginning, and they're looking at twenty years of asking some screw for permission to do every little piss-ant thing, they start rethinking their misplaced loyalties."

Pat sat rigid.

"Did you hear that, Reilly? Misplaced loyalties. Your chubby whore Pattie Cherrington, down in Chicago, Cherry is telling us all about you."

Pat stared at his bare feet.

"You were playing with the big boys at Little Bohemia. Flashing a wad, the way Cherry tells it."

Pat shrugged.

"Whose cash was it, Pat?"

Pat pursed his lips.

"Did it belong to little Johnny Dillinger?"

"Cherry is a liar. She'll tell you guys anything."

"Cherry's story checks out. Yours is a load of crap."

"I haven't said nothing."

"Correction. You admitted that you aided and abetted the Dillinger gang."

Pat wanted a Lucky Strike so bad, he longed for the harsh comfort of its fragrant smoke, that burning stick between his yellow-stained fingers, the wispy curlicues like a conjured-up genie.

As if he could read Pat's mind, the Fireman withdrew from his shirt pocket a pack of Luckies. He lit one up with Pat's Statue of Liberty lighter, and blew smoke toward the ceiling.

"Just happen to smoke your brand," he said. He stared at the cigarette burning between the thick uncouth knuckles of his right hand.

"And by the way," he said. "Thanks for the lighter. You didn't have to do that. Federal government, we're not supposed to take gifts, you know."

"I didn't give it to you," Pat protested. "You stole it."

He walked behind Pat and said: "Take a memo. When the

prisoner came to us, he had been tortured by gangsters. There were cigarette burns up and down his spine."

"What are you talking about?"

"The report I'm going to write. You already had cigarette burns when you came to me. Where is John Dillinger right now?"

"I don't know."

Pat flinched as he felt the heat of a cigarette approach the top of his spine.

"I don't know, I don't know," Pat said. Face contorted by fear, he squirmed to look at the Fireman. "You can't do this, I'm a citizen. I pay taxes."

The Fireman grinned. "You're not in the United States of America right now, you're in my country, and there are no laws. The only way out is to tell the border guards where they can find John Herbert Dillinger."

"I last seen him in Wisconsin."

"At the kraut resort Little Bohemia."

"Correct."

"And Baby Face and Van and Red and Tommy all were there."

"Yes yes yes and yes."

"And then where did Dillinger go?"

"I'm the errand boy, that's all. They don't tell me nothing."

The Fireman held the burning cigarette in front of Pat's eyes.

"Everybody scrammed," Pat said.

"If you had to find Dillinger..."

"I would wait for him to contact me. He don't give out his phone number. Let me go. Let me out and I'll bet he calls me."

The Fireman put the cigarette in his lips, hitched his belt. "Now we're getting serious. Where would you look for Dillinger right now, today?"

"Chicago."

The Fireman waited.

"He likes the North Side."

The Fireman tapped ashes into Clegg's wiped-clean ashtray.

"Maybe at a Cubs game."

"What about taverns?"

"I don't know his hangouts. I only been to Chicago once."

The Fireman ground out the cigarette.

"Okay, now the question is, how light a sentence can we get you in return for your cooperation. Where's Baby Face Nelson?"

"He's no good."

"We know that. He shot one of our men. Where is he?"

"He don't like me, he never told me nothing."

"Van Meter."

"He's with Dillinger. They're tight."

The door opened and Clegg put his head in, inclined it at the Fireman, and both agents retreated to the hallway, leaving Pat alone. His mind seethed with the idea of betrayal. He'd always feared it would be his mother-in-law but there was no denying the obvious: Opal. Nobody else knew where he was living. The stinking little waitress with the big innocent liar eyes.

I guess I deserved it, Your Honor, for cheating on my marriage.

He stood, barefoot, bare-chested, the beginnings of a pot belly on a skinny frame and looked out at the trolley traffic and at Rice Park. The ragged desperate fellows were assembling for another unemployed worker rally. The whole establishment and their crooked cops were against these guys and somehow the ordinary sap was winning. Which gave Pat hope, now if only he had a cigarette and some breakfast and a lawyer. He looked down and judged this second story, perched above a lobby, far too high for a heroic leap. His hands trembled. Along with everything else, he had disgraced the Reilly name, splashed all over the newspapers. To make it worse, the homes of his relatives had been tossed by policemen, his honest hard-working parents painted with the red brush of shame.

He needed a cigarette pretty bad. And he wanted his lighter back! In three lousy months he had gone from heir apparent of Harry's empire to a quivering half-naked bundle of nerves. This was the Pat Reilly he hated, Pat the coward.

The Fireman ducked in, followed by Coulter and Clegg. The Fireman had over his arm a starched white dress shirt and a red tie. He worked himself up, buttoning the shirt, looping the tie, grabbing a federal-gray suit jacket from the coatrack.

"Has the prisoner had breakfast?" Clegg asked.

"He refused it," said the Fireman.

"Put your shirt on," Clegg commanded, and Pat reached for it on the floor.

"Has he been advised of his rights?" asked Clegg.

"Repeatedly, and he has refused legal counsel," said the Fireman.

"Albert William Reilly," said Clegg, "you are under arrest for aiding in the murder of federal agent Carter Baum on the evening of April 23 in Vilas County, Wisconsin ... and you are to be transported to the Ramsey County Jail until arraignment tomorrow morning on charges of accessory to murder and harboring a federal fugitive."

Clegg inclined his head toward Coulter.

"Remove this sorry specimen from the premises."

Coulter on one side, the Fireman on the other, Pat was walked out into the gallery of the Federal Building. He was utterly astonished that they did not handcuff him. Maybe they were hoping he'd run so they could shoot him in the back like they done to Eddie Green. Well no thanks, Patrick Reilly don't end that way. Down the wide staircase he walked, between two G-men in suits, across the polished floors, out to the blinding sunlight.

They were calling his name, the reporters, all of them his so-called friends, freeloaders at the Green Lantern. They shouted questions, pointed cameras his way.

"Hey Pat," a reporter shouted, "did you ever rob banks with Dillinger?"

As the Feds hustled him away from the newshounds, he had a glimpse, over their shoulders, of Dolly. He raised a hand in greeting. She burst into tears. When they slipped him into the paddy wagon and the door clanged shut, Pat explained to his Judge:

I never meant to make her cry, Your Honor.

REILLY PLEADS
NOT GUILTY
OF HAROBRING DILLINGER

St. Paul Daily News
July 9, 1934

FATHER MACK

In his jail cell, Pat wore a white shirt and twill trousers. He paced barefoot on a concrete floor. A toilet, two bunks and a schoolboy desk were all bolted in.

"They're taking me out, Father. They're taking me to court today, I think."

Pat looked smaller and more harmless than ever. He engaged Father Mack with his hazy blue eyes.

"I don't have a chance, do I, Father?"

Father Mack saw a photo of Dolly on that schoolboy desk.

An old, skinny deputy came along with his ring of keys and let Father Mack into the cell without a word.

The cell door clanged.

"You been talking to them Father?"

"Of necessity."

Pat had been playing solitaire, a losing hand spread out on the bunk. His hair was wild uncombed. The smell of bad breath mingled with all the other acrid jail smells. Father Mack had long ago identified the typical Irish personality, good cheer struggling with black despair. It reflected the weather of that island nation, sunshine and clouds doing battle every day. But all the cheer had gone out of this Irishman, and he was sagging with defeat.

"Sit down Father, well, there ain't nowhere decent to sit."

Father Mack chose the end of a bunk.

Pat struck up a Lucky. "Cigarettes," he said, "they're like gold in here. If you want to do me a favor, Father, buy me a couple of packs on the way out. Camels and Luckies, they're the best."

He shook out the match, pitched it into the open toilet.

"The accommodations," he said, "stink."

He looked at Father Mack as if he had just now seen him.

"So where you been keeping yourself, Father?"

Father Mack felt flooded by a warm sorrow. Patrick might not be in this terrible fix were it not for the cynical greed of the Saint Paul police. Inspector Crumley, who had vowed to hold Opal away from the federal men, had broken his promise. Apparently he wanted his bribe, in the form of a refrigerator, delivered before he held up his end of the bargain.

"Patrick, the time to make a deal is running out."

"Oh," said Pat. "You been talking to my lawyer."

Father Mack nodded.

"Yeah, well I don't know who's paying him. Whose side is he on, Father?"

"Save yourself, Patrick."

"I ain't done nothing wrong, Father. It's the cops who should be confessing. Crumley and Big Ryan. We're the saints, they're the sinners." Pat blew a long stream of smoke toward the tiny barred window.

"Hey, I got a view of the Mississippi," he said. "I gotta stand on the toilet to see it, though." He demonstrated. "See?"

Then he dismounted. "Ah, truth is, I ain't doing too good in here, Father, not too good at all. These ain't my kind of people in here. I'm used to a higher class. I ran with Dillinger once."

He sighed.

"Before the bastards shot him in the back."

He blew smoke.

"And now they want Harry, so they can shoot him in the back like they done to Eddie and Tommy and Dillinger. Well I ain't gonna give up Harry to them murdering cowards. Bring J. Edgar

Hoover here and I'll spit in his face."

He scooped up his solitaire game.

"Dolly was here yesterday," he said. "I mean not here in the cell. In the visitors room, you know. Through the glass."

Father Mack saw him swallow the lump in his throat.

"Of course she wants a divorce now. Says I was cattin' around with Opal. But you know what the truth is, Father? I'm broke now. I ain't bringing in the coin. So all of a sudden Dolly ..."

He couldn't speak for a moment. He touched the photo of Dolly.

"Everybody's turned on me. And I ain't turned on nobody. There's no salvation, Father, like they taught us in Catechism. Is there?"

"Your mother," said Father Mack, and from his black trousers pulled a small leather pouch, "is paying for the legal services of Mister DeCourcy."

"My mother?"

"Your widowed mother. From the sweat of her labor at the laundry."

"I'm ashamed, Father."

"Such is a mother's love. But she does not want you to know she is paying the lawyer, so you must ..."

"I'll pay her back when I get out Father, I swear to God."

"Her heart is broken, Patrick."

He handed Pat the pouch.

"Pray."

Pat's face wrinkled in disappointment when he saw that the pouch contained rosary beads.

"I ain't a holy roller Father."

Pat held the rosaries up, black beads, silver links and crucifix in the light from the tiny window.

"You want me walkin' around praying the rosary in here? That's a sign of weakness, Father. Weak men talk and weak men don't last in here."

"A holy meditation," said Father Mack, "will lead to your personal salvation. And once that occurs, it won't matter what happens in the world around you."

Pat draped the rosary over Dolly's photo.

"Patrick as everyone seems to know, I was a young prizefighter once and on a damp Saturday evening in a ring in Cork City it went dark for me. One moment I was sitting in the training room with my hands and feet going cold, as they always did before a bout, and the very next thing I was staring at harsh ceiling lights and being carried off. They tell me the fight lasted five rounds, and yet I remember nothing."

"Bareknuckle days, eh Father?"

"In my knocked-out haze I encountered a figure who exuded kindness and soft light..."

"Jesus."

"No it was a female, St. Bridgid perhaps, but in truth she had no face to show, she was just a feeling, soft, womanly, green, sunny and misty at once like Mother Ireland herself."

"And what did she say Father?"

"Not a word. Perfect, stunning silence, she was. And in that silence I realized a prizefighter is like a thief, serving only his own ego, seeking to profit from the destruction of his opponent. When I came out of that hospital I had blurred vision in my right eye but clear vision in my mind's eye. Serving others is the only salvation. All else is a fool's errand."

"I've been a crook all my life, Father, how am I going to change now?"

"There's nothing more plentiful in this world, Patrick, than excuses."

Agent Guerrero appeared on the other side of the bars.

Patrick said: "Will you talk to Dolly for me? About the divorce, Father."

Father Mack surrounded Pat's hands with his own. "Good luck Patrick, and God bless you."

"Same thing ain't it, Father?"

Agent Guerrero escorted Father Mack down a long white-tiled hallway that smelled of antiseptic cleaner and vomit.

"I admire the man for his silence," said Father Mack. "He's only a grade school education, but not for him the naive reading of good and evil."

When they were around the corner at the guard's station, Father Mack said: "He believes his mother paid for his lawyer. It would be cruel to advise him otherwise."

Guerrero nodded and walked with Father Mack to the door that led to the sunshine of the main boulevard.

"It would be better for Patrick if he informed on Harry," Father Mack said. "But if he did so, he would lose his soul. Even a criminal has a soul, Mister Guerrero."

"Likewise a federal agent," said Guerrero. "May I have your blessing Father?"

Right there on the busy street, Father Mack indulged him with the Sign of the Cross.

FEDS PUT "END"
TO OUTLAW DILLINGER
AT CLOSE OF GANG FILM

WOMAN IN RED DRESS LED
DILLINGER TO DEATH
IN TRAP OF FEDERAL AGENTS

ONLY 3 OF DILLINGER GROUP REMAIN:
HAMILTON, VAN METER,
BABY FACE NELSON STILL ELUDE
U.S. GREATEST MANHUNTS.

St. Paul Daily News
Monday, July 23, 1934

FATHER MACK

The envelope was sealed with red wax, as it might have been in the Middle Ages. It lay on the Chancery library desk near the great globe, at the windows overlooking the Cathedral.

The Archbishop was seated in an antique brass chair carved with scenes from the Stations of the Cross. At his side, upright like a spear, stood his gold-and-ivory crosier. He adjusted thin wire rim glasses over his austere face.

"Father O'Sullivan, it appears your term as Provost has expired."

"I understand, Excellency."

"You have performed admirably, and so I trust you will enjoy your next assignment."

"And that is…"

"Your holy orders are contained in the envelope."

Father Mack picked up the envelope, understood that he was not to open it in the presence of the Archbishop. He folded it into his trouser pocket.

"Our shame must never happen again," said the Archbishop.

After a pause to let those words ring, the Archbishop resumed: "Father McCarthy. You are a Skibbereen man."

"Ballydehob," said Father Mack.

"Close enough," said the Archbishop. "It was your own

ancestors who starved, McCarthys and O'Sullivans both, and within living memory. As a people we have suffered our last humiliation."

Father Mack nodded.

"They rarely speak of it. They pretend it never happened. The Irish, for all their incessant talking, are struck dumb in the presence of profound truth."

He looked at Father Mack directly: "I understand you fought the British man to man."

"Once, for a bit, there was street fighting. In Cork it was, and long ago."

"A Fenian then. You stood strong for your people, Father O'Sullivan. The Irish people, who watched their children starve, who surrendered the lands of their ancestors, who groveled before the British jackboot, have regained their dignity here. This dignity and self-sufficiency we will preserve, no matter the price. *Salus populi, suprema lex esto.*"

"The health of the people, yes, I understand, Excellency."

"Every city in history has been run by a gang," the Archbishop said. "When such a gang is sanctioned, it is called the Police Department. The city below us is run by a gang which includes both criminals and policemen. That does make it complicated. But what is most important, Father, is that our good Irish people are running the taverns, patrolling the streets, manning the river docks and railroads, taking charge of the union halls. We've even elected an Irishman to run City Hall. I don't need to remind you what the stakes are, with men all over America begging on the streets."

He set his eyeglasses down on his nose, as if to see more clearly. "All politics is dishonorable, Father McCarthy, and whatever price we must pay, there will be no starving Irish in this country. God failed Ireland for six hundred years, Father McCarthy, mysterious are his ways. But we will never fail ourselves, never, ever again."

Father Mack bit his lip to check some dark emotion.

"You depart with honor," said the Archbishop. He lifted his crozier and tapped the priest on each shoulder. "Go with my blessing, Father O'Sullivan."

On his way to the door, Father Mack spun the globe.

Easter Saturday
April 16, 1938

PATRICK

It was night and cold and Saint Paul again.

Soggy snow had ruined the cheap shoes they had given him upon his parole from Leavenworth. His feet were so numb they didn't feel wet anymore. The trees of Rice Park were strung with lights, but said illumination only accented the cold night. Behind Pat rose the dark Germanic castle, lit only by the second floor offices of late-working G-men. They called themselves the FBI nowadays. But they were still a treacherous bunch of hard-hearted bastards.

They won, all right. But they cheated.

Pat, wrapped in a soggy gray overcoat, turned his back to that castle, best to forget what happened to him in there.

A streetcar picked up a scrum of shouting drunks from the Hotel Saint Paul. Though it would be warm and dry in the Grill Room, Pat didn't want to go in. What would be worse? To see some old pal and endure his questions? Or to look around and recognize nobody at all?

It was frightening how many things had changed in less than three years. Pat had missed all the big Saint Paul trials, reading about them in the prison library days later. He'd refused to see the G-men who wanted him to testify. But it didn't matter.

So-called reformers had run Big Ryan off the police force. Harry, Karpis and Doc were locked up at Alcatraz. Fred Barker,

Ma Barker, Tommy Carroll, Homer Van Meter, Dillinger and Baby Face had all been gunned down. Jack Peifer committed suicide rather than go to prison. Father Mack was coaching boxing at some rube Catholic college. Bess Green had served her time in the same prison as Billie Frechette, got sprung, and made herself scarce. Filben, never loyal to anybody but himself, had a mansion with a swimming pool in the California desert. Opal was waiting tables was over on the west side of Minneapolis, and was never seen in Saint Paul. Dolly was shacked up with a shoe salesman in Chicago.

Three years in Leavenworth, you did 'em level, and now nobody remembers your name. Pat Reilly, ghost in his own hometown.

A car crawled along Market Street, a Buick with Illinois plates. Pat stepped under a streetlamp, buttoned his overcoat, tilted his fedora over his head.

The car stopped, gagging him with exhaust. The driver leaned across the front seat and rolled down the window. He was alone in the car.

"You Reilly?"

Pat shrugged. A level gangster might shift the action to his own car, but Pat couldn't afford one yet.

He squatted to look the guy in the eye. It was hard to tell much with everything dark but streetlamps and speedometer.

"Looking for somebody special?"

"Like I said, a guy named Reilly."

"Maybe I can take you to him."

"Okay, well." The guy produced a five-dollar bill. "Take me."

Pat snatched the money and whirled around for a look. It rattles your mind, three years in Leavenworth. You realize there's no such thing as trust.

"Let's get a cab," Pat said.

"What?"

"Park it. We'll get a cab."

Did it make sense to waste money on a cab? No. But caution made sense. Technically, Pat was still in federal prison, his freedom a mere piece of paper that could be snatched by any bum cop any time.

He crossed Market Street and got into the first cab in the hotel's driveway. He waited for this Illinois guy to lock his car. He was a big, round, bulky guy, like he was raised on steaks and cocktails. He had a fat red face and dressed darkly. His heavy overcoat was thrown over his arm when he crossed the street and got in beside Pat.

"Cathedral Hill," Pat said. "The Dublin Tavern."

The driver was an old tired white-haired guy and his cab stank of cheap cigars. He took nearly ten minutes to drive uphill on slippery streets. Bits of icy rain sputtered from the sky. "Fixing to be an ice storm," the driver ventured, but got no answer from either passenger.

At the Dublin Tavern, Pat got out first while the Illinois guy paid off the driver. The two stood sheltered by the tavern's green canvas awning.

"Everybody says this Reilly," the Illinois guy said, "is the guy to see around here."

Pat struck a match, lit a Lucky, did not offer a cigarette to the guy.

"I heard he ran with Dillinger," the guy said.

"Yeah," said Pat. "I heard that too. Saint Dillinger, we called him. He stood up. He was one of us all the way."

"Reilly was at Little Bohemia, that's what I heard."

Pat blew smoke.

"We waiting for somebody?" the Illinois guy asked.

Pat nodded.

"This Reilly guy?"

"He'll be here," Pat said.

"Cold fucking town," said the guy.

"Don't say nothing about his weight," Pat said. "He's a great big fat guy. He's a whale, this Reilly."

Pat puffed his Lucky to a nub, pitched it into the rainy gutter. He flipped the flaps of his overcoat like a bird trying to fly. He let out a lungful of frustrated air.

"He's making us wait," Pat said. "Like it's a game."

"I figured," said the guy.

Both guys were shivering by the time a dark Packard pulled up to the curb. With a groan, James Crumley extracted himself from the passenger seat. He needed a cane to thump across the dark sidewalk toward the light of the tavern.

Crumley looked the Illinois guy up and down.

"You get in the car," he said.

The Illinois guy pointed to his own chest.

"Yeah, you," said Crumley.

The Illinois guy shrugged and walked to the Packard, sitting in the seat Crumley had just abandoned.

The Packard motored to the corner and turned right.

"I see you made it," Crumley said.

"You ain't on time," Pat said.

"Always make 'em wait," Crumley said. "You want to show 'em who's boss."

"I want a drink," said Pat.

"Good to see you home," said Crumley.

They pushed into the Dublin Tavern, which seemed bright compared to the spring night. Heads turned and acknowledged Crumley as he and Pat walked along the bar toward back booths.

Crumley removed his cashmere topcoat to reveal a beautiful vanilla suit and bright blue tie. Pat hung up his cheap raincoat and Crumley said: "That's the one the shills made for you?"

"Huh?"

"The suit."

"Oh yeah," Pat said. "The Leavenworth tailor. No wonder

he's in prison. His suits are a crime. I'm gonna burn it."

It did hang off him, shapeless, sleeves so short his shirt cuffs stuck out. Pat sat across from Crumley, and the bartender put a bottle of Old Crab Orchard whiskey between them, along with a bowl of ice cubes and two short glasses.

Pat poured. They drank.

"To the boys," said Crumley.

"To the old days," said Pat. "Fucking Alcatraz," he said. "Poor Harry."

"I tried to help him," said Crumley.

"Yeah," said Pat.

"I sent the Bulldog out there after him."

"Yeah, I know," said Pat.

"J. Edgar Hoover, Public Asshole Number One," said Crumley.

"I'll drink to that," said Pat, and they clinked glasses.

"So you went down to see Dolly in Chicago," Crumley said, "and you came back with this Illinois bum. Chicago. We'll call him Charley Chicago now."

"No, Charley Chicago drove up to see me. Because of my reputation."

"But first thing you got out, you ran down to see Dolly in Chicago."

"Yeah."

Crumley shook his head.

"What you got against her, Crumley?"

"She shut you out, didn't she? She took up with another man while you was locked up, didn't she? See I told you about women. But you never listened, Reilly. Where other people got ears on the sides of their heads, you got doorknobs."

Pat added whiskey and one ice cube to his glass. "Cures every Irish disease," he said. "Whiskey."

"What's Charley Chicago want?" asked Crumley.

"Yen shee."

"Jesus Patrick. That's federal language, now. Where'd you meet him?"

"I told you I got a reputation now, all the way to Chicago."

"Not like the old days. Not like Harry."

"They got Harry locked up pretty tight."

"See that's the most tight-assed of all the federal prisons."

"I know it."

"Can't get out of there without going in the drink."

"I heard about the sharks," Pat said. "It's way out in the ocean, right?"

"Federals? Yen shee? Jesus, Reilly, I can't swim a stroke. What's he want, now?"

"What's who want?"

"Charley Chicago out there."

"Protected deal."

"Maybe in Minneapolis."

"Do we know anybody over there?"

"Your girlfriend, Opal."

"Fuck that bitch."

"I heard she's waiting tables again. Don't think about it Reilly, the Feds will know who done it."

"I ain't thinking about her."

"You know with Big Ryan gone, you can't get a thing done in this town, but I might know a guy across the river."

Pat lit a Lucky.

"Jesus, you lost weight in there," said Crumley. "I know somebody on Uncle Sam's payroll. The old-fashioned kind, now, level from back in the day. Guy like us. Guy with a big heart."

"Like us?" Pat blew smoke away from Crumley's face.

"Yeah, us," said Crumley. "I ain't carrying a badge no more, you know that." Sweating, he shifted his weight like he couldn't get comfortable. "I can't guarantee what the nightsticks will do. This ain't the good old days, now. But my guy can steer a case should Charley Chicago get nailed. Sympathetic judge. That's all we can offer, now. Steerage."

"You ever see Bess Green around?" Pat asked.

"Are you kidding? She's laying so low the streetcar would run over her without mussing her hair."

"The mouth on that broad. J. Edgar Hoover wouldn't have known a thing if she'd only shut up."

"Yeah I know, don't be bitter Patrick, dames talk, they can't help it. That's why, ya know."

"Yeah I know."

"Forgive and forget Patrick."

"I'm trying."

"Think of all the people what done me wrong, and I coulda run 'em in and I didn't. People don't appreciate that about Crumley. They say he's this and that. But they don't know how bad I coulda been. I never left no bodies in the alleys now, like some cops I could mention. I ain't no murderer."

"Just Leavenworth makes you bitter and all."

Crumley began to unwrap a cigar just as Pat snuffed out his Lucky.

"I miss the action," Pat said.

"Well, you're back in it partner."

"With yen shee, though."

"What's the difference?"

"Well booze," Pat said, "booze was all right with me. Booze was Irish. Yen shee, that's Chinese, ain't it? Where's it come from, China?"

"Now don't go examining your conscience. It gets an Irishman in trouble every time."

"I can't help it."

"You're a goddamn Irish Catholic, that's why. The Sisters of Mercy, they beat it into you."

Crumley lit his cigar. "See if I was as bad as Big Ryan, I would be on easy street. He's up there at the lakes, running a tavern, I hear, going fishing every day, living off a police pension."

"How about this Chicago guy?"

"Charley Chicago? What's he got?

"Says he can put a package a week on the train."

"A Chicago guy is usually full of shit."

"Says he can pay up front, Jim."

"Now you're talking, partner."

"A hundred bucks."

"Why, that ain't a lot of money anymore."

"A month in, he's still going, we jack him up."

"Yeah, that's when things get tricky. Let's start him at two hundred right off."

"But it's dope though."

"You angling for a bigger cut?"

"No, Jim, it's dope, I mean, ain't that kinda wrong, maybe it's not a mortal sin, but still … ?"

"Reilly, in the old days, how many bottles of booze did you deliver?"

Pat shrugged.

"So what's the difference? People got a way of getting noddy, and nobody's going to stop 'em. Don't believe that stuff about yen shee, it's the liquor business all over again."

"How we gonna know?"

"The Bulldog is pulling Charley Chicago's prints right now. We'll know in two days whether we got a live one. You living on your own now?"

"Ain't found a place yet."

"Yeah, well your mother's a good woman, I'll tell you that. She got you working at the laundry?"

"Part time." Pat laughed. "Well, Jim, to tell you the truth, I already quit."

"Quit your own mother?"

"I can't take the steam, my lungs. Prison ruined 'em."

"It's only yen shee Patrick, the people that need it, need it. To them it's like potatoes and whiskey is to us. We can't take less than two hundred, I won't take no less, there's too many people to pay off."

"Yeah, I was gonna go see Harry in California, but you know, they don't let you into Alcatraz. It ain't like a normal prison. I was gonna save up the train fare. How do they take you out to see him? By boat, must be. It's an island, right, way out in the ocean?"

Crumley shrugged. "I don't know, partner. I don't want no part of Alcatraz. You know, the federals were out there, trying to get Harry to rat, he wouldn't say nothing."

Suddenly Pat was aware of Bulldog McMullen, passing bar stools, headed straight for them. The Bulldog wore a big bright smile on his craggy face.

"We'll see if the prints come back," said the Bulldog.

He fake-punched Pat on the shoulder, and sat across from him. The three men poured a good amount of whiskey each.

Said whiskey was beautiful, harsh and warm going down Pat's throat.

He began to feel like Pat Reilly again, a kind of a dark saint, sitting in the corner of a good Irish tavern, booze-warmed and working on a deal.

SEE THE OTHER BOOKS
IN THIS SERIES:

IF THE DEAD COULD SPEAK

As Prohibition ends, bootlegger Mick Powers needs to find another line of work. Papa Alt, millionaire brewer, sends him to snoop on two gangster molls. But the women, Sadie and Rose, are in more trouble than Mick imagines.

DEAD A LONG TIME

Mick Powers, behind on the rent, embarks on a desperate gamble. But the stakes are raised to the house maximum when Ma Barker and sons return to Saint Paul, with a spectacular bank robbery in mind.

DEAD LIKE LAZARUS

A gentleman gangster arrives from Chicago, claiming to be on vacation. Alvin Karpis and Fred Barker stalk a millionaire. And bootlegger Mick Powers gets mixed up in a crime that makes national headlines.

DEAD MESSENGER

Mick Powers, wanted in Saint Paul, is living on the lam deep in the quiet woods of Wisconsin. Just after New Year's, his phone starts ringing with phantom calls. Then one snowy afternoon, a dark sedan lumbers down his driveway. Mick's dogs go into a frenzy of barking, trying to tell him that the visitors are big trouble.

Out of that sedan pops Alvin Karpis, Fred Barker and his brother Doc. They say they only want a small favor.

So begins a dark adventure that finds Mick involved in the final crime of the Barker Gang's long and deadly career.

SECRET
PARTNERS

The Police Chief and the Barker Gang

This book of documented history, published by the Minnesota History Society Press, is the foundation work of "The Resurrection of Saint Johnny" as well as the four related books mentioned on the previous page.

Secret Partners reveals that the roll-call of Public Enemies has long been missing one important name. Alvin Karpis, Fred Barker, Doc Barker and John Dillinger are now joined by "Big Tom" Brown.

A gangster who was also chief of police, Brown was a secret partner of some of the most notorious criminals of the 1930s. Brown's hidden role in the kidnappings, bank robberies and murders of the Public Enemies era is fully explored for the first time.

The story is illustrated with more than 30 photos, many never before published.

Secret Partners is available in book stores, online, and as an e-book.

A preview of *Secret Partners*, and all its related works of fiction, is available at www.tpmahoney.com